A SECOND CHANCE

Chuck wanted to grab her and shake her, she infuriated him so. "Don't be coy, Toni," he pleaded. "I've been honest with you. Can't you let go of the past long enough to embrace the future?"

"Oh, that's rich!" Toni cried. "Coming from a man who ran from his past for thirty years!"

"That's good," Chuck encouraged her, hoping to open a dialogue of truth that would get them past the animosity and pent-up hurt both of them were experiencing.

Toni continued toward the exit. He grasped her by the arm, and she turned to look up at him, her eyes so sad. "I'm forty-eight years old. I don't need this sort of nonsense in my life, Charles Waters."

Uh-oh. She never called him Charles unless she was seething.

He let go of her arm but blocked her exit. "I need you, Toni. I need this kind of nonsense in my life. What are you afraid of? Are you afraid I'll hurt you again?"

Toni gave him a steely look. "You'll never get the opportunity to hurt me again, Chuck."

"Kiss me, Toni."

"What?"

"Look, if you can kiss me and then tell me there's nothing left between us, I'll let it drop. Otherwise, I'm going to court you whether you like it or not."

He got his kiss that day, but Toni wouldn't admit she had been moved by it. Or him. And he kept his word. He was in hot pursuit of her from the moment she went back to New Orleans. . . .

Other Titles by Janice Sims

AFFAIR OF THE HEART

"To Love Again" in the anthology,
LOVE LETTERS

ALL THE RIGHT REASONS

OUT OF THE BLUE

FOR KEEPS

A BITTERSWEET LOVE

"The Keys to My Heart" in the anthology,
A VERY SPECIAL LOVE

Published by BET/Arabesque books

A SECOND CHANCE AT LOVE

Janice Sims

ARABESQUE
BET
BOOKS

BET Publications, LLC
www.bet.com
www.arabesquebooks.com

ARABESQUE BOOKS are published by

BET Publications, LLC
c/o BET BOOKS
One BET Plaza
1900 W Place NE
Washington, D.C. 20018-1211

All Kensington titles, imprints, and distributed lines are available at special quantity discounts for bulk purchases for sales promotions, premiums, fund raising, educational, or institutional use.

Special book excerpts or customized printings can also be created to fit specific needs. For details, write or phone the office of the Kensington special sales manager: Kensington Publishing Corp., 850 Third Avenue, New York, NY 10022, attn: Special Sales Department, Phone: 1-800-221-2647.

BET Books is a trademark of Black Entertainment Television, Inc. ARABESQUE, the ARABESQUE logo, and the BET BOOKS logo are trademarks and registered trademarks.

First Printing: January, 2001
10 9 8 7 6 5 4 3 2 1

Printed in the United States of America

Thanks to Sabrina L. Demps, Internet wizard, who was able to find information on Ethiopia and fertility gods that I would have spent hours trying to find. Thanks to my loving family, who're always supportive of this crazy career of mine. Lastly, thanks to my editor for putting up with me. She deserves better!

In life you can either choose to be
an unanchored boat tossed about
by every wave of the sea
Or a tree with strong roots
that nourish and sustain you.
Which will you be
That boat or the tree?

—*The Book of Counted Joys*

One

The day Toni Shaw decided to stick her nose where it didn't belong, she received the second serious marriage proposal in her life. October in New Orleans was usually a month of promise for her. She enjoyed the crisp days. The summer months had been mostly hot and humid, or rainy and moist. A cool, dry day topped by a clear blue sky was a thing of beauty. Toni relished the change. Window shopping on a Friday afternoon in the French Quarter, she stopped in front of Mackenzie's, feeling the urge to press her nose against the bakery shop's window as she used to do when she was a kid, with her mouth watering for a turtle, a fat cookie made with pecans and smothered under thick, rich chocolate. How they used to melt on her tongue!

The turtles displayed in the window today looked no less appealing, but she was fifty-one now and had the willpower needed to resist the decadent treats. Sighing for old time's sake she moved on, hurrying now, because while she had been salivating over turtles, she had remembered her book signing tonight at The African Violet. Madelyn Simpson, the owner, had talked her into it in spite of the fact that Toni rarely did signings. It wasn't because she didn't want to meet the readers of her novels. It was more a case of not wanting to disappoint those readers. Before her incarnation as Serena

Kincaid, she had been Toni Shaw, social activist, single
mother of twin daughters and, generally, a hell raiser.
Sometimes she didn't know whether she was a different
person back then, or if it had been the times themselves. There had been something in the air in the sixties, a wild expectation that defined the era. No one
wanted to sit still and simply take what anyone was
handing out anymore. Toni had left New Orleans, the
city of the saints, for the University of California at
Berkeley when she was seventeen. A woman-child in
search of an identity apart from the one her parents
had imposed on her all her life. Not that Marie or
James Shaw had been overly strict. No, what they did
was raise their precious only child, Antoinette, in such
a way that she understood she was capable of anything,
and she was expected to achieve greatness in life. This
was driven home by the implicit faith they had in her.
No one ever had to discipline Toni. Even as a child she
knew more was required of her. *To whom much is given,
much is expected.* Those sentiments had been ingrained
in her from birth.

No wonder she went a little crazy once she was two
thousand miles from home. Her freshman year, the year
she lost her mind, she felt a bit like a pampered pooch
who had been let off its leash to explore a park with
myriad delights. In 1967, Berkeley was the place to be if
you were ready to experience life. Ready? Toni was long
overdue! She immersed herself in her studies—there
would be no half stepping where school was concerned.
She had come there on scholarship and wasn't about to
lose it over foolishness. It was her extracurricular activities that got her in trouble: If there was a grievance, she
led the charge. Her group addressed all forms of social
ills, from racial equality to sexual equality. She didn't play
favorites. A child of the South, which, when she was growing up, wasn't a place that encouraged free expression

from young black women, Toni found that here she had a voice and used it often and vociferously. The local news media ate it up. She was seen on television newscasts so often she became a celebrity in the college community. It wasn't uncommon to see her on the six o'clock news, huge Angela Davisesque 'fro framing her face, leading a mob of students up the steps of the administration building with the purpose of storming the chancellor's office. She was arrested seven times during her Berkeley days. She saw the brief stays in jail as badges of honor. It was only right to stand up for what you believed in.

After a summer of social activism fervor, something happened to take the wind out of her sails, for a while anyway: Toni Shaw fell in love.

She shouldn't have been attracted to him. Charles Edward Waters reminded her of a brown-skinned Robert Redford at the peak of his career. Growing up on the edges of black Creole society in New Orleans, where they had put the "class" in upper class, Toni was used to mingling with the wealthy. Neither of her parents chose to follow the traditions of their ancestors. But when you're born into a group, you're bound by their customs whether you wish to be or not. Toni had been introduced to society right alongside the other fresh-faced, white-gowned debutantes.

If the sisters of St. Mary's had foreseen what a hedonistic child I would become, they would've locked me in the attic and thrown away the key, Toni thought now as she crossed the street to stand with the small crowd waiting for the St. Charles streetcar.

Her fall from impending sainthood came, aptly, in the fall of 1967.

She, Margery Devlin and Connie Moore arrived at the mating ritual commonly known as a house party fashionably late. It was Saturday night, and it seemed like every single black male and female within a five-mile radius was packed into the ramshackle two-story house off campus.

When the girls walked through the door into the dimly lit room, they could practically smell the funky pheromones coming off those hot, sweaty bodies writhing to the beat of Aretha singing, "I Never Loved A Man (The Way I Love You)."

The moment the dateless guys spied the three unattached females, they made eager beelines for them. Margery, a petite theater major from Tupelo, Mississippi, went off on the arm of a football player who had been checking her out for some time but hadn't had the nerve to approach her. He did so tonight because he had been waiting for her to put in an appearance for more than two hours, and he wasn't about to let some other brother beat his time. Connie, a sensitive voice major from Birmingham, Alabama, was approached by two prospective dance partners. Making her decision, she swept onto the dance floor with the shorter fellow while the taller one shook his head in amazement at Connie's choice.

Surrounded by dancers, Toni stood rubbing her moist palms on the sides of her tight jeans. Because of her reputation as a take-charge rabble-rouser, she intimidated boys her age. She was about to exit the dance floor in favor of a quiet corner when from behind her a deep male voice said, "You're the Creole wildcat I've been hearing so much about."

Toni slowly spun on her heels and smiled even slower. She had to come within three feet of him to make out his features and boldly did so. Standing in front of him with one hand on her hip, giving him attitude with her gaze, she said, "You got something against Creoles?"

She saw now that he was an upperclassman. Twenty-one, maybe twenty-two. His handsome face was dusky brown, and his eyes looked like they would be either hazel or light brown in better lighting. He leaned down.

She felt his breath on her cheek and smelled the Dentyne on his breath as he whispered, "I've got nothing against them if they all look as good as you do. Dance with me." It wasn't a request. It was just inevitable.

Toni went into his arms, which were strong and sure. Her nose came to his clavicle. His chin could rest on her head. They fit well together. And they danced to the slow number for a few moments without saying another word.

When the deejay put on a fast-paced James Brown number and they moved into a sensuous dance, he said close to her ear, "Charles Edward Waters."

He twirled her around, admiring her lush hips and thighs, wondering how they would feel wrapped around him. Toni came back into his arms like a yo-yo on a string, smiled at him and said, "Toni Shaw."

"I know." He held her tightly against him. Looking deeply into her eyes, he murmured, "I'm too old for you."

"Then, what are you doing?" *Holding me like this?*

"I was standing across the street talking to a couple of the fellas when I saw you and your friends come in here. I've been watching you. You're loud. You're too bold for your own good. But you're damned fine!"

As she listened closely to his voice, she realized he sounded like Jack and Bobby Kennedy. However, that fact didn't work in his favor. To her he was just another horny senior testing the morals of a freshman.

Toni laughed shortly as she met his eyes. *And his rap ain't even tight.*

"I can see by the expression on your face that you think I'm full of crap," he allowed.

"You're perceptive." She saw no reason to be less than honest with him.

"It would be like robbing the cradle," he mused aloud, giving her an enigmatic smile.

"What?" Feigned ignorance. She knew exactly what he was referring to.

More and more men were dispensing with the pretense of falling for a woman's personality or her brain. It was the sixties, and free love wasn't just an expression. She knew the score, even if she hadn't yet racked up any numbers on the scoreboard.

"Seducing you."

"Why would you want to seduce me when there are so many other likely candidates out there?" Her eyes scanned his expensive attire. "Lots of women appreciate pretty boys like you."

He knew he was attractive to women; therefore her comment didn't rile him in the least.

"Unlike yourself?" he inquired softly, his fine brows slightly arched. "I don't think you know what kind of man you like, little girl. You look like a neophyte to me."

"Interesting choice of words, neophyte," Toni said, looking him directly in the eyes. "It means a new convert, a beginner, a novice." She paused in her steps and reached up to caress his freshly shaven jaw. Charles Edward Waters leaned in, expecting a kiss. Toni stood on tiptoe, her mouth only centimeters from his. "This neophyte doesn't wish to learn anything you want to teach her, *Chuck*. Nice try, though."

With that she smiled sweetly at him, removed his arms from her person, showed him her back and walked away. Amused, Chuck admired the hip action a moment or two, then followed. He spotted her as she stepped out onto the porch and into the cool night air. He hung back, watching her. The porch was deserted. Toni breathed in the fresh air, expelling the smoky air of the house party from her lungs. Imagine that preppy boy coming on to her like that! If they were in New Orleans, he would have been gingerly rubbing his face by now. Trying to soothe the sting of a right cross. She would never get used to how forward the boys were out here. If you as much as smiled at some of them, they took it as an invitation to bed you. That wasn't what she was about. She was here to get an education. To experience life, yes. But not *that* much life. Twelve years of Catholic school had not been for nothing. She knew how to keep her dress down and her legs crossed. Still angry, she spun around suddenly as if to peruse the scene of the crime, and saw Chuck leaning against the doorjamb. He pushed away with the intent of joining her on the porch. Toni immediately headed for the front steps. "Don't hassle me," she tossed over her shoulder. "I meant what I said. I don't want anything to do with you."

Chuck quickly closed the space between them and grabbed Toni by the upper part of her arm. "I just wanted to apologize . . . ," he began, letting go of her arm just as swiftly as he had taken it. "Please?"

They were standing on the lawn. Five feet separated them with Toni looking about them as if she were afraid of being alone with him. Their exhalations were visible in the cold air. "You know, you've got us all fooled. There you are yelling demands and inciting a riot at the student union—"

"That wasn't my fault," Toni jumped to her own defense. "Someone started throwing food, and before I knew it the whole place erupted into a huge food fight."

Chuck laughed. "I was there that day, trying to have lunch before going to my economics class. I wound up with chocolate pudding all over my mohair jacket."

"Honestly, I had nothing to do with it," Toni insisted. "But when you're known for being a troublemaker, you get blamed for everything whether you're guilty or not! Not the one with the Nehru collar?" The image of him covered in chocolate pudding popped into her head, and she laughed. She couldn't help it.

"That's the one!" Chuck confirmed, trying to keep a straight face.

It was his willingness to laugh at himself that won me over that night, Toni thought now as she boarded the streetcar for Poydras Street. The car wasn't crowded. Three rows down, she found an empty seat and moved over to the window, placing her packages on the seat beside her.

The conductor rang the bell signaling the car was on the move, and Toni settled in for the short ride. It felt wonderful being home again. But she wasn't the type to deceive herself. Where exactly was home? Her soul hadn't found that place yet.

New Orleans was her hometown, but could she claim it as her very own? Home was the place where you wanted to die. It was as simple as that for her. Macabre, but true. Home was a place you created with your own spirit and personality. It was the place you shared with the man who was your soul mate and where you had raised children together. Toni was perhaps being too hard on herself, but if that was her definition of a home, then she had never had one. Rootless. That was her. A nomad. Only visiting. Like now: Home to New Orleans to visit her elderly parents for two weeks. And while she was here, do a bit of shopping, drop by to say hello to school chums. Do a book signing to show appreciation for her fans. Then what? Back to her latest place of residence, an oldie but a goodie, San Francisco. She and the girls had been calling San Francisco home for a lot of years. Georgie and Bree had gone to elementary school and high school there. Toni's career had been launched there. She had built lasting friendships there, the most important being her best friend, Margery Devlin-Lincoln. Toni was happy in Frisco even if she couldn't, in her heart of hearts, honestly think of it as home.

Maybe I should just tell him yes and get it over with, she mused as she distractedly watched the scenery go past.

There was a longing in her. A sweet hurt that lessened only when he held her in his arms. How could she love him? After everything he had put her through? Why had her heart betrayed her? It made no sense!

Just like their breakup had made no sense.

They had met in early September, and by late November, Toni knew she was in love for the first time in her life. She wanted to constantly be with Chuck. The weekends were theirs: long drives along the coast, stays at quaint inns. Chuck was a gentle but passionate lover who showed great care when initiating her in the art of love. He made her feel as though she was cherished. As if what she gave up to be with him was well worth the sacrifice. Toni, in return, filled the emptiness in Chuck. Where he was bound by societal and familial restrictions, Toni's love freed him. With her at his side, he felt he could face down the world—and his parents, who stifled his growth. The mere fact that Toni loved him was proof that he had survived his parents' indoctrination. They would never have chosen a girl like Toni as a mate for him. Not with her outspokenness, her joie de vivre, her family background and, most of all, not with her dark brown skin. That same skin that called to him, made him want to feel it no matter how often he had already touched her. He loved the way the sun brought out the red undertones. The way the moon kissed it when they strolled the campus at night. How sweet it smelled, how warm and alive! He had never been happier. So when he phoned home to tell his mother he had met someone, and heard the excitement in her voice when she had asked him to bring his "friend" home with him for Thanksgiving, he had readily agreed.

It was on a cold November morning that Toni and Chuck were met at Logan Airport by the family's driver and deposited on the front portico of the Waters mansion in Beacon Hill. The four-story, red-brick home was as large as Toni's high school in New Orleans.

She thought it peculiar that Chuck would stand outside his own home and ring the bell. But he did, pressing the button like any common door-to-door salesman. She and Chuck were similarly attired in matching psychedelic dashikis. Her natural, wild and woolly, and free, flowed down her back, and Chuck had grown a goatee in the past few months. Each of them wore rose-colored granny glasses. No wonder his parents were taken aback after the butler, Carson, opened the door to them. It had been Chuck's suggestion to dress in that fashion. Toni had wanted to wear her best dress, a navy blue A-line in worsted wool. Regine Waters couldn't conceal her distaste as she nonetheless extended a hand in Toni's direction. Toni grasped the proffered hand, hoping that by her respectful behavior she would be able to dispel the woman's fears. Regine fairly yanked her inside the foyer. Toni had the fleeting feeling that Regine was trying to ensure that the neighbors didn't see her on their doorstep. Inside, Regine relinquished Toni's hand.

Regine was immaculately dressed in a Chanel skirt suit in pale blue. Her translucent, barely brown face was expertly made up. She had one-carat diamond studs in her earlobes, and a modest diamond necklace glittered about her swanlike neck. Her coal-black hair was done up in a bouffant the likes of which Toni hadn't seen since she had visited her maternal grandmother's farm in southern Louisiana and had found a beehive stuck in an ancient oak tree. Chuck's father, Charles, recovered first, giving Toni what could have passed for a genuine smile if it had only reached his light brown eyes. Chuck placed a supportive hand at the small of Toni's back. He knew his parents were erecting barriers between them and

Toni as they stood there assessing her appearance. It was at that moment that a horrible thought occurred to him: pure satisfaction. He was tickled to see the disappointment reflected in their dour faces. Enjoyed the nearly imperceptible anger building in Toni. She read them well. He knew she would. Knew she would take one look at them and recognize them for the elitist snobs they were. And he also knew, as always, she would rebel against the authority they thought it was their right to wield over her.

There were no warm hugs between son and parents. Not like the hearty welcome Toni would have gotten in the Shaw household upon returning from school for the holidays. Regine turned a stiff back on her and said in nasally tones, "Welcome to our home, young woman."

Charles the first nervously cleared his throat. He was a slightly built man in his late forties. His naturally wavy, dark brown hair was receding, and he wore horn-rimmed glasses. "Yes, come in. You must be tired after that long plane ride."

Chuck had to give it to her; Toni tried her best to please. "Oh, no, not at all," she said too brightly. "I'm excited to be here." Her dark brown eyes glittered with forced enthusiasm. And if Chuck was correct, hurt. His parents had wounded her with their lukewarm greeting. He kept vacillating between delight at seeing his parents horrified by Toni and his desire to protect her.

He grasped her hand as they followed his parents into the library, the informal room where they entertained friends and business associates alike.

The library was a large, book-lined room furnished with fine brown leather upholstered sofas and chairs that had been imported from Argentina. Regine and Charles sat on one of the sofas, and with a gesture of her delicate hand, Regine indicated that Toni and Chuck should sit on the twin sofa opposite her and Charles.

The interrogation commenced.

"Where are you from, ummm . . ."

"It's Antoinette, Mother," Chuck said calmly.

"Antoinette?" Regine said the name as though it was probably what all the ghetto people were calling their female children nowadays.

"My friends call me Toni. And I'm from New Orleans."

"What does your father do?" This from Charles the first.

"He's a car inspector for the Seaboard Coastline. He's been with them for more than twenty years." She was understandably proud of her father.

"I see," Regine said with a smug little smile. *More than twenty years as a car inspector for a railroad? The man must not have much formal education, if any.* "And what of your mother? Does she work for the railroad as well?"

Toni heard the taunting lilt to Regine's voice but chose to ignore it. She was hundreds of miles from home, dependent upon these people for shelter. This wasn't what she had expected, not from the description Chuck had given her. "They're strict disciplinarians," he had said. From that she had gleaned that they lived by the rules, as her parents did. As all good parents did. But there was an underlying meanness to these people that she wondered at. What had made them dislike her upon seeing her face?

Toni sat up straighter before replying. "My mother is a schoolteacher. She comes from a long line of schoolteachers. . . ."

"I suspect that's what you aspire to as well," Charles put in smoothly, leaning forward to look Toni in the eyes. "Being a teacher and returning to your quaint hometown. I suppose you miss small-town southern life, don't you?"

Toni smiled at him. "I miss my family and my hometown, yes. But I love going to school at Berkeley. And in answer to your question, no. I don't want to become a teacher, although it's a very honorable profession. I'm a writer."

Charles and Regine both smiled at her claim. Regine rose and walked over to a wall intercom unit, picked up the extension and spoke into it. "Yes, Cook. Would you have one of the girls bring a tray? Tea and refreshments." Returning to her seat, she looked at Toni. "A writer. Isn't that occupation somewhat like being an out-of-work actor? You never know where your next meal will come from. Many writers barely make a decent living writing. Did you know that?"

"I'm aware that it isn't going to be easy," Toni said, careful to keep the defensiveness she was feeling out of her tone. Aware that her body language could give away how uncomfortable she was at that moment, she sat with her spine erect, her hands folded on her lap.

It was clear to her who the powerhouse was in this marriage: Regine. Charles just sat there and let her run the show. "Perhaps you're counting on finding a rich husband," Regine continued as she sat down and crossed her slim legs. She laughed, a rather high-pitched cackle that sent chills down Toni's spine. "You wouldn't be the first female to go to college simply to snare a meal ticket."

"Mother!" Chuck angrily cried, getting to his feet. "You owe Toni an apology."

Charles the first, not bothering to rise, said sagely, "Now, son, your mother never accused the young woman of being a gold digger. Your mother was only illustrating her point that some young women go to college to find a husband."

"I'm sure that's true," Toni said. She had sized them up by now. Knew that she would be put on the hot seat for the entire weekend. Knew that no matter what she did, they would never like her. "I'm quite certain, in fact, that some tea-swilling, spoiled women who're raised to depend on Daddy and Mommy will be desperate enough to attend college in hopes of snaring a rich husband. But you don't have to worry about my being of that mind. Because, Mr. and Mrs. Waters, I have a mind and I know how to use it. I'd rather starve than depend on a man to give me everything." She ended with her gaze riveted to Regine Waters' face. Regine's golden-hued eyes narrowed. The little ghetto rat was calling her on the mat in her own home! Her nostrils flared in anger, and she had to breathe deeply before she once again had hold of her composure. She gained it, though, and smiled sweetly at the girl. "That's good to know."

The bitter harpy had much more in store for me before that *weekend was over!* Toni thought as the streetcar came to a halt near her home, which was three blocks over. She rose and got in line behind an elderly woman with a purple tam on her iron gray curls.

"Girl, you look *good*. What's your secret?" Natalie Winbush asked, bending over the table to lean close to Toni. Toni met her friend's eyes, an innocent expression in her own dark brown depths. "Why, Nat, I don't know what you're getting at! Are you saying I don't always look good?" She scribbled an amusing line or two on the title page of her latest novel, *Long Time Coming*, and signed her pen name, Serena Kincaid.

Handing the hardcover book back to Natalie, she said, "Speaking of looks, I like that cut on you. Makes you look like you did when we were at St. Mary's." The two had gone to high school together there in New Orleans more than thirty years ago. Natalie, a beauty, got married right out of high school and, with the aid of a devoted husband, managed to rear five children. Toni, on the other hand, had gone to college in California, gotten pregnant her freshman year and given birth to twin daughters. She had never gotten married. In spite of the disparate directions their lives had taken, she and Natalie always made it a priority to keep in touch.

Natalie humphed and whispered in Toni's ear, "Change the subject if you want to, but you know I'll get the truth out of you before long." She clasped her book to her bosom, straightened up and politely moved aside for the next impatient reader in line.

Toni laughed softly in Natalie's absence. It was just like eagle-eyed Natalie to notice the subtle improvements in her. Not just the physical changes such as a better-toned body due to power walking. Or the new short, tapered cut she had had her stylist give her the last time she had sat in her chair. No. Her whole attitude bespoke some deeper influence that had wrought this ebullience she was experiencing as of late.

"I just loved the way you described Ben's pursuit of Emma," the woman in front of her said as she handed Toni a copy of *Long Time Coming*. "Would you sign it to Doris?" She held another copy in her other hand. "This one's for my mother-in-law, Jean."

"I'm glad you enjoyed it," Toni thanked Doris. "It's about time an older woman got her own story, don't you think?"

Doris, who appeared to be in her early fifties, smiled. Dark eyes laughed in a warm brown face. "Absolutely! Who says a woman stops being sexy after forty, or fifty, or sixty for that matter!"

Toni laughed delightedly. "My mother's in her seventies, and you can't tell her she doesn't still have it."

"I heard *that!*" Doris guffawed, accepting the first book and handing Toni the second. She lowered her voice and said in conspiratorial tones, "I read the good parts to my husband." She gave a dramatic sigh. "The man was inspired by your words, girlfriend. And that's all I have to say on the subject."

Toni was laughing in earnest now. "It does my heart good to hear that, Doris."

Doris accepted the second book and stood smiling at Toni a moment. "If you keep writing them, I'll keep reading them."

"Well, I'm not thinking of quitting anytime soon," Toni assured her with a smile.

"You'd better not!" Doris joked as she moved on.

Toni spent the better part of two hours signing books, meeting and greeting new and old fans who had braved the inclement weather to support a hometown girl. The bookstore was so packed, Toni felt a little claustrophobic sitting behind the small table Madelyn had set up for her in the back of the store. Earlier in the evening, she had read passages from *Long Time Coming* to a rapt audience. Her parents had attended but had departed for home shortly after the reading. She kept scanning the room for Chuck. Last night, on the phone, he had hinted about being there—even though he was presently in Boston putting the final touches on a deal that would make Waters Foods the second-largest frozen foods manufacturer in the United States. Quite an accomplishment for a company he had practically built from the ground up and that he had nearly lost two years ago in an aggressive takeover bid.

The bookstore owner, Madelyn Simpson, came to stand next to Toni, her perfume wafting downward. "Toni, we're nearly done here. I'm going to go lock the door to discourage latecomers." She departed. Another customer stepped up to the table. Toni briefly glanced at her watch. It was nearly nine o'clock, closing time for The African Violet. She inwardly chided herself. She had been anxiously hoping Chuck would show up at the last minute, arms burdened by a dozen roses and with a beautiful smile on his face. If she wasn't mistaken, she had told him what time the signing would begin and end. Then, where was he?

She smiled as she accepted two books from a lone fan, a middle-aged gentleman of average height with salt-and-pepper hair and skin the color of sun-dried tobacco.

His clear brown eyes held an amused glimmer as he regarded her. "You look like you're expecting someone," he commented. "One's for my wife, Dana, and the other is for my daughter-in-law, Carmen."

"Aren't you thoughtful, buying books for them," Toni complimented him.

"I'm not being entirely altruistic," he avowed, warmly smiling into her upturned face. "Your books are a guilty pleasure for me. When I buy them I say they're for Dana, but I get into them just as much as she does."

Toni laughed softly at his admission. Men had often told her they enjoyed her books, but many of them didn't like others knowing they read romance novels. Closet readers. The thought amused her because she was of the opinion that a good book was a good book, no matter what genre it belonged to. It did sometimes irritate her that romance was seen as the stepchild of the publishing industry, even though the genre brought in nearly fifty percent of the revenue. However, she had learned to live with it years ago. She made a very comfortable living as a romance novelist. And although she wrote mysteries on the side under the pseudonym Julia Wentworth, she had no plans to give up romance.

After signing both books, Toni took another copy of *Long Time Coming* from the stack at her left. Looking up at the man, she said, "This is a gift from me to you. What's your name, sugar?" Her southern accent was clearly evident in her sensuous voice. Harmless flirting, really. A part of her personality she had never been able to suppress.

Surprised and delighted, the man broke into a wide grin. "It's Roman, Roman Duchamps."

Toni wrote, *Come out of the closet, Roman. It's your God-given right to read romance! Best Wishes, Serena Kincaid.*

Madelyn appeared and escorted Roman to the door with a sincere thank-you for attending the signing.

In Madelyn's absence, Toni rose and started collecting her signing giveaways—bookmarks, flyers, head shots—and putting them in her leather tote. As she was finishing, Madelyn returned and cleared her throat. She had a strangely serene smile on her pretty face. "Toni, there's a gentleman at the door who says he's a friend of yours."

Toni shouldered the tote and smoothed her smart pantsuit. "Oh, really?" She picked up her jacket and joined Madelyn. "By the way, Maddy, that last fellow amused me so much, I gave him a copy of the book. Please bill me for it."

"Don't be ridiculous, Toni. I can eat the cost this time. We nearly sold out!" Madelyn sincerely said. "I'm just so happy you decided to come. I know you don't do many signings. But the local fans have been behind me to get you in here for a while now."

It was true. For a long time, Toni had been content to simply write her Serena Kincaid novels and remain anonymous. However, many things had changed since 1997 when Chuck had finally bitten the bullet and faced her again after their tempestuous college romance that had produced their daughters, Georgette Danise and Briane Marie. The lengths Chuck had gone to in order to regain her trust had endeared him to her. She wasn't ready to admit that, though. Not by a long shot.

"Well, thank you, Maddy," Toni said. "I just thought it was time I got out and met the folks who've so generously supported me all these years."

The double glass doors came into view, and Toni paused in her steps as she got a good look at Chuck standing outside underneath the bookstore's awning, rubbing his arms against the cold and the dampness in the air. Her heart did a little flip-flop at the sight of him. She turned to Madelyn and gave her a warm hug. "Thanks again, Maddy. I had a good time."

As they drew apart, Madelyn said, "You're welcome." She cut her eyes in Chuck's direction. "You know him, then?"

"Oh, I've known him nearly all my life," Toni answered. She slipped into her jacket.

"Lucky you," Madelyn said, giving Chuck the once-over. "He's quite distinguished-looking.

"That, he is," Toni agreed as she walked to the door and pulled it open. A blustery wind hit her full in the face, bringing with it a sprinkling of rain. "I was beginning to think you were just pulling my leg when you said you were coming to town tonight."

Chuck was wearing a black overcoat and a black felt fedora. To Toni, he looked like the proverbial spy who had come in from the cold. "I was unavoidably detained," he said, his clipped Boston accent soft on his tongue tonight. His light brown eyes swept over her face as he bent to meet her mouth in a gentle kiss. "I missed you, too."

He looked up to see Madelyn smiling at the loving picture he and Toni made. Giving her a parting wave, he directed Toni to the waiting Lincoln Town Car he had hired for the duration of his stay in the city. Once he and Toni were wrapped in each other's arms on the backseat, he asked the driver to take them to the Hotel Monteleone, where he had reserved a suite.

Toni felt his enticing warmth envelope her. Their cheeks were touching as he told her of the difficulties he had encountered while trying to get there. "I would've been here sooner, but Daniel Youmans held out as long as he could. Being bullheaded. Thank God his advisers got him to see reason, and he went ahead and signed the contracts. Green Fields is now officially a subsidiary of Waters Foods."

Toni gave him a congratulatory buss on the cheek. "Good. Now you can devote all your spare time to me!"

Chuck squeezed her against his chest. "You are one greedy woman, Toni Shaw. So, you're actually admitting you missed me?"

"Kiss me again and test the waters," she challenged him saucily.

Chuck groaned softly, grasped her chin between finger and thumb and pulled her roughly toward his mouth. Toni grinned and met his lips.

Afterward, both a bit breathless, they fell back on the seat and just held hands. Toni cherished the feel of his big hand encircling her own. She wondered why she had resisted him for so long, now that she was reaping the benefits of his closeness. She knew why. It was a matter of trust. How could she trust her heart to a man who had abandoned her when she had needed him most?

Chuck enjoyed watching her. How her full lips appeared slightly puffed up after their kiss. The way her luscious brown skin cast an inner glow when she was happy, as if her spirit had turned on a light inside. *Toni's home now. Let's celebrate!* That was what he felt like doing whenever they were together, celebrating.

It had been a hard-won battle. Uphill all the way. He had expected it to be.

Five years ago, after losing his wife, Mariel, and son, Charles the third, in a freak accident, his guilt got the better of him, and he hired a detective agency to find Toni and the child she had told him about nearly twenty-five years earlier. He had done the unforgivable when Toni phoned him with the news: he had accused her of wanting something from him. He had known his words were a lie the moment they came out of his mouth. Toni had never wanted his money. Hell, she had left him when she was pregnant. If there was any time a young woman could extort money from a rich man, it was while she was carrying his child. No. He had behaved so abominably merely because he was scared. Scared to confess to Mariel that he had an illegitimate child out there. A child conceived in love while he was at Berkeley. And the mother was Toni Shaw.

Toni's career had just begun in college. After giving birth to Georgie and Bree, she stayed at Berkeley, earning a master's degree in literature—and an even bigger reputation as an activist who would go to any lengths to be heard. She made the national news in 1969 when she set fire to an American flag on the steps of the state capitol to protest the Vietnam War. She was arrested for that. It was illegal to desecrate the flag, the symbol of our great nation. After that, Toni went underground, and he didn't hear anything else about her for a long time—not until he was attending a party at a friend's home in Boston where, to his surprise, a mutual friend of his and Toni's was also a guest. Phil Rankin had pulled him aside and told him how Toni had redefined herself. She was now a serious writer whose first two books had garnered praise from critics and fans, alike. She was known as Serena Kincaid, and she and her daughters lived in the Pacific Heights area of San Francisco. Comfortable. That was Toni. She had made a comfortable life for herself and her daughters. It was then that it struck Chuck: daughters, Phil had said. Toni had apparently had a relationship with another man who had fathered her second daughter. But the first, Georgette, Phil had called her . . . Georgette was his, and by God he wanted to meet her! The desire blossomed in him and grew until it was a full-blown obsession. He had to see his daughter. He had no one else. Not really. There was his nephew, Benjamin, whom he had taken in when he was orphaned at sixteen. Back then it had seemed as if the Waterses were cursed. All that money and they had no protection from tragedy. First Benjamin's father drowned while sailing. Less than two years later, his mother lost her battle with cervical cancer. Then, only a few years following that loss, Mariel and Charlie were returning from a weekend at the lake, without Chuck, who had been bogged down with work as usual, and the brakes failed on the car. They collided with a tree and had both died at the scene of the accident.

Chuck fell into a downward spiral of self-pity. He immersed himself in work, making it his god since he had lost faith in the other one. For a short while rumors spread that he was dead, too. Stocks plummeted, and he had to put in an appearance at headquarters to squelch any further harm to the company. While he worked vigorously to preserve his birthright, his heart wasn't in it. What he wanted more than anything else was a family again. And he had a family . . . well, a daughter anyway. The only obstacle in his path was Toni, who would give him nothing when he contacted her and asked after Georgette. He stooped to employing private investigators who tailed Toni and took photos of her going about her everyday life, hoping to chance upon the moment when her daughters were with her. Catching Toni in an unguarded moment was difficult. However, as it turned out, the stack of photos provided Chuck with some insight. Toni and her daughters were an extremely close family. For three years, Chuck observed their lives through photographs. But by November 1997, he had endured enough of Toni's stubborn unwillingness to even talk with him, and he hired private investigator Clayton Knight to go to New Orleans, where Toni was living at the time, and get final and irrefutable proof that Georgette was his. Toni's father, James, had suffered a stroke some months earlier, and Toni had moved back home to help with his recovery.

From that point it wouldn't be an exaggeration to say all hell broke loose.

In his eagerness to finally meet his daughter, Chuck hadn't weighed the pros and cons of his interference in their lives. He sent Clayton Knight in search of answers, only to find more questions. Like, who in his camp would want to kill off his heirs and why? Clayton Knight had inadvertently led an assassin straight to his target: Georgette. By some miracle Clay was able to stop the would-be killer before he could harm Georgette, but from there a chase ensued that left them all emotional wrecks for months, until Anne Ballentine, who had been Chuck's personal assistant, was safely locked away in the Massachusetts State Prison for women. Yet another Waters family tragedy had occurred, for it came to light that Anne Ballentine was the birth mother of Chuck's nephew, Benjamin, the man slated to take over the reins when Chuck stepped down as head of Waters Foods. Chuck's head still spun whenever he thought about it.

Later, when things had settled down, Chuck went to Toni and sheepishly admitted he had had an ulterior motive when he sent Clay to New Orleans in search of Georgette: unfinished business with Toni. Toni had laughed in his face.

Now, as the car moved smoothly through New Orleans traffic on the way to the Hotel Monteleone, Chuck surreptitiously studied Toni's face as she sat looking peacefully out the window at the beauty of the city at night. His thoughts returned to that day in the greenhouse enclosure at Greenbriar, his family home. If anyone had told him he and Toni would be lovers three years later, he would have told them they were out of their minds.

He found her there alone with her nose inches away from a Peace rose, inhaling its delicately lovely essence. When she looked up and saw him, the expression in her eyes went from contentment to irritation. Toni blamed him for putting their daughters in danger, and it would be a long time before she forgave him for that.

He approached her cautiously, realizing that what he was about to say was going to shock and amaze her. So he started with some inane conversation opener, offering to cut some of the roses for her room since she apparently enjoyed them. Then things got tense when he brought up the fact that their daughters were reserving their acceptance of him into their lives until he and their mother worked out their differences. Toni surprised him by saying if that was the only obstacle, then he had her cooperation. But only for the sake of Georgie and Bree, who had made it clear to her that they wanted to get to know their father. Buoyed by the positive turn of events, Chuck then boldly confessed, "I'm falling in love with you all over again."

Toni stared at him a moment or two. "We had better get out of this enclosure. I think you could use some air."

Chuck wanted to grab her and shake her, she infuriated him so. But his right arm was in a sling due to being shot during a struggle with the gunman who had targeted Georgie. He could only gaze at her with woebegone eyes. "Don't be coy, Toni," he pleaded. "I've been honest with you. Can't you let go of the past long enough to embrace the future?"

"Oh, that's rich!" Toni cried, turning her back on him

and heading for the exit. "Coming from a man who ran from his past for thirty years!"

"That's good," Chuck encouraged her, hoping to open a dialogue of truth that would get them past the animosity and pent-up hurt both of them were experiencing. He knew he had been wrong. It was why he had sought them out. To make amends. Try, at least. Make up for the time they had lost—time that could never be recovered, for sure. But maybe, just maybe, he could atone for his sins, help make their lives better from this moment on. "Let it out," he told her. "Come on, Toni. Tell me how you really feel."

Toni continued toward the exit. He had to run in order to catch her before she got away. He grasped her by the arm, and she turned to look up at him, her eyes so sad. He almost let go of her when hit with the realization that he had put that pain in her eyes. "I'm forty-eight years old. I don't need this sort of nonsense in my life, Charles Waters."

Uh-oh. She never called him Charles unless she was seething.

"Let go of me."

He let go of her arm but blocked her exit. "I need you, Toni. I need this kind of nonsense in my life. What are you afraid of? Are you afraid I'll hurt you again?"

Toni gave him a steely look. "You'll never get the opportunity to hurt me again, Chuck. So stop dreaming."

"Kiss me, Toni."

"What?"

"I can't very well grab you and force myself on you with my arm in a sling," he joked. "Look, if you can kiss me and then tell me there's nothing left between us, I'll let it drop. Otherwise, I'm going to court you whether you like it or not. I'll show up on your doorstep in New Orleans every single day until you go out with me. And you know I'll do it. I'll pester you so badly, your parents

will toss you out the door into my arms to get rid of
me."

He got his kiss that day, but Toni wouldn't admit she
had been moved by it. Or him. And he kept his word.
He was in hot pursuit of her from the moment she went
back to New Orleans. His campaign was still under way.

Two

Georgie Shaw-Knight stood on the terrace of the loft in Jamaica Plain. The evening was shrouded in indigo. Sufficiently bundled up, she didn't seem to feel the cold. Inside, a Shemekia Copeland CD played. Shemekia's deep, powerful notes rose and fell with smooth fluidity. On the table in the dining room sat place settings for two and a good bottle of wine chilling. The smells from the kitchen were appetite-inducing. A little Cajun cooking. Her husband's favorite, jambalaya. She had had to phone her grandma Marie for the recipe. Georgie was a competent cook but not a seasoned one. And she wanted tonight to be special.

She hugged herself and smiled broadly, quelling the urge to jump up and down like a crazy woman. They had won the case! She had known from the beginning that they would, but it had still been the most agonizing case of her career.

Manfred Jones, a twenty-year veteran of the Cordone Refuse Company, which was contracted to collect garbage within the city limits for the city of Boston, fell while trying to climb onto the back of a garbage truck. He injured his coccyx and went to the emergency room only to be told that the Cordone Refuse Company had allowed his insurance to lapse. The hospital didn't refuse treatment but they had billed Manfred, who couldn't afford to pay. For as long as Manfred could remember, Cordone Refuse had been automatically deducting the cost of employee insurance benefits from his take-home pay once a month. Thinking there was an easily correctable error somewhere, Manfred took his saved pay stubs into the home office of Cordone Refuse. They told him his insurance had lapsed due to nonpayment. More than a year before, the company had sent out a form to its nearly six hundred employees stating that they now had the option to seek health insurance elsewhere. If they didn't return the form, Cordone Refuse would no longer include them in their employee health insurance plan. Manfred told them he had never received that form, and if he had, he most definitely would have returned it! Cordone Refuse offered their sincere sympathies but that was all. Manfred would have to pay his doctor bills himself.

Manfred returned to work but soon found that he suffered severe pain whenever he tried to hoist the garbage cans with his usual vigor. He went back to the home office and inquired about workmen's compensation. He had been hurt on the job. Wouldn't workmen's compensation take care of his bills? No, Cordone said. Since his insurance was invalid during the time of the accident, workmen's compensation didn't come into play.

That was when he went to Georgie.

And Georgie started digging.

"Something smells good."

Georgie turned and beamed at her man, her previous thoughts crowded out by new ones. *It's a sin for a man to look that good at the end of a long day.* She quickly closed and locked the terrace door, then ran and launched herself into his open arms.

At six-two and two hundred pounds, Clayton Knight was built to withstand the impact. Laughing, he wrapped her in his embrace, lifting her off the floor. "Damn, you smell better than that jambalaya," he said against her ear, his voice a sexy rumble. He set her back on the floor and bent his head to meet her mouth in a slow kiss. Georgie's hands were in his closely shorn hair as she went up on her toes, trying to compensate for their difference in height. Clay's hands were full of her waist-length braids as he firmly held her, giving her the succor she had been waiting for all day. And taking some for himself.

He hadn't bothered to remove his black duster. Still, Georgie could feel his warmth through her wool overcoat. Clay raised his head a moment to bury his face on the side of her fragrant neck. "You did it, baby. It's all over the news."

With her head thrown back to allow him full access to her neck, Georgie moaned and reached for the lapels of the duster. "I'm tickled pink. But right now all I want is you out of those clothes." She gazed up at him, her dark brown eyes drunk with passion. "I'll draw you a bath." She reluctantly let go of the lapels and began to turn out of Clay's embrace, but he held on to her.

"Not unless you're in it with me." Picking her up, he placed her across his shoulder and fairly ran with her to the master bedroom. Georgie laughed all the way.

A few minutes later they were sitting, facing each other in the sunken tub Clay had had installed as a second anniversary gift for Georgette. Candles were strategically placed around the room. The first year they were wed, he had observed how Georgette cherished a good soak, and was desirous of joining her in one of her favorite pastimes. So he had had the workmen tear down a wall, extend the size of the master bath and put in a tub that would accommodate both him and Georgette. The best investment he had ever made.

She was addictive, his Georgette. Like bottled water. You couldn't live without water, but did you really want to pay exorbitant prices for something that should be free? Before you knew it, though, you were throwing back six bottles of the stuff a day and it became habitual. Looking at Georgette now, he knew it was a sorry analogy. She was much more precious than water. But she did quench his thirst.

She had pinned up her braids to keep them from getting wet, and the hair piled on top of her head resembled Medusa's nest of snakes. "Know what I want to do now that Manfred Jones is a rich man?" she asked, grinning impishly.

"Stay home and make love to me all day and all night?"

"No. Leave the city. Maybe go to Daddy's cabin for the weekend. Just the two of us. And then make love to you all day and all night!"

Chuckling, Clay reached for her and pulled her closer to him. Soapy water escaped over the rim of the tub as Georgie's body touched his.

"You know, this is not a good venue for wrestling. Too slippery," she warned, giggling as he continued to pull her on top of him until the entire length of her body covered his.

"Wrestling wasn't what I had in mind," said her amorous husband.

Georgie kissed his chin. Peering into his hazel eyes, she murmured, "I'm getting chilled half out of the water like this."

Clay grasped her buttocks with both hands and pressed her close to his distended member. "I'll warm you up."

"Knew you had a plan," Georgie confidently said, and straddled him.

Later, as Clay lay watching Georgie sleep, he marveled at the fact that she loved him. Most of his formative years had been spent searching for affection. First from his parents. His father was a merchant marine and cared nothing for hearth and home. He went from one port to another, never satisfied with his surroundings, and ended up stabbed to death in a bar fight in Nepal. Clay and his mother had never even recovered the old man's body. His mother was an alcoholic. A disease that grew worse the longer she was married to his father. She was a needy woman married to a selfish man, a horrible match that neither of them took the time to evaluate. Clay supposed they had stayed married only because of him. If he had been given a say in the matter, he would have voted for a divorce.

After graduating from high school, he joined the Marine Corps. He was smart, could have gone to college, but back in 1977, and in his part of Boston, nobody cared enough to give a poor kid like him any solid career advice. He aced the Marine Corps entry exam, both physical and academic. He was a big kid even back then, already six-two and built like a stevedore. His father's genes had been good for something. He went into the Corps a raw recruit and seven years later came out a captain with the potential, if he had stayed, to become a major. Though that wasn't for him, he wasn't yet finished punishing himself. He became a Boston cop.

Clay was a good cop. The job suited his no-nonsense, by-the-rules personality that had been honed in the Marine Corps. Content to live his life being of service to others, making a difference in the city of Boston, he learned to expect nothing more. Especially not love, a special someone he could come home to. He coasted like that for some time—Until he met Josie and fell hard. She was an elementary schoolteacher. They met when he pulled community duty and went to her school to give a speech on stranger danger to her second-grade class. Clay was instantly smitten but would not ask her out. It

was Josie who came by the precinct a week later to thank
him for coming to her classroom and, as a calculated
afterthought, invited him for coffee.

Clay asked her to marry him six months later.

They had two good years together. A blissful two years
during which Clay finally knew what it felt like to be
loved, wholly loved, by someone. Two years that almost
lulled him into thinking that maybe Clayton Knight was
meant to be happy after all. Maybe the gods had smiled
on him. He began to build his dreams around Josie,
found himself thinking of having children for the first
time in his life. Just because his own parents had been
failures didn't mean he would be also. Josie, who loved
children, wanted a houseful. She was just waiting on him
to give the go-ahead.

He never did, though. That was one of the things he
regretted most. He never told Josie how much he wanted
a child with her. His reticence kept him from opening
up, completely sharing himself with her. He held back
until it was too late. Until a mugger's bullet took Josie
from him.

He reclined now, laying his head on a pillow, fluffing
it just right, settling in for the night. But his eyes were
still on Georgie's face. She was unaware of his fear of
losing her. He would not give voice to the dread he had
acquired upon the arrival of their second anniversary.
Not to Georgie or anyone else. To actually speak of it
might make it come true. But the theme played over and
over in his mind. He had lost Josie after two years. What
if it happened again?

Georgie suddenly opened her eyes and saw him watching her. "What are you doing still up? You're a growing
boy. You need your rest."

Clay gathered her in his arms and gently kissed her
forehead. "Just watching you sleep, babe. Go back to
sleep."

"If you insist," Georgie said in muffled tones, and closed her eyes. In a little while she was softly snoring. Clay reached up to run his fingers along her smooth brow. Shortly, his eyelids grew heavy, and he fell asleep with her in his arms.

Georgie awakened to find herself in the crook of her husband's arm. She rose slowly, not wanting to disturb him. It might be her imagination, but she could have sworn he was smiling in his sleep. The way his generous mouth curved upward at the corners, he must be dreaming about her. That was just the way she thought. Confidently. Georgie was confident in their love and in their weathering whatever storms life might visit upon them.

She backed away, her eyes trained on him. She still thought his dark brown skin was like chocolate left at room temperature: warm and inviting. It had been the first thought that had come into her mind when they had met three years ago in the lobby of the Hotel Le Pavillon in New Orleans.

In the bathroom, she splashed cold water on her face and dried it with a clean towel. This done, she gazed into the mirror and worked the matter out of the corners of her eyes with her forefinger. She had her mother's coloring: rich dark brown, with red undertones. Georgie had never thought of herself as beautiful, even though men seemed to contradict her opinion. She, instead, liked to think of herself as enduring. Her skin type rarely started to crinkle until late in the wearer's twilight years. And that was her goal, to grow old gracefully . . . with Clay.

As she brushed her teeth, she wondered what her baby sister was up to in Addis Ababa. The last time Bree had phoned—it was always next to impossible to catch up with her; therefore Georgie usually waited for Bree's call—she had said they were in the last week of on-location shooting. Bree rarely complained about the sometimes stark locations she must visit in her career as an actress. But there had been something in her tone that had made Georgie wonder at her state of mind. She knew Bree and Dominic were having problems because Dominic, whom Bree had been dating the last year and a half, had commitment issues he needed to work out. That much Georgie had been able to discern from the conversation she had had with Bree last week. Dominic wanted Bree to move in with him. Bree, like the other Shaw women, didn't live with a man unless she was married to him. All the years their mother was raising them, not one time did a favorite "uncle" even stay overnight, let alone several years with her. Toni didn't play that, and she had drummed it into her daughters as well. "Why buy the cow when you can get the milk for free?" It was a saying her own mother, Marie, had liked to quote when Toni was in her teens and all the boys were trying to turn her head with sweet words.

I'll call her, Georgie decided as she left the bathroom.

Passing through the bedroom, she glanced at Clay. He had rolled over but was sleeping soundly. She would go start his favorite breakfast of blueberry pancakes and sausages and see if the aroma roused him.

"Look what I found," Chuck said as he joined Toni at the breakfast table the next morning. In his hand was a section of the *Boston Globe.* Toni took the paper from him and read the article he was indicating: FERTILITY GODDESS STOLEN FROM MUSEUM, the headline read. Toni smiled as she quickly scanned the article and grinned even broader at Chuck when she was finished. Slapping the paper onto the tabletop, she regarded him with keen eyes. "He's stealing fertility gods from major museums around the world. And his collection is nearly complete."

"He?" Chuck asked. "You can't be sure it's one person behind the nefarious deeds." He had tried not to be drawn into Toni's latest "mind exercise," her term for the act of trying to figure out a mystery, but he had been caught up nonetheless. Especially now that the number of thefts totaled six. Toni had a theory that whoever was making off with the fertility gods was trying to complete a collection of seven gods and goddesses. There was a little-known North African myth that promised the birth of a special child if the seven fertility gods from various African nations were brought together. She hadn't arrived at this belief on her own. Since her days at Berkeley, Toni had maintained a network of friends, many of them scholars. Her good friend, Johnathan J. Crenshaw, retired University of California at Berkeley English professor, had a friend in the archaeology department who did some research in her off time that connected the previously stolen fertility gods to the myth. Whoever gathered all seven authentic gods and goddesses would be assured of conceiving or siring a godlike child. Supposedly, Makeba, the Queen of Sheba, had first used the spell to conceive Menelik I, the first King of Ethiopia and son of King Solomon. Did Toni actually believe the myth? No. But she did believe whoever was behind the thefts believed in it. And she could guess just where he would strike next. "The University of Miami," she told Chuck. "They've acquired the final idol. Dr. Wang says a young archaeologist who works there discovered the idol on a trip to Burundi several months ago. A Dr. Solange DuPree. She and Dr. Wang have been corresponding via e-mail. Dr. DuPree has agreed to let me have a look at the idol if I can come before the seventeenth, when she has to go out of the country."

"So you're going to Miami," Chuck deduced.

"I'm going to Miami," Toni confirmed.

Chuck let out an exasperated sigh and threw his cloth napkin onto his nearly empty plate. "Why are you getting so deeply involved in this, Toni?" He held her gaze, daring her to look away. "Are you going to write a book about it? What?"

"I might," Toni hedged.

"Don't lie, Toni," Chuck cried, rising. He glared at her. "You're only doing this to avoid the issue."

"What issue?" Toni said sharply. She didn't appreciate his tone of voice, even though she knew good and well to what he was referring. She maintained eye contact with him, feeling justified in her stance.

"We are the issue," Chuck said simply. Needing to burn off frustration, he paced the room. "We have been behaving like a couple of hot-blooded teenagers who have no place to consummate our passion. Hotel rooms, for God's sake! My cabin in the woods. And your place in San Francisco, on occasion. But that's not good enough for me." He met her eyes from across the room. "I don't want to do this anymore."

The muscles in Toni's stomach constricted painfully. For a moment, she felt the loss of him. Her mind fast-forwarded to what her life would be like without him—how her life had been before he came back into it. Busy, yes. Interesting, yes. But missing the bare essence of true contentment. He had given her that.

It took a great deal of strength to ask, "What do you mean?"

Chuck came to stand before her and spread his arms wide in a gesture of capitulation. "I give up, Toni. Are you kidding me, or are you being purposely obtuse?"

He knelt in front of her and clasped her hand in both

of his. Looking into her eyes, he said, "Marry me, Toni. Stop chasing after a myth and face up to reality. I love you. You love me. We should have been together years ago. Let's do it."

Relieved that he wasn't searching for just the right words to call off their affair, Toni felt the tension slide away. Running her free hand along his stubble-covered jaw, she smiled warmly. "Chuck, why do we need to get married? Everything's perfect just the way it is. . . ."

His lips set firmly, Chuck let go of her hand and rose. He had had enough of coddling this woman. He loved her. But she had to face up to some serious insecurities. He held her gaze. "Admit it, Toni Shaw, you're scared witless of looking like a fool to your friends and relatives. And that's why you won't marry me. You're so afraid that they're going to say, 'What happened to Toni? Marrying the man who abandoned her and those girls years ago. Whatever possessed her to stoop to such a thing?' Or . . . 'Toni must be desperate, taking a man back who dogged her like that. Poor thing.' Which is it? Are you afraid of looking foolish or desperate? Or both?"

Toni's heart rate had accelerated, and her breathing was shallow. He had definitely struck a nerve. Shame? Of course she felt shame for having an affair with him. She had vowed that she would never let him near her heart again and look at her! Copulating with him every chance she got. Reveling in the joy he brought her. Greedily accepting all the sweet adulation he laid at her feet, damn it! And why shouldn't she? She was a woman who felt deeply and needed the kind of stimulation he offered.

The ironic thing was, if their affair were public, she wouldn't have felt any shame. And if he were any other man on the face of the earth, their affair would be public. But because he was the man who had betrayed her, she felt compelled to hide it from family and friends.

And if he didn't understand that, then too bad!

Toni got to her feet and faced him. "What's the matter, Chuck? Being a kept man disturbs your Ivy League sensibilities?"

"That's old, Toni," Chuck told her. "You're not going to throw our backgrounds in my face anymore because I know for a fact that it doesn't bother you. What bothers you is to admit defeat. Admitting that you have fallen for me again, against your better judgment, I might add. You love me, Toni. You love me more than you did that Ivy League boy you met at Berkeley thirty-four years ago. And you know why? It's because I'm a man now, Toni. Not a boy who couldn't, or wouldn't, stand up to his parents. No one dictates my actions any longer. I don't give a damn what anyone else thinks. And I could give a rat's ass what my so-called friends are going to think when I marry you and take you to live at Greenbriar as my wife! So run if you want to. Run to Miami and confirm the existence of some artifact that is so important to you at the moment. More important than what we have here. Run to *Africa* if you have to, and collect all the fertility gods you need to in order to satisfy your lust for knowledge. Just know this, when you return I'll be here, and the 'issue' will still not be resolved!"

"I will," Toni shouted at him. "I'll go to Africa if that's where this leads me, because a man has never controlled my life and no man ever will!"

Chuck turned away in a huff. "I never thought I'd live to see the day when you would be afraid of anything. I guess everyone has his Waterloo."

Toni had no reply to that. She sat back down, tears misting her eyes. But she refused to let them fall, willing them to halt at once, before she turned into a weak-willed idiot and ran after him.

Chuck continued to the bedroom, where he shut the

door and went straight back to the bathroom. He was going to shower, dress and get the first plane back to Boston. October in Boston was warmer than the reception he had gotten in New Orleans on this ill-fated trip. Let her go to Miami. Let her go to Africa. Life was a circle, and she would end up right back here whether she knew it or not. What was between them wasn't going away. Ever.

"You're not always an angel, baby. And I ain't no saint," Keb' Mo's gritty, sexy voice came through the headphones of Bree's Sony Walkman. She was sitting in a director's chair on the set of *The Queen of Sheba,* waiting for her assistant, Paula, to come for her. Paula always raced across the large set to collect Bree when it was time to go before the cameras. Bree was dressed in a period costume, a flowing white gown made of the finest Egyptian cotton and bordered in gold. Her black hair was done in braids that spilled down her back. Although the apparel was cumbersome, Bree liked it because it put her in the right frame of mind for the role. In it, she felt like a queen.

While she listened to music, she was reading the script over again. She had already read it at least a dozen times, but she liked being well prepared. A professional, she hated flubbing her lines, or holding up production because of lack of preparedness. Since becoming an actress, she had found that nothing could get you blackballed in this business swifter than being a pain to work with. Laymen might think of movie making as being a wide-open profession, but in reality, it was a rather closed and tight-knit community of people. If you did something detrimental within the confines of the business, eventually everyone heard about it.

Bree felt a hand on her arm and looked up to find her aunt Margery smiling at her.

She turned off the Walkman and smiled back. "Hello, my queen," she said. Margery was portraying the mother of Bree's title character. Her costume was a purple wrap dress that clung to her slender, petite figure and was so tight, she had to take baby steps in order to get around while in it. "Hi, sweetie," Margery said, "I'm going to get out of this mummy's shroud. I just wanted to warn you: that man of yours is in a snit today. He's yelling at everybody!"

"He didn't yell at you, did he?" Bree inquired, frowning.

"Darling, he knows better than to raise his voice to me!" Margery assured her with an imperious toss of her braids. "It's the other cast and crew who've been subjected to his abuse today. What happened between you two?"

She tried to wiggle onto the director's chair next to Bree's but found that try as she might, the dress was not going to let her. She had no choice but to stand.

Bree rose out of deference to her aunt, who was actually her mother's best friend; but she had grown up calling Margery Devlin-Lincoln aunt, so she wasn't about to stop now. "We decided that our relationship would be strictly business from now on," Bree told her, her voice low so as not to be overheard by members of the crew. Gossip circulated like wildfire on the set. "He won't commit, and I won't move in with him until he does. We're at a stalemate, Auntie. So I told him it's over." Her light brown eyes held a sad expression in them. "And know what he did? He begged me to reconsider. Told me he loved me but he couldn't marry me. Then he went into how his parents divorced when he was five years old and he had gone through hell because of it. All the acrimony, high drama. He never saw his father again afterward. His mom remarried numerous times. Going from one toxic relationship to another." Bree groaned. "I don't know what else to do. I love him, but I'm not going to sit around waiting on him to get over thirty-five years of a bad childhood. Come on, either he's going to rise above his upbringing like the rest of us, or he'll remain stagnant and not grow as a person. I'm thirty-three. My Mommy Clock is ticking so loudly, it keeps me up nights."

Margery could only shake her head in commiseration. She had been there. Her husband, Daniel—actually, if you got technical, he was her second husband because she had married him twice—had cheated on her during the first go-round. She had thrown his sorry behind out and had to withstand a decade of begging and pleading from him before she was persuaded of his sincerity. Men could change their stripes. However, it took desire, strength and perseverance in order to effect those changes. Daniel was willing to do it, but was Dominic?

"You're really certain about leaving him?" Margery asked. "Because I was just as adamant when Daniel and I broke up. And look at us now."

They had been remarried since June 1997. The second time around had been the charm for them. Margery cocked her head to the side and sighed as she looked into her niece's lovely face. In some ways, Bree was more like her than Toni. Bree was sensitive and artistic. She wore her heart on her sleeve more often than not. And because she did, her heart had been broken several times by men she trusted before it was wise. "Don't throw the baby out with the bathwater yet," she advised Bree. "Dominic loves you, I know he does! Give him a little more time."

"How much time?" Bree plaintively asked.

"I can't tell you that," Margery admitted as she pulled Bree into her arms for a warm hug. "All I'm saying is, life isn't cut and dried. Dominic might be hesitant about a wedding and family today and tomorrow decide he can't go another day without putting a ring on your finger and a child in your womb. There are no absolutes. But I'll tell you this; if you're certain of Dominic's love, then you can afford to be generous awhile longer." Margery frowned and held Bree at arm's length, peering into her eyes. "But about that baby: If you're bent on becoming a mother, then do it. Don't wait on that, because you could wind up in my boat and never have the experience of giving birth."

Margery was grateful to have her adopted daughter, Alana, in her life. Alana was the child of Margery and Toni's friend Connie, who died suddenly when Alana was sixteen. Connie had indicated in her will that in the event of her death, she wanted her only child to be cared for by her best friends, Toni and Margery. The details of who would take full custody were to be left up to Toni and Margery. Since Toni had Georgie and Bree and Margery had no one, not even a husband, at the time because she had divorced Daniel, the women decided Alana would become Margery's adopted daughter. Alana was now wed to Nicolas Setera, an inspector with the San Francisco Police Department, and they had given her three grandchildren, a boy and twin daughters. Margery was truly blessed to have them.

She wouldn't have traded the experience for anything, except the return to health of her dear friend Connie. Still, she regretted never having given birth to her own child, Daniel's child.

Clasping both Bree's hands in her own, she said, "You're going to be a wonderful mother, Bree. Just like your mother before you."

At that moment Bree's assistant, Paula, sprinted up to her and between breaths announced, "They're ready for you now, Bree." She was a tiny girl of twenty-two with dark cinnamon skin and black eyes. Her short brown bangs lay limp against her sweaty brow. Bree immediately gave Margery's silken cheek a parting kiss and whispered, "I'll give some thought to what you said about me and Dominic."

Margery gave her hand a squeeze. "You do that."

"Nothing has pleased him all day," Paula said of Dominic as she and Bree hurried off. On the way they passed various members of cast and crew on the large soundstage. Some of the crew pushed wheeled racks laden with wardrobe, while others hurried about with clipboards in their hands, worried expressions on their faces and, it seemed, invisible wings on their feet. Just another day on the set. Except for Dominic's behavior. Dominic was normally known for his patience. He was a hard taskmaster, for sure. A perfectionist, he wanted things done right and done right the first time, not the second. But those who worked with him had come to expect that of him. He had gotten exceptional work out of them before, without being a dictator. Bree felt he should suspend the Mussolini act and get on with the job at hand.

When she arrived at the spot where the set had been staged to look like the bedchamber of Her Majesty the queen, Bree walked straight up to Dominic, who was giving directions to his lead cameraman, and said, "I'd like a word with you in private, please."

Eddie Perez, the cameraman, looked eager to give the two all the privacy they needed. Bree assumed Dominic had been particularly hard on Eddie that day.

Dominic dismissed Eddie with a curt nod of his head. Eddie hastily retreated, leaving the two of them alone.

Dominic was six feet tall to Bree's five-eight, so she had to tilt her head back a little in order to sternly look him in the eyes. "If you're angry at me, then take it out on me," she said in low tones. She moved even closer to him, until her cotton-sheathed thigh was touching his denim-clad one. Dominic bent his head to rest his mouth on her forehead, but he didn't kiss her. His lips simply touched her warm, jasmine-scented skin. "You're driving me crazy," he said hoarsely.

"That isn't my intent," Bree told him truthfully. "All I want to do is love you properly. Give you that home and family you've never had. Be the port in the storm for you, baby." The consummate actor, she straightened and took a step away from him, her golden-hued eyes smiling. "But now we have work to do, Mr. Director." She gave him a seductive smile and went to join her acting partner, Ward Stone, who was portraying King Solomon. Dominic, who had felt as if his head were about to explode from the stress only moments before he saw her, now relaxed and let go of the poisonous mood in which he had been. He watched her as she sauntered up to Ward and flashed a smile. God, he loved her so much it hurt. He turned away, the sight of her giving her time and attention to another man inspiring fierce jealousy. Besides, they had a film to shoot.

"You've been stirring that oatmeal without eating a bite of it for the past five minutes," Marie Shaw told her daughter Sunday morning. They were Catholic and had attended Mass earlier that morning. Now their pace was more leisurely.

Toni and her mother were alone in the kitchen since her father had already eaten and left the house to join his friend, G-Boy—real name Gerald Montrose, son of Gerald Montrose, Sr., hence G-Boy, as in Gerald's boy— for a round of golf at the formerly whites-only country club on the outskirts of town. Toni's father, James, and his cronies rarely missed a tee-off time, thinking it was their civic duty to represent the "old school" among the black New Orleanians.

"I haven't had a decent conversation over breakfast since your papa took up golf," Marie said, a twinkle in her chocolate brown eyes. Her hair was silver now. She had stopped coloring it when she turned seventy. By then she figured she had earned every silver strand up there. James proudly called her his silver fox. When Toni still didn't respond, Marie reached across the table and placed a gentle hand atop her daughter's.

Toni dropped her spoon and raised her eyes to her mother's. "When does life start getting easier, Mere? When do the choices we have to make come to us instantly and stop eating at us, causing us to second-guess ourselves?" She hesitated before adding, "I think I may have made a big mistake."

"With the man you've been seeing?" Marie asked, placing her fork on her plate and giving Toni her full attention.

Toni's brows arched in surprise. "I haven't told you I'm seeing anyone. . . ."

"You didn't have to, *mon petite*. I've known you all your life. Don't you think I'd recognize when you're happy or when you're sad? You've been happy the last few months. Flitting through life with nary a complaint on your lips. Remember those long phone conversations we used to have about The Pause? You were so apprehensive about that time of life. Thought you were in the midst of it when your periods started coming some months and not showing up others. You dreaded the onset of hot flashes and night sweats. Said if your mood started swinging more than it already did, you'd wind up in the crazy house. Remember that, *mon petite?* Then, suddenly, you stopped mentioning The Pause. You were cheerful, mellow at other times, and you invariably wore a smile or a contemplative look. . . ."

"You studying to become a detective, Mere? You're very observant these days."

Marie laughed shortly. "Just 'fess up, Antoinette Shaw, and tell me I'm right. It's a man. Who is he? Has Spencer come back for another go-round? Poor thing, doesn't he know when to call it quits?"

Toni had to laugh. Little did her mother know, the last time she had been out with Spencer Taylor, the jazz pianist she had dated off and on for nearly three years, was the same night Chuck had seduced her.

She could see it all as clear as day: Elian's, a posh San Francisco supper club, was alive with the sights, sounds, and smells of people having a good time. Jazz music, played by a five-member band, floated on the air, as did the tinkle of cutlery and glasses, and the slight buzzing sound of myriad voices being used all at once.

Toni and Spencer were seated at a table in the center of the dining room. They were nearly finished with their meal and had ordered coffee, neither of them desiring a rich dessert. Spencer's dark eyes had been lovingly caressing her face all night. He made her feel as if she were the most fascinating woman in the room. She didn't love him, knew she would never love him. But at their stage in life, love wasn't so important to either of them. They had laid the ground rules early on. Toni wanted a companion. A discreet lover. Spencer said he wanted the same, although he did admit to being more taken with her than she was with him, which made things a bit awkward sometimes. But as long as Spencer didn't pressure her into a commitment, Toni was content to maintain the status quo. Therefore, depending on their schedules, they were the fashionable couple out on the town two or three times a week. They had fun together. And that was enough.

That night, Toni was wearing a black sheath with a square collar that revealed her bosom to perfection. Her short black hair was combed away from her face, the silver streaks in it glittering. Pink diamond stud earrings were in her ears, and a single pear-shaped diamond in the same hue hung suspended around her neck. Spencer was especially debonair in his dark suit with crisp white collar and no tie. The dark skin glimpsed at his throat excited Toni. She knew how he liked her to undress him, and she always started with the buttons on his shirt. . . .

"Well, if it isn't my old friend, Spencer Taylor," a masculine voice said.

Toni drew her eyes away from Spencer's and peered up into the face of Charles Edward Waters. Her gaze narrowed. Apparently he hadn't gotten the message she had sent him with the emerald necklace he had messengered to her that afternoon. When she returned the necklace a few minutes later, she had written, *The answer is still no. I will not go out with you. Give it up, Chuck.* She had thought her play on words, up Chuck for upchuck, was pretty amusing. His being there proved he hadn't agreed.

Not knowing the dynamics of the relationship between Chuck and Toni, Spencer saw only Charles Edward Waters, a patron of the arts—a man who had, in fact, sponsored a concert in Boston that had helped propel him to the level of success he was presently enjoying. He owed Charles a debt of gratitude.

He rose and offered Chuck his hand. "It's a pleasure to see you again, Charles."

Toni didn't know what to do. Should she pretend she had never met Chuck before? She had not seen fit to drag her past with Chuck into her relationship with Spencer. There had been no press conferences after Chuck came back into their lives. So no one except the family knew that Chuck was the father of her daughters. Toni liked it that way. The fewer people who knew, the better. Chuck wanted to shout it from the rooftops, but out of respect for her, he had agreed to keep the news within the family unit.

"Let me introduce you to my lady," Spencer said proudly, gesturing to Toni.

Toni smiled at Chuck and surprised herself by saying, "We've met."

A nonplussed expression fleetingly ran across Spencer's features, but soon he was his amicable self again. "I didn't know," he said. Then, gentleman that he was, he offered Chuck a seat. "Please join us, Charles. I'd like to hear where you and Toni met."

"I'd be delighted," Chuck returned, his light brown eyes raking over Toni's face, causing her to blush against her will.

Chuck sat on Toni's right. Spencer was on her left, leaving her in the uncomfortable position of being in the middle of two men whom she had had as lovers.

The waiter who was servicing them that night appeared and asked if he could bring Chuck anything. Chuck ordered a coffee and settled down to tell Spencer where he and Toni had met.

"We were college sweethearts," he informed Spencer, sitting up straighter on his chair and defiantly looking Toni in the eyes as if to say, *Deny it!*

She calmly turned her head to smile at Spencer. "It was short-lived."

"But memorable," Chuck countered.

Toni leaned toward Spencer. "I was young and foolish."

"You were younger, but you've never been foolish, Toni," Chuck said. His smile had never left his face, though it was calculating. Toni wondered just how far he was prepared to go in order to make his point.

The waiter arrived with the coffee she and Spencer

had ordered before Chuck had horned in, and Chuck's as well. They remained silent until the waiter departed.

"Well," Spencer said, trying to keep the nervousness out of his voice, but failing. "It must be pleasant seeing each other after all these years."

"Oh, it is indeed," Chuck said. It was the tone of his voice, soft and filled with longing, that made her turn. His eyes pierced her soul with their intensity, and she couldn't look away. "I was wondering, Toni, how are your daughters, Georgette and Briane? Did their father ever come forward and claim them, or did he remain an abject coward?"

He wasn't telling Spencer anything he didn't already know. Toni had explained to Spencer about the circumstances surrounding the birth of her daughters. But with his bold words, Chuck was putting her on notice. He was finished beating around the bush and was declaring all-out war. No. He would not embarrass her in front of her erstwhile paramour, because that was how he thought of Spencer—as a former lover of Toni's, not as anyone to think of as the competition for her affections. She felt the confidence coming off him like waves of emotion that night. That was how he seduced her, with his intentions.

"The girls' father did step forward. It seems he actually grew a backbone after slithering like a snake on his belly for years." She said it without malice. A statement of facts. Just two long-lost friends making conversation.

Crossing her legs, she turned toward him. "And you, Chuck? What have you been doing with yourself? Still in the family business?"

"Someone had to continue the legacy," Chuck said, his tone light. He glanced at her long, smooth brown legs. And smiled.

With Toni's back to him, Spencer wasn't able to see her eyes in order to read her emotions, but he hadn't missed the covetous look Chuck had given his lady. Clearing his throat, Spencer said, "Are you meeting someone, Charles?"

Chuck raised his eyes from Toni's legs to regard Spencer. "As a matter of fact, I did come here to see someone. That business has been concluded, and I was on my way out when I spotted you and Toni." He paused to sample his coffee. Placing the cup back on the saucer, he said, "I must be going now, though."

He rose and bent to brush his lips against Toni's cheek, lingering a moment to inhale her essence. As he straightened up, he purposefully met Spencer's glare. "I don't know how she does it, Spencer, but Toni only gets more beautiful every time I see her. You're a lucky man."

The muscles worked in Spencer's jaw. "I'm well aware of that, Charles. Good night."

Chuck left without another word. But when Toni and Spencer called for the check, they found it had already been taken care of. Spencer thought of it as the final insult from the inexplicably bold Charles Edward Waters. Toni agreed with him on principle but was unable to suppress a secret delight at Chuck's interest. From that moment on it became increasingly difficult to ignore him.

On the drive home, Spencer asked Toni, point-blank, how well she knew Charles. Toni chose to tell him the whole truth. When he walked her to her door, he didn't try to kiss her good night or press her for a nightcap, which sometimes led to lovemaking. He did none of those things. He leaned close to her, clasped her hand in his and said, "I won't be back this time, Toni. I suppose I like my women a little less mysterious. I'm afraid the next revelation will be the death of me. Perhaps you and Charles are meant to be together after all."

Toni couldn't muster up regret as she watched him climb into his car and drive away. They had been way stations for each other. Only a stopping-off place. Toni had not found a home in his arms. And she hadn't been willing to pretend to find it in order to have a safe haven when the world turned mean. Apart, Spencer might find someone who would complement him.

She wished him well.

Three

"I'm sure Spencer would be pleased to know he's the source of such amusement," Marie said testily after watching her daughter laugh so hard, she had dissolved into tears. "Especially since you never really gave him a fair chance."

That wiped the grin off Toni's face.

She took a napkin and patted her wet cheeks with the corner of it. "Let's not get into your grand theory of the reason why I'm still single, Mere."

Marie sighed and picked up her coffee cup. The chicory-laced brew's aroma filled the air. She took a good sip, her eyes boring into her daughter's over the rim of the mug. Swallowing, she said, "I could never understand why you keep secrets from me, Antoinette; although I have a theory. . . ."

"Oh, you always have a theory," Toni said, sounding put upon. She ran long, tapered fingers through her short locks. A nervous habit. One that her mother, she realized in the midst of doing it, was very familiar with. Slamming her errant hand onto the tabletop, she cried, "All right, Mere! It's Chuck. I'm seeing Chuck."

"Seeing him, *mon petite?*" Marie asked, her tone inviting further elucidation.

"I'm dating him. . . ."

Marie sat for a moment, still as a statue, her mouth

slightly agape with surprise. She clamped her mouth shut. Blowing air between full lips, she asked, "For how long?"

"Nearly a year," Toni said quietly. Fifty-one, and she was worried about what her mother thought of her lover. She should be past that. Not the part about valuing her mother's opinion, because she loved and respected her mother above everyone else. What she should be past was feeling the need to sneak around and hide the identity of her lover from the people she cared about most. It was childish, and she felt ashamed for having done it.

Silence held sway for a few minutes.

Then Marie reached over, caressed Toni's hand and asked, "Do you love him, Antoinette?"

Meeting her mother's eyes, Toni said, "I love him, Mere."

"How much do you love him?" Marie wanted to know. She had to ask because she knew that if her only child had been hiding an affair with the father of her children for nearly a year, then there was a problem. Whether the problem was a perceived one or a real one, she hadn't figured out yet. She knew that by Toni's silence, Toni believed her choice would displease her family. Otherwise, the affair would have been out in the open. The question was, did Toni love Chuck enough to bear the public humiliation that would surely come when, or if, they announced their status as a couple?

"I'm ashamed to say, I love him so much I'm afraid of losing him," Toni frankly admitted. She shook her head and momentarily closed her eyes. Meeting her mother's warm brown gaze again, she continued, "I feel as if I've betrayed myself, Mere. All those years of hating him for what he did. Dreaming up ways to exact revenge. Making him pay for the pain he put me through. Now, it's like he's a whole different person. He's not the Chuck I knew back then. I look into his eyes sometimes, and I don't recognize the soul that's looking back at me. He's become this wonderful, strong, capable, vibrant human being. But there's something inside of me that doesn't want to own up to that fact. Some petty part of me that isn't finished living in the past still wants him to suffer for what he did."

Marie's heart went out to Toni. Hadn't her child been through enough because of Charles Edward Waters? A mother of twins at eighteen. No visible means of support from a spoiled rich boy who was too much of a coward to even accept culpability when Toni told him they had a child together. Yet, the experience had made her stronger, given her a mind-set that held her in good stead all the years she was raising her girls by herself.

The heart is a treacherous thing! Marie thought sadly.

"When I told you you had things to settle with Charles, I never expected I was right!" Marie said now. "After everyone was out of danger and he went on to become a part of the girls' lives, and you went back to your own life, I thought, 'And never the twain shall meet.' It was over between you two." She reassuringly squeezed Toni's hand and smiled at her. "You're well over the age of consent, my dear. If Charles is the man you want, then you should take him. Don't worry about what your family or friends are going to think; because when it comes down to it, he's the one you'll be sleeping next to every night . . . if you're lucky!"

Astonished, Toni cried, "Mere! Do you really mean that?" She didn't give her mother time to reply, however, as she went on excitedly, "What about Papa? He said that if Chuck ever crossed this threshold, he'd shoot him where he stood!"

Marie chuckled softly, her eyes sparkling at the memory. "He did, didn't he? And he meant it thirty years ago when you came home with infant daughters! Hell, I could have shot Charles then myself! But a lot of things have changed since then. Among them, apparently, Charles. Life has a way of seasoning a person, *mon petite*. Of course, some people just get worse. But, sometimes, they actually do progress and climb another rung up the evolutionary ladder."

Toni got up and moved around the table to hug her mother. "Oh, Mere, that's a load off my mind."

"And your heart?" Marie asked knowingly.

Toni kissed her mother's forehead and hugged her tighter. "And my heart."

What's her problem? Chuck asked himself as he approached the two-mile mark while swimming laps in the heated pool at Greenbriar. He had gone back home to an empty house. And now that the merger with Green Fields had gone through, he wasn't needed at headquarters for a while. He had been "retired" for several months. However, his nephew, Ben, who was now CEO of Waters Foods, was forever consulting with him for one thing or another. Chuck was beginning to suspect Ben only called on him to help keep his mind occupied. Chuck had been a veritable workaholic before deciding to hand over the reins to Ben. Of course, his plans for retirement hadn't materialized yet because they all hinged on one thing: winning Toni. He had single-mindedly gone after her, with both barrels blazing! He smiled, just thinking about the early days of their courtship.

Pulling himself out of the water, he sat on the edge of the pool a moment, getting his breath. He was in better shape now than he was three years ago when he had been a desk jockey. Today he lifted weights, courtesy of his health-conscious son-in-law, Clay, who had put him through his paces in the gym. Weight training, laps in the pool and jogging a couple of miles around the estate, Chuck staggered the exercises so he wouldn't get bored.

At five-eleven he had good muscle tone: well-shaped biceps and calves women enjoyed ogling whenever he wore shorts on the golf course, arms Toni didn't mind having around her, and a chest she could appreciate. But it wasn't enough. And he knew why. No matter how many times he apologized to that woman, it would never be enough! *Get a grip, Charles.*

He rose, wondering how he had gone from congratulating himself on his physique to grousing about Toni . . . again!

Because he loved her. And he missed her.

The indoor pool made it possible for him to swim year-round. Swimming was his favorite sport. It made him feel limber and weightless, as if his body was a malleable instrument that he could mold to his liking. On land, he noticed his physical limitations more. He wasn't one to pull the wool over his own eyes. Time was running out . . . fast.

He had been the dutiful son. His first marriage was good, even though he knew he could have forgone business and spent more time with Mariel. And he had been a loving father to Charles III . . . Charlie. He experienced no guilt regarding Charlie. He had loved him with his whole heart, bestowing on him the extra love he felt he would never get the chance to show the child he and Toni had brought into the world.

As he entered his suite of rooms, the phone rang. He waited for Carson to get it. Carson was getting so persnickety about his duties that whenever anyone performed a task assigned to him, he sulked. Chuck humored the elderly manservant. Carson had been loyal to the family for more than fifty years. The least Chuck could do was allow him some dignity in his waning years. The extension buzzed in the room now, and he strolled over to the desk to answer it, dripping water and drying his hair with a plush white towel as he did so. "Hello."

"Miss Georgie is on the line, sir," Carson said in his cultured Boston accent.

"Daddy!" Georgie said. She didn't stand on ceremony. "Thanks, Carson old buddy!"

"Miss," Carson acknowledged, and was gone. He might not show much enthusiasm, but he was quite fond of Georgette and her sister, Briane.

"Daddy," Georgie said again. "What's this about Mom going to Miami? What happened between you two?"

"How did you know she's going to Miami?"

"She phoned me and told me all about the fertility gods and her hypothesis that the thieves will strike next at the University of Miami. She's leaving for Miami tomorrow morning. I thought you were going to convince her to marry you and you two would be on your way to some desert isle by now."

"You know your mother, stubborn," Chuck said, his voice soft and more relaxed than he had previously felt. Georgie had that effect on him.

He had taken Georgie and Bree into his confidence when he had decided that Toni would be his within the year. That was two years ago. They were in his corner all the way—providing advice when needed, and encouragement when Toni left him in the cold, as with recent events. The girls let their mother believe they knew nothing of her relationship with their father. However, they were secretly wishing for a wedding.

"I can't understand it," Georgie went on. "I know she loves you! I've seen the way she's blossomed the last few months. You must be doing something right!"

"Baby," her father said wearily, "I've stopped trying to understand your mother. I just go with the flow. It's easier that way, and much safer."

Georgie laughed. "Know what? You ought to get on a plane and go to Miami, too. Meet her there and see how she likes it. She retreats, you advance."

"That's your strategy, huh?" Chuck asked. "You didn't hear her. She as much as told me to stay out of her life. No man has ever controlled her, she said. And no man ever will."

Georgie guffawed. "That's my mother! But listen, when have you ever let her attitude chase you away? You're nearing victory, Daddy; I can feel it! Don't let her think that she's won this battle. You know how aggressive she can be, how competitive. She'll lose the only man she's ever loved over her need to conquer you!"

"If she really loved me, she wouldn't mind being conquered by me," Chuck reasoned.

"Do I hear logic in your tone of voice?" Georgie joked. "This isn't a war that will be won with logic, Daddy. Logically, Mom shouldn't be giving you the time of day. But she's drawn to you against her will. Work on that. Make her suffer with the want of you. Go to Miami. Bug the heck out of her. Charm her clothes off!"

This time it was Chuck who laughed. "You're too much, Georgette Danise."

"That's what my husband tells me," his saucy daughter replied. "And speaking of husbands, mine is crooking a finger at me right now. Good night, Daddy. I love you! Go to Miami!"

"Good night, sweetheart. I love you, too. And I just might."

After Chuck hung up the phone, he strolled into the walk-in closet to pick out a change of clothing. It was eight-fifteen on a Monday night. With a few phone calls, he could be in Miami in a few hours. If he really wanted to be.

* * *

Because of her previously hectic schedule, Georgie had been missing her Monday night judo classes at the dojo of a friend. So, she had learned to improvise a series of exercises at home in order to stay in shape for the time she would be able to resume her classes.

Tonight, wearing only the pants of the pajamalike *judogi* and a tank top, she went about the *atemiwaza*, which were techniques used to kick and strike your opponent. As always, all her concentration was on the task at hand. Breathing deeply, enjoying the feel of the sweat trickling down her face, she kicked at an unseen assailant, her movements sharp and precise. At five-eight and one hundred and forty pounds, she made a formidable sight going through the motions.

Unseen, Clay watched from the doorway. He was supposed to be watching a football game, but he thought his wife made a more enticing figure with her gleaming skin, determined eyes and that strong, fit body moving with such fluid power.

Georgie threw punches, holding nothing back. She knew that if she failed to follow through in practice, if the time should ever come when she would truly need her skills, she wouldn't be properly prepared. Her best friend, Sammy Chan, a jujitsu master, had taught her that. Always give your best. Sammy adopted the teachings of the founder of judo, Jigoro Kano, whose slogan was, "Maximum efficiency with minimum effort." Therefore, Georgie's exercises were performed in such a graceful fashion that they resembled a dance. She made it appear effortless.

To Clay, she was as beautiful as any ballerina who had ever stepped on a stage. He entered the room. He was barefoot, so not even the sound of his ever-present cowboy boots on the hardwood floor would alert Georgie to his presence. Nonetheless, she looked up at him as he approached. He didn't know how she did it. But he could never sneak up on her. It was as if she had a sixth sense.

Georgie smiled and continued with the exercises, throwing punches at her imaginary assailant's head, ducking when the apparition returned the favor, and executing kicks that would put the average man out of commission for a week.

She halted for a moment when Clay stepped onto the mat. Breathing hard, she faced him. The both of them bowed briefly, and Clay, the aggressor, threw a punch at Georgie's solar plexus, which she blocked and quickly moved in to adeptly trip him. Clay went down hard on the mat but was up in an instant.

They faced each other again, circling, looking for the advantage. "Lucky shot," Clay said, smiling.

"If you say so," Georgie replied. She didn't like engaging in conversation while in combat. She liked to maintain concentration, and talking wasn't conducive to good concentration. Clay knew that about her and played on her weaknesses.

"You're damned sexy when you sweat," he said. And just as he noted a softening in her eyes, he struck, pushing her down onto the mat and straddling her. His weight fully on top of her, he said, "Let's hope your next opponent doesn't know you fall for flattery every time." And then he kissed her.

Georgie drew her lips from his and looked into his eyes. She pushed him onto his back and climbed on top. Languidly rotating her neck as if to get the kinks out of it, she stretched like a cat, then peered down at him. He was wearing jeans, and she felt his erection through them. She patted him there and smiled. "My, my, aren't we horny tonight?"

Clay had gotten comfortable with one hand behind his head as he lazily regarded her.

"Baby, you know you turn me on whenever you don that suit."

Georgie reached down and undid the top button on his button-fly jeans. Then she ran her right hand up and under his T-shirt until her palm was flat against his chest. She felt the thump of his strong heart. The steady rhythm soothed and excited her. He was a warm and vibrant man, her husband. Steady as a rock. And, now, as hard as one, too.

Her nipples grew tumescent at the thought of his hands, his mouth, on them and then, as if she had willed it, Clay gently pressed his palms against the cloth of her top, exciting the nubs even more. He pulled the edges of her top out of the waistband of her pants. "Let's see what surprises my Georgette has in store for me tonight," he said. Pulling up the top, he saw she was wearing a white support bra. He tugged at the clasps at the front of the bra until they came apart. The separated parts fell open and Georgie's full, creamy brown breasts spilled into his eager hands. Clay raised up and, pulling Georgie toward him, bent his head to suckle one breast until she moaned loudly. "Don't be shy, baby. Just let me know what feels good to you."

Georgie felt as if her eyes would roll back in her head with ecstasy. Feel good? Everything he did to her felt good when they made love. From the very beginning Clay had made it his business to become an expert on Georgette.

"Free me, baby, it's getting a little close in there."

Georgie moved down a bit on her husband's thighs so that she could reach the remaining buttons on his jeans. After undoing them, she took the waistband of his briefs and pulled it down. Then she reached in and held him a moment in her warm hand. Clay was busy untying the string at the waist of her pants. "I hate these draw-strings," he complained. His fingers simply weren't nimble enough to do the deed quickly enough for him. Giving up, he kissed her between her breasts. "You do the honors while I get out of these jeans."

He rose with care and peeled the jeans from his long legs and thighs. Off came the T-shirt and the briefs. Georgie had risen but had barely gotten the drawstring untied because she was so busy admiring her husband's dark, muscular body. His thighs were powerfully built from all the lunges he did. Chestnut brown all over. Darker in the place that was steadily growing. His chest was smooth and hard, the nipples dark brown and at this moment standing at attention just as hers were.

Clay enjoyed the expression on his wife's face. Each time she saw him in his birthday suit, it appeared as if she were seeing him for the first time. A look of astonishment coupled with breathless anticipation crossed her face. He saw, with satisfaction, that she had managed to get the drawstring untied. He stepped forward and stayed her hand as she began pulling down the pants of the judogi. "Let me," he said, as he walked behind her and grasped the waistbands of both her pants and her panties and slowly pulled them down. Georgie stepped out of them, and Clay pressed his warm body against hers from behind, pulling her into his arms, his hardened penis against her buttocks. Georgie closed her eyes and gave herself over to his sensual ministrations. In Clay's hands, she knew two things: she was safe, and she was as close to heaven as she would ever get on this earth!

Clay nuzzled the side of her neck, then trailed kisses down her spine, ending with a kiss to each of her beautifully round, lush buttocks. On his knees, he turned her around to face him, and then he did penance as any grateful man might. He ran his tongue along her inner thigh, the faint taste of salt on her skin due to perspiration. He didn't let that deter him, though. He loved the taste of her skin and had been known to kiss her tears away. And they were saltier than her skin was at this moment.

Georgie moaned softly as Clay manipulated her navel with his tongue. Before she had met him, she had no idea a navel could be an erogenous zone. He had charted places on her body that no other man had ever touched. And now she was glad of her lack of past extensive sexual experiences. She could indulge in delights with her mate for life—the only man who had ever brought her to such orgasmic heights.

"Come a bit closer, baby," Clay murmured as he grabbed her derriere with both hands and coaxed her forward. He buried his face in her womanhood, his tongue flicking out to probe deeper into her warm center.

"Oh . . . ," Georgie cried as her legs quivered. She tried to push him away, but knew that was only part of the game between them. She wanted it as much as he wanted to give it, and they both knew it. It wasn't something the good Catholic girl in her could reconcile, even if it was her own husband who was doing it. Some part of her thought it was devilishly sinful.

Clay glanced up into her face, saw the pain of indecision and the mounting joy residing there, too. He continued until he had brought her to the peak and she had fallen into his arms on the mat, spent and weak kneed. He held her a moment. Then he felt her reach for him, her hands doing wanton things to him that brought his manhood immediately back to its full size. She fell onto her back, her legs open to him, and he took his time pushing inside of her where he claimed her tight sweetness, reveling in her soft gasps of pleasure.

Georgie bucked beneath him, meeting his thrusts with enthusiasm, until Clay suddenly pulled her hard against his chest, breasts meeting muscle, and groaned deeply. "Oh, God, oh, God." He spilled his seed inside of her and held her close until the both of them stopped trembling. Finally, they lay on the mat with Georgie's head in the crook of his arm. The room was silent except for their breathing and the ticking of the clock on the wall. Georgie turned her back to him, and they lay in spoon fashion. She was in no rush to hurry to the bathroom. She wanted his seed to fill her with their child. A child of their love. A child they had been hoping for since their first wedding anniversary.

Early Tuesday morning, using her key, Dr. Solange Du-Pree entered the three-story brick building that housed the archaeology department at the University of Miami. A petite, attractive Haitian-American woman of thirty-two, she was dressed in casual clothing of khaki slacks and a white T-shirt with brown leather boots encasing her small feet. No sweater, as it was already seventy degrees in the city and would be eighty by noon. They had been experiencing an unseasonable warming trend in the South. Normally, in October, the high would be around seventy-two degrees.

The key felt peculiar in the lock. It wouldn't turn easily, but with some effort, she finally got it to turn, and she was inside the darkened building. Placing the heavy tote bag she carried on the floor inside the door, she reached for the familiar spot where she had thrown the switch every morning for the past four years and found the cover plate was wet. She clicked on the light anyway, walked fully into the room, then examined the cover plate. If she wasn't mistaken, that already thickening, red-brown liquid was blood. She examined the hand that had touched it and had to resist wiping it off on her pant leg.

Alarmed now, she thought to exit the way she had come and go to a neighboring building for help. Then she heard a moan. A human in trouble, somewhere deeper in the dark recesses of the building. Her mind raced. The only person it could be was Jack Cairns, the security guard. Jack had been the midnight-to-seven shift guard ever since she had been at the university. If it was Jack making those sounds, she had no choice but to investigate further. "Jack?"

Solange walked down the corridor, slowly passing the first three doors, which were closed, realizing that there was no way she was hearing that voice so clearly through a shut door. She stopped before she came upon the fourth, which was hanging open. She cautiously moved nearer to the open door. "Jack?"

"It's me, Dr. DuPree," Jack said weakly from inside the open door of the office. *Her office.* Emboldened by the desire to help a friend, Solange quickly stepped through the threshold and momentarily froze when she saw the carnage that greeted her: overturned filing cabinets, her desk's drawers all removed, the contents strewn about the floor. Then her gaze fell on Jack. Sprawled on the floor next to the desk, his head a bloody mess, he looked up at her, his brown eyes clouded with pain.

She knelt beside him, her two years of medical school coming to the fore. He tried to sit up, but she coaxed him back into a prone position. "Don't try to sit up, Jack. You could have internal injuries." She drew her attention away from Jack long enough to survey the room, looking for the telephone that was usually on her desk. She saw it lying near the foot of the desk. It had been ripped out of the wall. Then she remembered: she had a cell phone in her tote. Rising, she said, "I'm going to phone for help, Jack. Lie still."

Ten minutes later, the police arrived, followed by a team of paramedics. Jack was carried out on a stretcher with Solange solemnly following the procession out the door. She felt strong fingers on her upper arm just as she stepped down onto the sidewalk with the intention of accompanying Jack all the way to the waiting ambulance. Peering up, and up, into the face of a tall, dark-skinned man with eyes the color of burnt caramel, she frowned. "Let me pass."

"Dr. DuPree, you can't do the security guard any good by getting in the way. Let the paramedics do their job." He had a deep, resonant voice with a distinct British accent. She had not expected that, although in Miami there was a generous mixture of cultures. Dressed in an expensive dark suit and white, long-sleeve shirt with gold cuff links that sparkled at his wrists and wearing highly polished wing tips, he appeared to be a bank president. Not a cop, which she assumed he was.

His short, natural black hair was combed away from a square-chinned, clean-shaven face. "Do you have any idea who would toss your office?" he asked her as he pulled her aside. They stood on the grassy slope between the back door of the building and the sidewalk. "Any rivals who'd like to get their hands on your work?"

Solange's attention was on the paramedics as they transferred Jack to the back of the ambulance. When they closed the door, she looked up at the man next to her. "My work is not of a sensitive nature. I'm presently doing research on the ancient African kingdom of Kush. And, besides, I don't keep anything of value in my office. All artifacts are locked in storage cells located in the basement."

"Information?" the man inquired. Squinting in the bright Miami sunshine, he leaned in. "Are you working on anything that others have shown an interest in?"

His eyes bored into hers as if by their determined expression he could get information out of her that she normally might not be willing to give him. He enjoyed the view while he waited: She was tiny, maybe five-four at best. Her brown skin looked as if she spent a lot of time outdoors. He could detect her tan since he was a sun worshipper himself. He hailed from Guyana, that ill-fated island that was known more for the Jim Jones atrocity than for its natural beauty. After Guyana, he had gone to London where he was adopted by a British couple who didn't know how to show affection the way most parents did. Both university professors, they gave him love in the form of education. He recognized in the comely doctor a kindred spirit. He, too, had had to prove his self-worth in order to get where he was. Of course, that was then. Today, he didn't have to prove anything to anybody.

"I've been corresponding with Dr. Victor Wang, a colleague from the University of California, concerning a statue I discovered while in Burundi a short while ago. . . ."

His brows arched with interest. "What sort of statue?"

"An unnamed fertility goddess. It stands about eighteen inches. Made of some type of wood. Actually, the department hasn't classified it yet. We don't know how old it is, or if it has any intrinsic worth. . . ."

"But Dr. Wang believes you've chanced upon something?"

"Yes. He told me about an obscure myth that strangely coincides with the thefts of six other fertility figures. Dr. Wang believes the figure we're in possession of completes a set."

The man suddenly tensed. "Dr. DuPree, was there anything in your office that might indicate the location of the fertility goddess?"

A look of horror spread over Solange's face. "The log to the storage cells was in my desk drawer. I, regrettably, am in charge of inventorying the cells periodically."

Not caring about propriety, the stranger grabbed the doctor by the hand and said with urgency, "Take me to your storage room immediately, Doctor!"

Solange led him, both of them sprinting now, back into the building and to a set of stairs adjacent to the entrance. They descended two flights. "I don't have my keys." Solange shot a warning over her shoulder as they ran. "We won't be able to get into the cells."

"If I'm right, Doctor, we won't need keys," her companion said grimly.

In the dank, dark, stale-smelling basement, Solange led him along the corridor until they reached the end of the hall. She stepped on broken glass three feet from the storage cell door. The stranger stepped in front of her, placing her protectively behind him as he withdrew a blue-steel automatic weapon from a shoulder holster Solange hadn't even noticed until now. "Wait here," he told her.

He entered the darkened room with his weapon drawn. The large room, characterized by steel mesh cages the size of closets was empty, but the locks on each of the cages had been broken off. And none too neatly. He suspected a crowbar had been used to do the deed. "Come on in, Doctor," he called. He walked back to the entrance and switched on the overhead light.

Gingerly stepping over papers and more broken glass, Solange came into the room. She went straight to the seventh cell, entering it. Going to the back of the small area, she bent and rapped on the wooden floor. The sound was hollow. Pushing the spot with her thumb, a section of the wood popped up as if on a hinge. A secret compartment. She reached in and removed a twenty-inch-long box. Smiling, she turned to tell the detective that the fertility goddess was safe, but he wasn't there.

Shaken to the core, and unwilling to let the goddess out of her sight again, she clutched the box to her chest and went back upstairs.

As she entered the first-floor corridor, someone shouted her name. "Dr. DuPree?"

A Hispanic man of average height and weight hurried to her side. "Dr. DuPree, isn't it?" He extended a hand. "I'm Detective Raul Montez of the Miami Police Department. I'll be investigating the break-in. I'd like to ask you a few questions if I may."

Four

Toni had been in the backs of cabs in cities all over the world, but she didn't believe she had ever been more terrified than she was right now. The driver drove like a bat out of hell. He didn't know the purpose of a turn signal. He followed cars in front of him so closely that he had been forced to brake sharply often to avoid rear-ending them, causing Toni's feet to be planted on the back of the driver's seat in order to brace herself for the impending impact.

Reggae music blasted from the speakers, and he was trying to talk over it. "Yo furst time in Miami, heh? You need a guide, lady. Purty lady like you needs a man to show her 'round. Won't charge much neither. . . ."

Toni's mouth was agape as she watched the car approaching a busy intersection. The light was yellow and due to turn red any second. "Light!" she screamed.

The driver put his foot down hard on the accelerator, and Toni was thrown backward on the seat. "Dat was close," he said with obvious relief.

Toni could have grabbed him by the throat and throttled him, she was so angry.

"Look!" she shouted—had to in order to be heard over the music. "That's the Marriott ahead on the right."

He was up to fifty-five in a forty-mile-per-hour zone. "Why didn't you tell me dat was where you goin'?" He

cut the wheel sharply to the right and nearly sideswiped
a tractor-trailer. The driver of the truck blasted its horn
and shot him the bird. But the taxi driver was in the
turning lane now and was grinning to beat the band,
and still bobbing his head to the reggae.

Screeching to a halt in front of the Marriott, burning
rubber as he did so, he looked back at his ashen passen-
ger and said, "We here, lady. Dat'll be ten-fifty."

Toni threw a ten and a five across the seat and hastily
abandoned the cab, dragging her bags with her. Standing
on slightly wobbly legs, she straightened to her full height
of five-eight and took inventory. Yeah, she was still intact.
While he dug in his pocket for change, Toni said, "Oh,
keep the change, baby; and don't take this the wrong
way, but whoever gave you a driver's license should be
committed. And you right alongside him!"

The driver threw back his dreadlocked head in laughter. "You one funny lady!"

With that, he put the car in gear and sped off, leaving
a plume of exhaust in his wake.

Coughing, Toni resisted the urge to fall on her knees
and kiss the ground and turned toward the entrance of
the Marriott. It was a beautiful sunlit day. A breeze was
coming in off the gulf, and she was alive! Glancing down
at her watch, she saw that it was eleven-sixteen. She had
an appointment with Dr. DuPree at twelve forty-five. She
had just enough time to go upstairs, freshen up, get another cab—which she wasn't looking forward to—and
meet the doctor at her office on campus.

The lobby was fairly crowded with tourists and business
people alike. Toni walked up to the front desk and gave
the clerk, a young African-American man with a neat,
trimmed moustache over full lips, her name. He smiled
a greeting. "Miss Shaw. It's a pleasure. We'll have you all
set in no time."

His name tag read Will Monroe.

In under five minutes, Will had placed a key in her palm and was directing her to the bank of elevators off the lobby.

Toni hurried toward them. She could use a drink of water. Fighting for her life in the back of a gypsy cab was thirsty work! She knew the Marriott supplied bottled water for their guests since she often frequented the chain in her travels.

She was standing, alone, in front of the closed door of an elevator, her eyes downcast, when a man came to stand beside her. He had on a pair of highly polished, brown wing tips, and his expensive slacks had cuffs in them. For a moment, she thought she was imagining things, but she could have sworn she had seen those particular wing tips before. Nah, it couldn't be. . . .

"You gonna admire my shoes all day?"

Toni had swung her carry-on bag up and around before she knew it. She hit Chuck squarely in the stomach with it. "How dare you sneak up on me like that! I've already had one scare today!"

Laughing, Chuck grabbed the offending bag and wrenched it from her hand. "Give me that, woman."

Toni let him have the bag and stood back, looking at him. Not a hair was out of place. He was impeccable as usual, in his brown double-breasted suit. His light brown eyes held an amused glint. And he was giving her that crooked smile that turned her insides to mush. "Oh, Chuck!"

She went into his open arms, burying her face in his chest. "I'm so glad to see you."

Chuck continued to laugh softly. "I'm glad to see you, too, my love."

He stepped back to tilt her head up. "Now. What was that all about? What sort of scare were you referring to?"

Toni's nearly black eyes were misty, a nervous reaction to seeing him there when she hadn't expected to. "A crazy cabdriver," she told him, her voice low. She relaxed in his arms.

"Ah . . . ," Chuck said. "Now you know why I always use a car service whenever I travel."

"Yes," she said, as she reached up to caress his chin. Her almond-shaped eyes were suddenly full of sensual fire. "I didn't mean what I said. I know you're not trying to control me."

The elevator doors opened, and several passengers spilled out of it. Chuck and Toni waited until the car was empty, then stepped inside where they were once again alone.

Chuck placed Toni's carry-on bag on the floor and pulled her into his arms. "Don't you realize I know how frightened you are of what we have?"

"You can't understand what I'm going through. You've never been abandoned. Yes, you've suffered, but it wasn't the kind that makes you wary to trust again . . . to believe in love again."

"Think again," Chuck told her quietly. "Do you think I want to risk losing another wife? Child? There is no fiercer cut to the heart than having a child die before you. Believe that." He looked deeply into her eyes. "We have a choice: grab life by the throat and hold on for the ride, or sit back and watch others live. I'm tired of being a spectator, Toni. I'll risk anything to be with you. Your parents' wrath. In your father's case, buckshot in the ass. Hell, I've already been shot once and survived. A little buckshot can't hurt that much."

"My parents just want me to be happy," Toni told him, her smile lighting her eyes. "I'm the one who has been standing in the way of our happiness, Chuck."

Chuck reached up to run his hand through her short, silver-streaked hair. It was soft and silky, and he loved playing in it. "Are you saying you're done fighting the feeling, Toni Shaw?"

"That's right," Toni said with a rakish grin. "I ain't fightin' the feelin' no more, baby!"

With a groan, Chuck pulled her against him and kissed her hard on the lips. Their bodies pressed closer together. When they came up for air, Toni laughed and said, "Okay, now. Come clean. Who told you I'd be here? Mere? Georgie? They're the only ones I told I was coming to Miami."

The elevator came to a stop on the third floor. Chuck picked up Toni's bag and allowed her to precede him off the conveyance. "You also told me. And I have a son-in-law who's a detective. It didn't take much time for him to track you down."

"Especially since he's sleeping with his best source," Toni quipped. In the hallway, she turned to regard him. "How long has Georgie known about us?"

"Since the beginning," Chuck admitted, figuring all the secrets should be told now, as they were starting fresh. "She's been a staunch supporter."

Toni didn't even look surprised. With a hand on her hip, and lips pursed, she said, "Mmm-huh. Bree?"

"Yeah, she knows, too."

"Anyone else?"

"Clay and Dominic. The girls can't keep a secret like that from their significant others. Then, of course, there's Margery. . . ."

"Of course!" Toni turned and began walking in the direction of her room. Chuck explained how Margery had come into his confidence. "I phoned Bree in San Francisco one day when Margery was visiting. She had no idea Bree was on the phone, so when she picked up the extension in her room to make a call, she overheard us discussing you. And you know Margery. She couldn't hang up the extension without finding out what was going on. That night I showed up at Elian's—"

"She told you about that?"

"Told me where you would be, who you would be with. It wasn't my intention to hurt Spencer. He's a decent man. . . ."

They arrived at the room, and Toni slipped the key card in the door. "If it wasn't your interference that night, it would have been something else that would have broken us up. We weren't right for each other."

Toni backed into the room, looking at Chuck the whole while. "He married a cabaret singer seven months later. She's twenty years younger than he is. Now he's a first-time father at fifty-two. More power to him!"

Chuck closed the door and handed Toni her carry-on bag. Toni took it and tossed it and her shoulder bag onto a nearby chair. She stepped out of her pumps and placed them underneath the same chair. Rising, her eyes raked over Chuck. "Do you know what you did to me that night? You made me recognize the possibilities. I started wondering what it would be like to make love to you again. After thirty years!"

"I'm a better lover today than I was back then," Chuck stated. He wasn't bragging. It was simply a fact. When he was younger, lovemaking was a means to an end: orgasm. And the faster he reached it, the better. He had learned a few things in the intervening years, like putting your partner's pleasure before your own had inherent benefits. A satisfied woman was a happy woman. And a happy woman was who you wanted in your bed. He circled Toni now, remembering how it had been between them when they were both young, with their sexual energy barely contained. After she had been introduced to physical love, she became a willing student. And like everything else Toni did, she gave it her all.

Toni raised her head proudly, her hand on the top button of her blouse. She backed away from him as he came toward her. "Look all you want, Charles Edward, but I have an appointment in less than an hour, and—"

She was unable to finish her sentence because Chuck
had covered her mouth with his own.

Twisting her head to the side, Toni reluctantly broke
off the kiss. "I'm serious, Chuck. I promised Dr. DuPree
I would be there by twelve forty-five."

Chuck's big hands were on her hips as he inched her
skirt up past her knees. He kissed her high on her neck,
near her ear. "All right, I'll be a good boy if you promise
to let me take you to dinner tonight and, afterward, to
Paradise."

Moaning softly, Toni said, "We can skip dinner and go
straight to Paradise."

After Detective Montez and the other members of the
police department left, Solange's office looked even
worse than it had before she had phoned them. Now,
dark powder dusted her desk and every other surface
where they thought a fingerprint might be found. She
had pulled Detective Montez aside and asked him if they
had found any prints. He had shaken his head in the
negative. "Gloves," was his one-word explanation.

She had to duck under the bright yellow crime-scene
tape they had placed across the entrance when she left.
She would get no work done here today. In her tote,
she had the box with the fertility goddess in it. She
hadn't told Detective Montez about the goddess. Why
hadn't she? One reason was that she feared he would
take it as evidence. There was a possibility she would
live to regret her decision. The goddess might be safer
in police custody. But if she did that, she would never
find out who the tall, mysterious stranger with the British accent was. She hadn't mentioned him to Detective
Montez either. Two infractions in one day. Dr. Solange
DuPree, upstanding citizen, was becoming a regular law-
breaker!

She was in her car driving home when she remembered the writer, Toni Shaw, was supposed to be coming to her office to have a look at the fertility goddess. Glancing down at her tote, lying on the car seat beside her, she laughed shortly. "You're one popular little lady."

If she had known, eight months ago, how much trouble the small wooden statue would bring her, she might have passed on it when she went into that shop in Burundi.

The capital city, Bujumbura, was densely populated. The two main groups of people, the Hutu and the Tutsi, who had been bitter enemies throughout history, were making an effort to cooperate, so the university had condoned her visit there.

What lay people didn't understand about archaeology was that it wasn't all excavating and digging up old bones. Many finds were brought about quite by accident. It was definitely Providence that brought her into that fetish shop in Bujumbura that day. Sorcia Gilbert, another American archaeologist, was with her. Sorcia spoke a bit of Kurundi, and being Haitian-American, Solange spoke a bit of French, though not fluently.

The shop was located at the end of a city street, tucked out of the way. When Solange and Sorcia pushed the door open, a ripe, offensive odor assailed their nostrils. It smelled like rotten eggs, or as if an animal had died in there and they were letting the carcass rot. Solange's first inclination was to turn around and leave right away. Coming from the bright sunlight outside into the darkness, they had to let their eyes adjust.

Sorcia called hello in Kurundi.

A feminine voice replied in the language.

Then the two women heard a light being switched on, the kind that had a chain at the end. The bulb must have been forty watts, or less. It didn't illuminate many corners in the dark shop. But the woman standing underneath was visible now. To say she was old was an understatement. She was tiny and so withered, her wrinkles had wrinkles. Her skin looked like aged cowhide, very dark brown and ashy. The pupils of her small eyes were so cloudy, Solange couldn't tell what color they had been in her youth, black or brown. Her solid white hair was thick and vibrant, though, appearing like thick ropes spilling down her back. She was dressed in the traditional sari the native women wore. It was faded and worn thin in spots, but clean. "One of you is here for the goddess, yes?" she said in Kurundi. "You long for children, but haven't been blessed."

Solange had felt her chest grow tight when Sorcia translated what the old woman had said. Solange had known since she was a teenager that she could never bear children. Underdeveloped ova, the doctor had said. She had been born with compromised eggs that would never be able to merge with sperm and produce a zygote, which would eventually become a child.

"Speak up," the old woman continued impatiently. "I'm a busy woman. Do you want to see the goddess or not?"

The two archaeologists had converted to English in order not to be understood by the proprietor.

"This is a fetish shop," Sorcia said. "You aren't going to find anything here except herbs and smelly potions that are supposed to have magical powers. It's a bunch of crock. Let's go, Solange."

"It couldn't hurt to take a look," Solange said. It was hot outside. The shop felt as cool as a cave. She could stand the smell long enough to cool off. "Tell her we'd like to see this goddess."

"You can tell me yourself," the woman spoke up. "Americans. You think everyone is as backward as you are!" She laughed then and turned her back to them. "Follow me, then. I haven't got all day. As a matter of fact, I'm so old, I might not have the next five minutes." She laughed harder, ending with a wheeze and a short bout of coughing.

Solange came forward to pat her on the back. "I'm sorry if our comments were insulting. We didn't mean anything by it, I assure you."

Pausing to stare up at her, the woman said, "I can tell by your voice that you meant no harm. Do you have a name, child?"

"I'm Dr.—"

"I don't care about titles. Your *name*, child!"

"Solange DuPree." Solange was duly chastened.

The woman humphed and continued toward the back of the store. "You're the one who wants a child, yes?"

Sorcia was right behind them, and Solange didn't feel free to discuss her problem within earshot of a colleague who was not a personal friend.

The woman sensed her reticence and dropped the matter.

Pulling a curtain back, she led Solange to a room deeper in the shop. Once in there, the woman reached up and pulled a chain, lighting another dim bulb. Solange heard the shuffling of sand on the floor and realized they now stood on packed earth. She looked down and saw that the old woman was barefoot. Most likely the skin on the bottom of her feet was so thick from years of going barefoot that she did not notice the floor's rough texture.

The woman was reaching up to grab something from the top shelf. "Help me, Solange DuPree," she said. When Solange stepped forward to assist the woman, she inhaled the woman's body odor, which was a mixture of snuff and sweat.

"If you reach up, you will feel a box," the woman instructed. "Get it down and hand it to me."

Solange stretched. She wasn't that much taller than

the old woman, but she did feel something. . . . Suddenly a creature slithered across her fingers, and she yelped and withdrew her hand. When she did that, a box fell from the shelf, and with an alacrity she didn't know she possessed, she caught it.

The old woman was chuckling. "Probably just a wood snake," she said. "More frightened of you than you are of him!"

"I wouldn't go that far!" Solange told her, handing her the box. "I hope this is what you were reaching for because I'm not putting my hand back up there."

"Yes," the woman said, accepting the box as though it contained something precious. She walked over to the table that was directly under the dim bulb. Setting the box on the table, she pried the lid off and stood the box up on the tabletop. Inside was a carved wooden figure in the shape of a nude woman. Its breasts hung to its distended belly. It stood in a defiant stance, arms raised, legs spread and in a slight squat. Solange stared at it. Sorcia had come into the room and joined them at the table, too. She was frowning. It must have been the ugliest thing she had ever seen. There was a pained expression on its face, as if it were straining. . . .

"It's giving birth!" Solange exclaimed, realizing how preposterous her comment had sounded as soon as it had issued from her mouth. A statue . . . giving birth?

Sorcia laughed, her blue eyes dancing. "Yeah, any minute now it's going to have a toothpick!"

Solange felt an overwhelming desire to touch the figure. However, when she went to place her hand on it, the old woman cautioned her with, "Do not touch the goddess unless it's your desire to bear children."

Sorcia nearly burst her sides laughing when she heard that. "Then, keep it away from me!" she cried, doubled over. Making her way to the exit, she added, "Solange, I need some air. I'll wait for you in front of the shop."

"Good riddance," the old woman said irritably. Her eyes shot daggers at Sorcia's retreating back. "The goddess doesn't abide unbelievers."

She looked at Solange, who, by that time, seemed to have snapped out of a spell. She allowed her hands to fall to her sides and regarded the woman with clearer eyes. "Does she have a name?"

"A name? Yes. But it's only known to a few of the living, and I'm not among them. Why do you need a name? Does the Creator have a name?"

"Yes, as a matter of fact, He does. Depending on what part of the world you're in, He's called Yahweh, Jehovah, Allah, and many more names," Solange said. She turned to leave. "If this is a ploy to get me to buy something that has no value, I'm afraid I'm the wrong person to scam. I'm just an untenured professor. I don't have money to be throwing after bad."

"I don't want your money," the old woman told her, her voice surprisingly calm, since Solange had just accused her of being a con artist. "You came in here. The goddess drew you. If you want her, she's yours. I'm getting too old to hang on to her. But if you do decide to take her, remember, no one must touch her unless they desire children. Her magic is powerful."

Solange had then examined the statue more closely. The wood appeared to be ebony; it was black with age but had reddish undertones. The artisan had been extremely talented. The features weren't at all exaggerated as were many African statues she had seen. The facial features could have been those of any modern-day African woman. It appeared she was in pain, but if those muscles were relaxed, she would be quite attractive for a wooden statue about to give birth.

Standing there, drinking in the beauty of the object, Solange accepted it for its aesthetic worth, denying the claims of the old woman who had no doubt imbued it with magical powers to pique her interest.

"All right," she said, smiling down into the old woman's upturned face. "Thank you! I'll take it."

Now, driving south, Solange wondered if she had made a huge mistake by taking the statue off the old woman's hands.

Her cell phone rang. Keeping her eyes on the road, she reached into the tote, removed the phone and flipped it open. "Dr. DuPree."

"I'm sorry I had to leave so suddenly," said the deep, British voice. "But since you were still in possession of the goddess, I saw no reason to linger—"

"Who are you?" Solange interrupted him.

"Who I am isn't important. What's important is, a guard was nearly killed by whoever is after the goddess. Try as I might, I can't be two places at once. Watch your back, Doctor. And don't trust anyone!"

"Are you with the government?"

"Whose government?" he asked cryptically, and hung up.

Solange hung up the phone and placed it on the seat beside her. Putting on her left turn signal, she waited while several cars passed, then turned into the parking lot of the main branch of her bank. If the people in search of the goddess came after her, they wouldn't get their hands on it. Not when there were safety deposit boxes just waiting to be filled with treasures.

As documented in the Bible, the Queen of Sheba visited King Solomon around 1000 B.C. And although Yemen was her true homeland, Ethiopia was regarded as her home since her son, Menelik I, was the first emperor of Ethiopia, ruling from about 982 to 957 B.C. Consequently, Dominic chose Ethiopia as the location to film

his definitive *Queen of Sheba*. It was a country that could
document its history going back five thousand years. It
had survived Italian occupation from 1936 to 1941, several social revolutions, and lately, the unenviable image
of being the poorest nation on earth, a nation that
couldn't feed its people due to repeat famines.

There were various logistical problems that came with
filming on location. Among them were all the local of-
ficial palms you had to grease with cash in order to by-
pass all the ordinances against filming in a foreign land.
Dominic didn't mind the payola, especially if he got to
shoot in locations that were authentic and appeared so
on film. He would do just about anything to produce a
fine piece of work.

But he tried to put all the problems of filming on location behind him as he sat across from Bree in the hotel
dining room. Besides, the producer should handle most
of those problems, freeing him up to create. Even though
that wasn't always the case. . . .

"Stop thinking!" Bree ordered petulantly. She threw a
piece of bread at him. "I take the time to get dressed
up, and you spend most of the evening thinking about
work!"

Dominic smiled at her. She did look good enough to
eat. Mindful of the local Islamic rules, she was covered
from neck to feet, but the white tunic she wore set off
the golden brown of her skin to perfection.

He reached across the tiny round table to rub the back
of his hand against her cheek. "I'm sorry, my queen.
You know how I get when I'm working."

"Yeah, I know how you get," Bree said, grasping his
hand and placing a kiss in his palm. "That's why I regret
blowing up at you the way I did. It wasn't fair to you to
bring up personal problems when we're working."

"So, you'll wait to skewer me once we're back in
Frisco?"

Although many who worked in the film industry made L.A. their home in order to be in the midst of the action, Bree and Dominic both lived in San Francisco. Bree had moved there more than two years ago to be closer to her mother. And Dominic had moved there to be closer to Bree. It still rankled that she wouldn't move in with him, but he had made a promise to himself to stop trying to persuade her to change her mind. He knew Bree was the woman he wanted to spend the rest of his life with, but he couldn't bring himself to propose marriage. Fear gripped him whenever he thought about marriage and everything it entailed. His mother had suffered because his father had found the institution so intolerable he had abandoned not only his wife, but his three children. The children had suffered when their mother became an embittered woman always seeking what she never really had with her first husband. Last count, she had gone through four other husbands since his father left.

A waiter strolled up to their table with a bottle of the restaurant's best champagne. "From Mr. Makonnen, with his compliments," he said.

Bree followed the waiter's line of sight. At a corner table sat a handsome man in his mid-thirties. He wore a tailored dark suit with a gray silk shirt underneath. Bree assumed he was a local. He had the dusky skin and shiny black hair of an Ethiopian. Back home, she would have taken him for a brother. His black, curly hair was cut short, tapered at the back of his well-shaped head. He smiled, revealing straight white teeth in his brown face. He raised a champagne glass in greeting.

Bree smiled at him.

She looked at Dominic, who was frowning at Makonnen.

"What is it?" she asked under her breath.

"Yusef Makonnen. He has a reputation for being a ruthless businessman, among other things."

Bree discreetly rolled her eyes in the waiter's direction, denoting the need to be more circumspect. The waiter could go back to Makonnen's table and tell him exactly what the "ugly Americans" had said about him.

Dominic chilled. "Express our thanks for his generosity," he instructed the waiter, who appeared relieved. Bree supposed he didn't want to return to Makonnen's table with a blunt refusal. That could cut into his tip.

He happily went off to give Makonnen the good news.

In his absence, Bree asked, "What 'other' things?"

"He's a collector of sorts. Art, women, companies. Whatever suits his fancy at the moment. Born rich and blessed with business acumen." He met her eyes. "Why are we talking about him?" He grasped her hand. "If you're finished, I suggest we find someplace a bit more private so I can show my appreciation for your patience tonight."

Bree dropped the cloth napkin onto her plate, and she and Dominic rose, her hand still clasped in his. Dominic grabbed the unopened bottle of chilled sparkling wine Yusef Makonnen had sent over, and they walked from the dining room arm in arm.

Makonnen followed their progress across the room, and when they were out of sight, he reached inside his coat pocket and retrieved a slim cellular phone.

Pressing a button, he waited until the phone was picked up on the other end.

"Status?"

By the time the person he had phoned had finished giving him the information he had requested, his dark eyes were narrowed into slits. Breathing hard, he closed the phone and returned it to his pocket. Incompetent people were the bane of his existence. He had given someone a simple assignment, and it appeared as if they weren't going to be able to carry out his orders. He had come to Addis to handle a few business concerns and to enjoy the various restaurants he and Salah frequented while here. He missed his wife. Seeing Briane Shaw here in the hotel dining room was a delightful surprise. Salah would be disappointed she hadn't been with him when he told her about it.

Bree and Dominic weren't sharing a room at the hotel, where the cast and crew took up the entire seventh floor of the grand hotel. But Bree's room was at the opposite end of the hall from Dominic's. It wasn't as if everyone working on the project didn't know they were a couple and would have raised an eyebrow if they did share a suite; it was just that Bree felt it was more professional to maintain separate quarters.

After dinner, they had gone back to her suite of rooms. She had one bedroom, a sitting room, and a bathroom with a sunken tub. All the luxuries befitting the star of the film.

Upon entering the suite, Bree had taken the bottle of champagne over to the bar and poured two glasses. Dominic was sprawled on the couch, watching her. Deep-set black eyes, in his medium-brown face, possessively raked over her. Bree handed him one of the glasses of champagne and sat next to him. She took a sip of hers. It was tart, but good. She gave him as sensual a perusal as he had given her, then placed her glass on the coffee table. Slowly unbuttoning the tunic, she removed it, revealing a sleeveless white T-shirt underneath. Her eyes remained locked with his throughout her striptease.

Wanting his hands free for more pleasurable endeavors, Dominic put down his glass, too. He absentmindedly removed his loafers, tossing the shoes aside.

Bree suddenly got up on her knees and reached over to rub his shaved head with both hands. His nose was in her cleavage. She lovingly kissed the top of his head.

Pulling her into his strong arms, he said against her ear, "Do you know what I love best about you?"

Bree lazily reclined her head. "Could it be my neck?"

Dominic kissed her there. Her warm, silken skin smelled faintly of jasmine and a citrus fruit he couldn't place at the moment. Not when he could concentrate on little else but getting her out of that head-to-toe get-up she had on. The jealous man in him could get used to Islamic customs. He didn't want other men eyeing his woman. But that was as far as his preference for the custom went. Still, it wasn't his job to come to a foreign country and free its female citizens from hundreds of years of ingrained restrictions. No. That was a job for a woman from their own ranks. A woman with the dedication of Susan B. Anthony and the fierce determination of Toni Shaw. Dominic was in awe of Bree's mom. In fact, he liked her entire family.

The hair extensions were getting in the way as Bree tried to pull the T-shirt over her head. Dominic lent his assistance; but when his hand touched the skin on her midriff, his eagerness heightened and he wound up snatching the T-shirt off and flinging it across the room. "No wonder those Victorians were so damned lusty, what with all the clothes a woman had to get out of in order to get to bare skin," he said roughly as he pushed Bree backward on the couch and buried his face in her cleavage.

Giggling, Bree said, "Anticipation is part of the enjoyment." She kissed his forehead. "Now, get up and let me watch you slowly remove your clothing."

As he rose, Dominic rained kisses from her firm, round breasts to her flat belly, making hungry noises as he did so. "Slowly?" he asked as he gained his full height of six feet. He rubbed his short beard as if he had never heard the term before. Then he reached for the buckle of his leather belt.

"Shirt first," Bree said as she sat up, wearing only a bra, her slacks and a lascivious smile. "Work it, boy!"

"Actresses," Dominic joked. "I always knew it was your secret desire to make the director perform for you. Mind you, no matter how cruel you are to me, you won't make me cry!"

Bree got to her feet and walked around him as he removed his long-sleeve black shirt. Dominic wasn't a weight lifter. He didn't jog five miles a day. He practiced what he called free weights. Lifting his own body weight with sit-ups, push-ups, rowing. It was working for him because his body was fit, if not bulky. And his six-pack was awesome. Bree went to him and ran her hand across his stomach. Placing her arms around his neck, she drew him down for a kiss. His full mouth covered her smaller one, and tongue touched tongue. He tasted clean and, faintly, of the sparkling wine. To Dominic, Bree was a compelling combination of softness, firmness and sensuality. To kiss her plump, sweet lips was to experience sheer bliss. And what she did with her tongue, the thorough plundering of his mouth, his body, made him forget every other woman he had ever kissed. Bree was his longest relationship, the only woman he felt he could grow old with. He had never quit being surprised by her and delighted with her! He suddenly felt a guilt trip coming on. Why couldn't he commit to this woman? He drank of her generosity like a man dying of thirst, but couldn't give her the one thing she wanted: marriage and family.

Bree was busy twirling her firm tongue around his areola. Then she took the nipple between her lips and treated it to the tongue action, too. Dominic abandoned the guilt and immersed himself in the moment from that point on. He bent his head and kissed her mouth, tasting his own skin on her tongue. There would be time enough to examine his motivations tomorrow. But for now, pleasure only.

Five

Simpletons, he thought as he trained the binoculars on the two beefy fellows who were breaking into Dr. Du-Pree's modest home in a quiet suburb of Miami. He knew the doctor wasn't there, so he was in no rush to apprehend the bozos. Broad daylight. Didn't they even know to wait until dusk or dark? Even in this sleepy neighborhood, they were bound to be seen by someone, a nosy neighbor, or the driver of a passing car. . . .

Wait a minute! More participants in the game.

Oh, no, it was the doctor pulling into the driveway in that black sports car she drove—a rather racy vehicle for a professor—and behind her was a stately black Lincoln Town Car. Sighing, he reached for the door's handle and got out of the rented Lexus.

When Toni wasn't able to get Solange on her office phone, she dialed the cellular phone number the professor had given her and reached Solange as she was leaving SunTrust Bank. Solange told her about the break-in at the office and suggested they meet somewhere. Toni agreed, saying she should choose the location. At that point, Solange remembered she had all her notes about the goddess, plus the e-mails she had exchanged with Dr. Wang, at home. She told Toni she would meet her at the Marriott; then Toni could follow her back to her home.

As the driver of the hired Lincoln Town Car pulled in behind Solange, Toni turned to Chuck. "I know you think I should leave this alone, but after what happened at Solange's office today, I'm more curious than ever. I mean, come on, what kind of man will stop at nothing to complete a collection? He's got to be stopped before he hurts somebody!"

"That's the authorities' job," Chuck reasoned with her. "From what we've already learned, statues have been stolen in five different countries. Don't you think *someone* is on the case by now? They don't need us interfering with their work."

Toni was pumped. Her dark eyes gleamed. On the hunt. That was how she thought of her love for solving a mystery. And the richer the mystery, the better.

She leaned close to Chuck. "Admit it, you're excited about this, too."

Chuck grimaced. "I've had my fill of mysteries, thank you. All I want to do is go home to Boston, with you, and get married. But if it'll make you happy, I'll go along for the ride. If only to keep you out of trouble."

Toni was excited enough for the both of them. "All right, I'll accept that!"

She opened the door and stepped out of the car, followed by Chuck.

Solange was walking toward them. She smiled. She had instantly liked them upon meeting them at the Marriott. She knew Toni from her books. She had read all of them with the exception of the last one. She had had little time for personal reading lately. And she knew of Charles Edward Waters from articles in national magazines. Her curiosity was piqued. Why were the two of them together?

To be truthful, she was flattered that Toni wanted to

do research on her and the fertility goddess with a mind to writing a novel about the recent events.

It was now after one o'clock in the afternoon. The sun was high in the sky and the temperature was in the eighties. Solange wondered how Mr. Waters stayed so cool-looking in his tailored suit. However, Toni looked acclimatized in her white, sleeveless pantsuit.

"Right this way," she invited them.

The house was a small green bungalow on a corner lot. Nothing special, really, but neatly kept. The lawn was lush and healthy. Solange enjoyed gardening, so she had flowers native to the area: hydrangeas, azaleas, and orchids—the most delicate of plants—which were her pride and joy. Her friend, Gaea, often said that Solange treated those orchids like the children she had been denied: with patience, care and an abundance of love.

As the three of them stepped onto the front porch, Solange stopped suddenly. The door was open, by only an inch or so, but open nonetheless. She looked back at her guests, alarm mirrored in her eyes. "Someone's been here," she said in a low voice. She immediately turned and ushered them back down the steps. As their feet touched the front walk, Solange saw the stranger from that morning hurdling over the hedge that separated her yard from the Stevensons' on the right. She was amazed by his physical prowess. He wasn't even breathing hard when he got to her. "Good thinking, Doc," he complimented her as he pulled her around the side of the house where there were no windows. Taking his cue, Toni and Chuck followed suit. "You have company inside," he briefly explained. "I suggest the three of you stay here and let me handle this—"

They heard a crash from inside the house.

Simpletons and buffoons, he thought as he turned and ran up the front steps. Not only were they going to toss the doctor's bungalow, but they were intent on destroying her property as well. He would just have to teach them a lesson.

In the stranger's absence, Toni asked, "Who was that?"

Solange could only shake her head. "I have no idea who he is." Then she told them about her first meeting with the black James Bond. That was how she had begun to think of him. He was obviously some sort of law enforcement agent. He was as handsome and dressed with the same sartorial splendor as any James Bond ever conceived on the silver screen. And then there was the accent.

When he went into the house, it didn't take long to locate the culprits. They were both in the living room of the house. One was methodically pulling everything off a built-in bookcase—books, glass figurines, family photos. The crash they had heard was the sound of the doctor's figurines being thrown to the floor. The other man was cutting the cushions of a sofa that must have cost the doctor a good portion of her hard-earned money. Both men were more than six feet tall and bulky. Hired henchmen, he would guess, former military men who had given in to their mercenary inclinations and now sold their services to the highest bidder. They were, undoubtedly, upset over not finding the goddess when they had broken into the doctor's office that morning and were now taking their rage out on the doctor's possessions. They didn't even stop in their headlong destruction when he entered the room.

He walked up to the one who was ripping up the sofa cushions and kicked the knife from his hand in one smooth movement. No need to fight a man with a weapon when you could just as easily disarm him.

The knife flew eight feet across the room and landed against the wall.

"You won't be needing that."

Now he had both men's attention.

The fellow he had disarmed growled and lunged low for him, as if he had played football sometime in his former crimeless life. He got a knee in the face for his troubles and a karate chop to the back of the neck. He went down hard and looked as if he would need help getting back up again.

The second fellow was more wary. He circled his opponent, trying to feel him out.

"Who are you?" He looked him up and down. "You're not a local cop. Interpol?"

"Are you going to fight, or talk? I could use a little physical activity after trailing you two dolts all the way from Boston and watching you fail time and time again. Your boss should hire more intelligent people to do his dirty work."

That got his goat. He threw a punch at his tormentor's right jaw, which didn't connect because his target calmly ducked, went low and gave him a debilitating punch to the liver. And when the intruder's chin went south, as it was inevitably certain to do, he got a right cross to the jaw that left him senseless. Wobbling, he collapsed to his knees, and because he no longer could balance himself, he fell on top of his partner.

"I'm always the one left cleaning up the mess after a party," the stranger groused as he reached behind him and removed a pair of cuffs that were attached to the utility belt on his holster. He cuffed the two men together at the wrists, then went into the doctor's kitchen to see if she was like millions of other Americans and kept a junk drawer where she stored things like duct tape. She was.

Returning to the living room, he taped the legs of both men together, hobbling them. After that, he thought it was safe for the doctor and her companions to enter the house. He stuck his head out the door and called to them, "You can come in now."

Upon seeing the doctor's lovely face again, he smiled. "I'm afraid I'll have to leave the garbage collecting to the local police, Doctor. I suggest you phone them right away and explain the situation."

Solange noticed he had ripped the sleeve of his jacket in the struggle. She touched his arm. "Are you all right?" She glanced at the two unconscious men on her floor. The only things they had in common were size and occupation. One was apparently Caucasian while the other was of African ancestry. "They're big guys."

"Doctor, the bigger they are . . ." And with that he turned and left.

"I'm getting a little tired of these quick exits!" Solange said, going after him. She could have saved her energy. He kept walking.

Toni put a comforting hand on the younger woman's shoulder. "I have a feeling you'll be seeing him again, dear. Let's get these two carted off to jail; then we need to put your place back in order. After that we can have a long talk."

"Pierre, Pierre, come here this very second," Bree cried impatiently. It was Friday morning, and she was standing on the grounds of the hotel after taking Pierre for his morning walk. While she was depositing his offering in a blue plastic bag and putting it in the nearby wire mesh trash receptacle, she allowed him off his leash for his customary romp. Now he didn't want to return to her. The more she called for him to come to her, the farther away from her he ran. She knew his moods and was aware he was paying her back for neglecting him lately. As he got older, he was less inclined to chew up her shoes, or leave less-than-welcome gifts on her pillow.

His revenge of choice nowadays was pouting, which made her feel guilty. After all, she had had him for nearly six years now, and he had been a faithful companion, cheering her, giving her unconditional love, even guarding her with his life. A tall order for a toy poodle, but he had heart!

Bree placed her hands on her hips, the southerly breezes whipping her sheer tunic about her long, slim legs. She was wearing a white shell and slacks underneath, so she was sufficiently covered. "Go ahead, have your fun, mister. But remember, I give you your kibble. Ungrateful wretch!"

Pierre glanced back at her and kept running.

Resigned, Bree began jogging after him. "I don't have time for this, you rugrat. I have to be on the set in less than an hour!"

Pierre ran around the corner of the gazebo. Beyond the gazebo was a man-made pond. Bree picked up her speed. Pierre wasn't averse to a morning dip. He loved the water and would probably enjoy making her come in after him . . . the little devil.

She passed a couple of white-jacketed hotel employees. "Good morning, missus," they called to her. Many of the staff referred to all the female guests as missus. Bree assumed it was a blanket title of respect. "Good morning!" she called back, pumping her legs. Pierre was out of sight by now.

As she turned the corner, she had a clearer view of the pond. Three or four long-necked swans floated on the placid surface of the water. The hotel management tried very hard to create a pastoral setting for the guests. Standing with his back to her was a tall man in a dark suit. "Excuse me," she said, as she approached him. "But did you see a small black dog come this way?"

"You mean this dog?" the man said as he turned.

Yusef Makonnen smiled warmly at her as he gently

stroked Pierre's furry head. "I heard you calling him when I was out for my morning constitutional and snatched him up before he could get to the water. He looked as if he was headed straight for the pond."

Bree gave him a grateful smile as she took Pierre from his arms. She hugged Pierre to her. "Knowing him, he was! Thank you. You're very kind, Mr. Makonnen."

"Oh, it was nothing. I have pets. I know how recalcitrant they can be. Like naughty children. Do you have children, Miss Shaw?"

Disarmed by his kindness, Bree easily replied, "No, but I do want them someday."

"I haven't been blessed in that way yet either," he said. "Too busy working, I suppose."

They began walking back in the direction of the hotel.

"What do you do?" Bree asked. It was obvious he knew what she did for a living. The story of the film production company's presence in the area had made all the local papers. And Yusef Makonnen appeared to be a man who liked to keep abreast of the news.

"My family is in oil; however, I've been known to dabble in various other ventures," he stated. Bree wondered where he had grown up. He didn't have the unique lilt the other locals had to their voices. She had been told Amharic was the language the locals spoke; however, she had not learned much of it during the six weeks they had been there. She knew how to ask the cost of an item while shopping in the street marts: *sint no wagaw?* And knew a few numbers like: *assr,* ten; and *haya,* twenty. Yusef Makonnen spoke with a slight British accent; however, she couldn't tell whether it was natural to him or practiced. If she ever tried to speak Amharic, he would be able to tell immediately that she was an American trying to fake the local language.

"Do you make Addis your home?" Bree asked.

"No, as a matter of fact, the only place I consider home these days is Djibouti, which is south of here."

"Djibouti is pretty desolate, isn't it?" Bree queried, hoping the information she had heard about his desert home was correct and she wouldn't wind up sounding stupid.

"It is true that from June to September it is very hot in Djibouti, and, unfortunately, in July there are the Khamsin winds, which make it the hottest month of all! But when you live there, you learn to adjust. And, I assure you, my home is comfortable year-round."

Bree was nodding. Of course it was. If he was as rich as he was reputed to be, he could have a veritable palace in the desert.

"Perhaps you and Mr. Solomon would like to visit sometime," Yusef casually offered. Then he quickly added, "When you get a free moment. It's an extremely short trip by helicopter. You could come to dinner, and my pilot would fly you back afterward."

Bree was adventurous by nature. The thought of seeing the desert compound of Yusef Makonnen intrigued her. But she didn't think Dominic would go for it, so she said, "I'll mention it to Dominic. It's kind of you to invite us."

"I would be honored to have such a beautiful, talented artist in my home," Yusef said humbly. "And Mr. Solomon, too." He actually blushed at nearly excluding Dominic.

Bree laughed delightedly. They arrived at the back entrance to the hotel. "Well, thanks again. It's off to work for me. I hope you have a pleasant day, Mr. Makonnen."

"I already have, Miss Shaw." He patted Pierre on his head. "You be good for your mistress."

Pierre snapped at his hand.

Quickly jerking his hand back, Yusef laughed. "You

don't think he's angry at me for preventing his morning swim, do you?"

"Bad boy," Bree scolded Pierre. "I'm sorry. He doesn't usually do that."

"No harm done." Yusef dismissed her apology with a shrug of his shoulders. "Good day to you then." He turned in the direction of the hotel gardens while Bree clipped the leash to Pierre's collar and set him on the tile floor. They entered the building. She had to put Pierre in the suite, then meet her driver downstairs in twenty minutes.

My guardian angel is slipping up. He neglected to give me a cover story, Solange thought irritably as Detective Montez drilled her about the two assailants his men had already taken out to a squad car. The detective's brown eyes had a hangdog expression in them. He was probably weary after a long day of investigating break-ins, first at her office, now at her home.

Cocking his head to the side as he looked down at her, he sighed. "Do you know how incredible your story sounds, Dr. DuPree? A man you don't know rides to the rescue, dispenses with two men who're probably professional killers, handcuffs them and then disappears without telling you anything about himself."

"Well, he must have been a law enforcement agent of some kind. He had a gun, and those are his cuffs. They certainly aren't mine! You've already taken statements from my guests, and both of them corroborate my story. What else do you want from me?"

He wasn't the only one weary. She had never been the subject of such interest before. She led a fairly sedate life. What with her work hours and her penchant for leaving the country at the first sign of a find that could prove interesting and possibly further her career, a personal life was out of the question. She hadn't been on a date in nearly nine months. And that had been with a colleague while in Burundi. He hadn't even kissed her good night. *Whoa! Where did that come from?*

Her cheeks grew hot. The stranger. He was getting to her.

"I don't mean to badger you," the detective said. "I'm just trying to get all the details I can in order to piece this case together."

"I understand your position, Detective Montez. I guess I'm just a little upset. . . ."

"Of course you're upset, you poor child," Toni cried as she stepped between the detective and Solange. She put a comforting arm around Solange's shoulders and glared at the detective. "Don't you think she's been through enough? She walks in and finds her friend near death—"

"Good news there," Detective Montez said, his haggard face appearing refreshed when he smiled. "Mr. Cairns is going to make it! He'll be laid up for a while, but the doctors say it looks as if he has no brain damage from the beating he took to the noggin. He's one lucky fellow. . . ."

While the detective was busying extolling the virtues of modern medicine, Toni leaned close to Solange and whispered, "Faint."

Solange's legs immediately grew too weak to hold up her body, and she faltered. Toni grabbed her about the waist, supporting her. "Oh, God! Help, Detective!"

Detective Montez easily swept Solange into his arms and carried her to the sofa where he gently laid her down with her head lower than her feet. He had read somewhere that this was the best position for a fainting victim. Concern was written all over his pecan tan face. Solange's eyes fluttered open. "Are you all right?" he anxiously asked.

"I'll be fine," she assured him in a feeble voice. "Too much excitement. . . ."

Toni came around and placed a hand on the detective's shoulder. "I'll take good care of her, Detective. Don't you worry."

Detective Montez reluctantly backed away. "I suppose you've told me everything you know. We'll be taking photos of the assailants to Mr. Cairns to see if they're the same men who beat him. I'll check back with you later, Dr. DuPree."

"Thank you," Solange said, and, with some effort, managed to give him a weak farewell wave. Toni sat down next to her on the sofa and clasped one of her hands. "You rest now, sugar."

"The coast is clear," Chuck said a few moments later as he returned from the front door after watching the detective's car, plus three black-and-whites, pull away from the curb.

Solange sat up and grinned at Toni. "You're devious. I like that!"

"Oh, darling, I could tell you stories," Toni said, smiling. "But right now, we need to get your place picked up."

"And lunch," Solange cried as she sprang to her feet. She looked around the room with dismay. "Have you had lunch yet? I'm starved! I have some shrimp in the freezer."

"We're both partial to shellfish," Toni said as she bent and began picking up books and cracked photo frames from the cluttered floor. Chuck removed his jacket in preparation for lending a hand. He righted an overturned straight-back chair that was part of the dining set and used the chair as a coat rack.

Solange went into the kitchen and removed a package of frozen jumbo shrimp from the freezer. She would make shrimp fried rice for her guests. It was quick and easy, and she had all the ingredients for the dish in her refrigerator. "I'm glad you're here," she called from the kitchen. "My nerves are a little on edge, and it helps to have company."

"Anyone's nerves would be on edge after what you've experienced the last few hours," Toni said knowingly. "Remind me to tell you of an adventure we had about three years ago. It'll make your hair stand on end."

Solange's laughter felt foreign to her. She hadn't laughed in a long while, it seemed. Some of the tension melted away. She tiptoed and got a deep, copper-bottomed frying pan from the rack overhead. "I grew up in Key West," she said conversationally. "I've heard some unusual tales in my time. But it's hard to believe that someone wants to collect all seven fertility gods in order to create a godlike child."

Toni appeared in the doorway. "Where's your dustpan and broom?"

Solange pointed to the utility room at the back of the room. "Switch on the light and you'll see them hanging on the wall. To the right."

"Keep talking," Toni said as she went to retrieve the items she would need in order to sweep up the broken glass. "I'd also like to hear how you found the goddess. Dr. Wang told me you found it in a shop in the capital city of Burundi, and that's all."

"Now that's a weird tale," Solange said as she rinsed carrots at the sink under a cool stream of water. Finished, she began scraping the skin off one of them with a vegetable peeler. She went into her story, starting when she and Sorcia walked into the shop that day.

Toni went back into the living room, but it was a small house, and they had no trouble hearing one another. By the time Toni returned to the living room, Chuck had all the books back on the shelf and held the sofa pillow that one of the miscreants had taken a knife to in his hands. "This is a goner," he said. He walked over to the sofa and placed the section with the other two that hadn't been ruined.

". . . Don't touch the goddess unless you want to bear children. . . ."

Toni hurried back to the kitchen, the dustpan filled with broken glass and other debris. She stood in the middle of the room, dustpan held aloft, her eyes trained on Solange. "Any woman who touches the goddess will get pregnant? Is that your understanding of what the old woman told you?"

Solange had been stir-frying the shrimp in peanut oil. She turned the gas flame down and faced Toni. "Mmm-huh. She was very adamant about my warning anyone of the danger."

Toni smiled at her. "Have you ever touched it?"

A brief look of embarrassment crossed Solange's features. Then she grinned. "Absolutely not!"

"Do you believe, or are you being cautious?" Toni asked softly. She went to the wastebasket next to the back door, stepped on the foot lever, and when the lid popped up, she emptied the dustpan.

Solange's brows knitted together in a frown. She realized, at that point, that she hadn't taken the time to evaluate her reasons behind not touching the goddess. For some strange reason, it simply felt natural not to touch it. Perhaps the old woman's warnings had gotten to her subconscious and planted an aversion to crossing that line.

She laughed now. "You know, I don't know why I haven't touched it. It isn't as if archaeologists pay heed to the talk of curses and such. God knows, archaeologists would be dropping like flies if all the curses attached to artifacts were genuine!"

"Well, I'm not asking all of those foolhardy archaeologists," Toni told her, meeting her eyes from across the room. "I'm asking you. Think about it. Why do you suppose you've never touched the goddess?"

Solange paused a long time. Then she said, "I believe it's because when the old woman told me about the goddess's powers, I didn't, for one moment, hear a note of insincerity in her voice. She might have been just a crazy woman. I'll never know for sure because she died the very next day. I know because I went back to the shop to give her something for the goddess. I didn't have a lot of money; but after a closer look, I was convinced the goddess was ancient, and I felt guilty for accepting it as a gift. Even though she'd told me she no longer wanted responsibility for it, I thought she should be compensated. I'd gotten together two hundred in cash. When I got to the shop, there were around ten women inside. They'd opened the windows and doors, and were sweeping out the shop, cleaning the shelves, and storing jars and bottles with her potions in them in boxes. And I knew, standing there in the doorway, she was dead. One of the women who spoke French told me when they discovered the shop hadn't been open for the day—it seemed she never let a day pass, except Sunday, without opening—they knew something was wrong. They had a man force the locked door open, and they found her dead in her bed in the little room she lived in out back. After the woman assured me she was related to the old woman and was in charge of the funeral arrangements, I gave her the two hundred, told her I hoped it helped and I left."

"She passed it on to you," Toni said, walking to the utility room to return the dustpan and the broom to their proper places. Closing the door, she looked at Solange. "It seems to me that the goddess was a personal gift to you. Why did you bring it back and store it with other artifacts belonging to the university? That was pretty generous of you since, judging from what you've told me, the goddess could be priceless."

"If it is priceless, it belongs in a museum, not on my curio shelf," Solange said as she turned the shrimp. "I've never been one to acquire much. I think it goes back to my childhood. My parents divorced when I was young, and I was passed back and forth between them and their families. Some weeks, I wouldn't know where I'd be staying. I got used to living out of suitcases and claiming only those things that were most precious to me. I don't need much to be happy."

Toni joined her at the sink. "We're practically done in there. I'll wash up and help you with lunch."

"Good," Solange replied, feeling comfortable with Toni already. "You can use the liquid soap there. And salad makings are in the vegetable bins: lettuce, cabbage, tomatoes, cucumbers, onions if you like, and radishes."

Chuck stood in the doorway. He had rolled up his shirtsleeves, and Toni's heart skipped a beat when she saw his hairy forearms—another part of his anatomy that turned her on. She sometimes wished she could switch her attraction to him on and off at will. But so far, no luck with that! "Is there anything I can do to help, ladies?" he asked, eyebrows arched questioningly.

Solange actually blushed. Toni smiled at the younger woman's reaction to Chuck. It only proved she was one hundred percent female.

"I've got a bottle of Chardonnay in the fridge." She pointed to the cabinet next to the entrance. "And the wineglasses are on the bottom shelf in that cabinet."

Soon, they were seated at the dining room table enjoying the shrimp fried rice and poring over the notes Solange had taken about the seven gods and goddesses the thieves were after.

"The first statue was stolen from a museum in Cairo," Solange told them. "It was Amon. He was the Tameran, or ancient Egyptian, god of the wind, fertility and, for some reason, secrets. He's usually depicted with the large, curving horns of a ram. In the form of a man, but with horns."

"I did a bit of research on fertility gods after you and Dr. Wang got my juices flowing," Toni said. "I learned that there are fertility gods in practically every culture on the planet, from animists in Africa to Native Americans in North America. The Greeks! One of their fertility gods, Priapus . . . Yikes! I'd say whoever first imagined him must have been suffering from phallus envy, big time!"

Solange laughed. "You're right. The first time I saw an etching of Priapus, I thought to myself, *You mean they even had pornography back then?* It's too much!"

Chuck cleared his throat. "Have you forgotten you're in mixed company, ladies?"

Solange and Toni burst out laughing.

"I'm sorry, sweetie," Toni offered, her eyes tearing up she was laughing so hard.

"We'll keep the conversation clean from this point on."

"But the African gods," Solange explained, "are usually not too exaggerated. Many of them are female because, as we know, the Africans by and large believed the female spirit was the creative force in the universe. So like the goddess in my possession, African fertility gods are often depicted with pendulous breasts and distended stomachs. Although my goddess is unique in that she's squatting and is about to give birth."

"I was wondering about the myth that states if all seven gods and goddesses come together, a special child will be produced. Exactly where did it originate?" Chuck asked. He took a sip of the Chardonnay as he awaited Solange's reply.

Solange had to finish chewing a mouthful of food,

swallow, and drink some of the wine to wash it down before saying, "Now, that's interesting! It seems that it originated with the Queen of Sheba. She got all her sorcerers together and told them to concoct a surefire way of getting with child. She wanted to ensure that she would bear Solomon a son. The sorcerers searched the entire continent of Africa until they came up with seven gods and goddesses. These they placed in their queen's bedchamber. When she seduced Solomon, it wasn't long before she learned she was expecting a child. Menelik I was that child."

"The first king of Ethiopia," Toni provided. "Dr. Wang wrote of it in one of the e-mails. Has any of that story actually been documented?"

"Of course not," Solange said. "It's been passed down for generations, but it can't be corroborated. As some experts have griped about Ethiopian history, much of their five-thousand-year-old history is only documented by the Ethiopians. However, can't that be said of the history of many countries? If blacks in this country hadn't documented their own history, they might've been nearly excluded from the history books. The writers of history tend to be biased."

"That said," Toni put in, "do you believe the Ethiopians are actually in possession of the Ark of the Covenant?"

"According to legend, ancient Ethiopians were Jews. Remember back in the eighties when Falashas, the last of the Ethiopian Jews, were airlifted to Israel? That was proof in and of itself that they existed. I'd say there is a distinct possibility that the Ethiopians are in possession of the Ark of the Covenant. If you can take the Bible literally—and, let's face it, millions of Christians do—then we know that the Ark of the Covenant was to be handled solely by the priestly class, the Levites. Sometime after 642 B.C.E., it turned up missing. Solomon's temple was supposed to be its permanent resting place, but it fell into the hands of subsequent kings, some of whom weren't devout Jews. The Bible doesn't say when or under what conditions the ark disappeared," Solange said excitedly.

"Fascinating," Toni said, smiling at Solange. "You certainly know your history. Is that what drew you to archaeology, your love of history?"

"That and my need for permanence in my life," Solange said, and immediately wished she hadn't said something so personal. After all, she had just met Toni and Chuck that day.

Seeing her discomfiture, Toni changed the subject. "I don't think you ought to stay here tonight." She looked over the house. Although back in order now, it had earlier been the scene of much chaos. "Why don't you pack an overnight bag and get a room at our hotel for the night at least? My treat."

"I know you're only thinking of my well-being," Solange said, her dark eyes grateful. "But I think I'm perfectly safe. They've arrested the two men who broke in here and, I suspect, into the office. And I've got an alarm system."

What she didn't intend to add was that she was hoping a certain mystery man would put in another appearance some time tonight. She wanted to be right here waiting when he did. Curiosity was eating her up. Who was he?

Yusef Makonnen had grown up in a wealthy Saudi family near Riyadh. He attended boarding school in Switzerland and, when he was in his teens, Britain. He spoke six different African dialects as well as English, Spanish, French, Italian and German. It was good to know what your enemies were saying when they spoke in front of you, believing you didn't understand their language.

In his thirty-eight years he had never been faced with a challenge he couldn't eventually conquer. He knew what some people were saying about him: he was ruthless, aggressive and competitive to the point of obsession. All true. But there were other sides to him. When he loved, for example, he loved with his whole heart. And there was nothing he would not do to please the object of his affection. His wife, Salah, was Sudanese. She had led a much different life from his. Orphaned at seven, she had nearly starved on the streets before she had been rescued by a Christian-based organization that found her a spot in an orphanage, and Americans to sponsor her upkeep. Yes, there were actually legitimate organizations that spent the money they collected on the children. He donated thousands to the same organization every year out of thanks for saving his Salah.

He met her nearly ten years ago in New York City where she was a well-known runway model studying economics at NYU. For him it was love at first sight. He had to grow on her. Eventually, though, he managed to win her, and they married. Now there was only one thing standing in the way of their perfect happiness. Because of years of bad nutrition, Salah could not conceive. Fertility experts the world over were consulted, but no one could give them hope. The answer was always adopt. Salah was heartbroken because she wanted to bear Yusef's child. She became despondent to the point of talking about leaving him so that he could marry a woman who could give him children.

From his perch in the company helicopter, the landscape below blurred into one continuous line of sand. Blue sky and sand for miles around—until you came upon his estate, which was like an oasis in the desert. He had paid a dear cost to have the land irrigated so that for two miles there was a green island in a sea of sand. That was how he thought of his compound, as an island, a separate place where he and Salah could do as they pleased without interruption.

He spied the spot of green far on the horizon now. They would soon be there. But Salah wouldn't greet him at the door attired in a diaphanous caftan, as was her practice. She was in San Francisco consulting another fertility specialist. She had been away nearly two weeks undergoing exhaustive tests. He cringed whenever he thought about everything she had undergone for him, all because she would not give up on the notion of giving birth to his child. He had enough money to last several lifetimes, and he couldn't buy her that one wish.

He now directed his attention to the man seated to his left. "All right, I'm ready to hear your report."

The man was Ethiopian, small-boned with deep-set, dark brown eyes, a rather long, hooked nose and prominent teeth in his thin face. He reminded Yusef of a ferret.

He cautiously eyed Yusef a moment. Then Yusef remembered, "Arabic."

His pilot was British and didn't speak a word of Arabic.

The man started speaking in rapid Arabic, "Hyde and Omoro first went to the office of Dr. DuPree and did not find the statue. A short while later, they entered her home, and while they were in the middle of a search of the premises, they were interrupted by the insurance investigator."

"He trounced them, I gather?" Yusef said, bored with the proceedings. They hadn't found the goddess, and that was what mattered. According to Mubara, all the gods and goddesses must be in place by sundown on the twenty-seventh of October, which was only five days away. Five days. Salah was expected back from the States then, so if the fools he had hired to collect the statues hadn't fouled up, everything would have gone like clockwork.

Now he had to regroup, or give up on his plans alto-
gether, which wasn't an option. He had lived too many
years being a witness to Salah's sadness. If there was a
chance, however small, of the process actually working,
he had to take the risk.

"While Hyde and Omoro were in the doctor's house,
Ishi stayed outside as a lookout—"

"Not a very good one."

"Yes, sir. At any rate, when Dr. Dupree arrived—"

"You mean the doctor was there?"

"With two guests, a man and a woman." He went into
his black briefcase and produced several eight-by-ten photographs. He handed the photos to Yusef one at a time.
"This woman is Toni Shaw; she's a popular writer of fiction. The gentleman is Charles Edward Waters of . . ."

"Formerly of Waters Foods," Yusef supplied. "Curious.
What does a businessman of his caliber have in common
with a writer and an archaeologist?"

"You know him, then?"

"I know *of* him. I've read articles on him. Tell me more
about the woman. Have you any idea how she and Waters
are related to Dr. DuPree? Good friends? Could they be
blood relations?"

"I don't know how they're related to the doctor. However, I did some digging into the woman's background.
She's the mother of two adult daughters. One is an attorney in Boston, and the other is an actress. You might
know her. Her name is Briane Shaw." He smiled after
revealing that tidbit to Yusef. He knew he had just saved
his job.

Yusef neither congratulated him on having the presence of mind to utilize the photos, nor on the third man
getting away and forwarding valuable evidence. "Hire an
attorney for Hyde and Omoro. One that will get them
released long enough for them to get on the next plane
out of Florida." He turned hard eyes on the small man.

"And make certain the paper trail doesn't lead back to me. Do you think you can handle that?"

The man's head bobbed up and down like one of those toy dogs in the back window of a low rider. "Oh, yes sir! It will be done exactly as you say."

"It had better be."

With that Yusef returned to his private ruminations, and the man next to him tried not to breathe too loudly.

Six

Solange immediately woke when she felt something crawling on her cheek. Her bedroom was at the front of the house. A slash of light from the street lamps came in through the slit in the curtains. The room was pitch-black aside from that bit of illumination. She, naturally, ran her hand across her face to dislodge whatever night creature had invaded her bedroom. A strong hand grasped hers. "Don't be alarmed."

How could she not be alarmed? She abruptly sat up, and the covers fell away from her body. She reached for the lamp on the nightstand. "I wouldn't turn that on if I were you, Doctor. My eyes have grown accustomed to the darkness, and that gown you have on leaves very little to the imagination."

Solange jerked the covers back up to her neck. "This is a bit unorthodox, isn't it? Breaking into a woman's house in the middle of the night? Or am I about to be invaded by brutes again?"

"I do apologize for letting myself in, Doctor. I simply wanted to speak with you about something that could prove important to you and the two who were here earlier today."

Solange could make out his profile, and the warmth emanating from his strong, vital body, coupled with the scent of his sandalwood cologne, spoke to the woman in her. He hadn't let go of her hand, and now he inched closer to her on the bed. Solange scooted over so that she was nearly sitting in the middle of the queen-size bed. "My robe is at the foot of the bed. If you'll hand it to me, I'll get up, and we can talk in the kitchen over coffee."

"It's sweet of you to want to entertain me, Doctor. . . ."

"Solange. My name is Solange," she firmly told him. "It seems we're going to keep running into one another. The least you can do is call me by my name."

"Solange. . . ." He tried it out. Leaning close to her, he murmured, "You'll distract me with your kindness if you're not careful." He placed the hand he held atop her flat stomach and patted it for good measure. "So behave yourself. I've a job to do." He cleared his throat. "This afternoon, after leaving you, I did a reconnaissance of the area to be certain the two who were arrested didn't have a partner. I found evidence of a third party. In his haste, he left behind the cap from his camera lens. Do you understand the import of that piece of information, Solange?"

Solange was too busy trying not to breathe in the male scent of him. Her pheromones had undoubtedly been activated, because her body was in the process of readying itself for lovemaking. The tips of her breasts had hardened, her female center throbbed . . . and he was asking her to consider the importance of a camera lens cap? It took all her willpower not to grab him by the shirt and pull him on top of her.

"Are you married?" she shocked herself by asking.

The question didn't seem to surprise him. His tone remained neutral. "No."

"Engaged?"

"No."

"Gay?" *Please, God, no!*

"The last time I checked, no," he replied with a hint of laughter in his voice.

Solange hesitated. She gently touched his chin with her right hand. "Am I correct in assuming you find me attractive?"

This time she did rattle him somewhat. He breathed in deeply and exhaled. "More than I have a right to be. Hey, where are all these questions coming from?"

Sighing, he reached over and switched on the bedside lamp. The crewneck, short-sleeve shirt, pleated slacks with a thin belt at the waist and expensive rubber-soled boots were all black. He looked like some suave cat burglar. He smiled down into her upturned face. "You're lovely even when you've been startled out of sleep."

Solange moistened her lips. "I'll have to take your word for it."

His warm brown eyes caressed her face. "Oh, yes. It's true. You remind me of the women on the island I grew up on. Beautiful brown skin. Body, healthy and womanly. Lips like plump plums. You could make a man forget himself."

Solange was getting warmer by the second. She raised her eyes to his. "Long enough to tell me your name?"

"Believe me, it isn't in any way romantic. It's just a plain, old British name. My parents didn't have great imaginations. When they adopted me, they wanted me to have a name that would help me fit in with the rest of the children at my boarding school, most of whom were British. . . ."

"Come on, it can't be any worse than Solange."

"Solange is a lovely name," he said. He had moved a bit closer to her on the bed, and Solange had to resist reaching out and touching his muscular chest.

"Let's not forget I entered your house illegally in order to impart important information. Shall we get back to the matter at hand?"

Solange laughed briefly. "You're so evasive. What harm

would it do to tell me your name? Your first name. A nickname. Something!''

Solange was so intent on persuading him to open up to her, she had forgotten to keep a tight grip on the covers. She only became aware of her slipup when she noticed the expression in his eyes go from amused to covetous. She wasn't so much out of practice that she could no longer recognize the look in a man's eyes when he wanted her.

She momentarily held her breath, and then she was up on her knees reaching for the robe lying atop the covers at the foot of the bed. She fell on top of him in her rush to get to the robe. She felt how hard he had become while they had been sitting there chatting, and the knowledge rocked her. With her mouth only inches from his, she said, "I'm sorry."

"I'm not," he replied, and placed a big hand behind her head, pulling her down to meet his mouth. Solange let out a soft sigh as she fell into him. His mouth was firm on hers, demanding, yet gentle, and he tasted clean and sweet. His tongue plundered her mouth, inciting, enticing, claiming her sweetness. He branded her with his kiss. When they drew apart, she knew she must appear drunk with passion. His own eyes were smoky with desire. "I won't make love to you, although I want to. It wouldn't be the right thing to do. Not now." He was a man at war with his baser instincts.

He gently rolled her over onto her side, and then he got to his feet, pulling her up with him. Holding her gaze, he demanded, "Listen to me, you have to be careful. The third party took photographs this afternoon. The purpose behind the act, I can only guess at. But if the photos can be used against you in any way, they'll do it."

Solange casually slipped on the robe and tied the belt. "Blackmail?"

"Possibly. I don't know. Toni Shaw and Charles Waters need to be warned, though. I won't tell you the name of the man who's behind the thefts of the statues. That would only compromise your safety further. I will tell you that his time is nearly up, and if you can keep the goddess out of his hands for the next few days, the situation will diffuse itself."

"He actually believes the myth, then?" She laughed briefly when she saw the incredulous expression on his face. "It wasn't that difficult piecing together what the culprit has in mind for the statues. I just didn't believe it, that's all."

"In the year 2000, it is hard to believe someone would put much store in magic. But you know, all magic is is one part desire and one part belief."

Solange turned to leave the room. "How about that coffee?"

He shook his handsome head. "Not for me. I'm going."

He paused long enough, however, to grasp her by the shoulders, glance down at her mouth, then back up to her eyes. "One more thing, though. When this is over I'd like to call on you properly."

Solange gazed up at him for a long while. "Do you really mean that?"

"I would be a fool not to. And I'm no fool." That said, he bowed slightly from the waist. "Until next time." He walked through the doorway.

"Wait a minute!" Solange hurried after him as he swiftly traversed the hallway and turned right to go into the living room. "It's Ethiopia, isn't it? Everything's going down in Ethiopia. They're trying to re-create the first spell that Makeba's sorcerers cast eons ago. . . ."

"When I return, we must discuss your alarm system. It's sorely lacking," he tossed over his shoulder. Then he was through the front door and had disappeared into the night.

Solange closed and locked the door. She threw the dead bolt into place, for all the good it would do. In the space of twenty-four hours, her home had been broken into twice.

Georgie didn't know why she had become lactose intolerant. Lately, every time she ate cheese, whether it was atop a cracker, or a pizza, or in Mrs. Hughes' baked macaroni and cheese—Mrs. Hughes, her father's cook for many years, was the best cook this side of the Mason-Dixon line—she invariably experienced a sour stomach.

As she sat at her desk in the office, going over the depositions of several city workers who claimed they had been treated as shabbily as Manfred Jones had when they tried to get their insurance to pay for medical treatments, her stomach felt as though she was going to heave. All because of a glass of skim milk she had drank with her toast that morning. She had rarely been ill in her life. Her grandmother said she had the constitution of a mule: strong as a horse and too damned stubborn to get sick. Therefore this stomachache was more irritating than painful. It was a monumental inconvenience for her to have something taking her attention away from her work.

She had a storefront office in Roxbury. Clay had tried to talk her out of hanging her shingle in his old stomping grounds. He had bad memories of a neighborhood where he had to fight nearly every day of his life. Georgie assured him the spot she had chosen was in a nice neighborhood and in the midst of renovations. It was true that some of the businesses close by were run by folks who were interested in giving back to the neighborhood and in seeing the area progress. To the left of her office was a cafe run by an elderly couple. It was a mainstay on her street. Many of the locals dropped by Fisher's Cafe for their morning coffee or the generous helpings of soul food they served for lunch and dinner. On her right was a small real estate office. It was owned by an unscrupulous con man by the name of Percy Handler. And that wasn't just her opinion of him. He was presently buying out local home owners for ridiculously low prices. It seemed like every time Georgie drove through the nearby neighborhoods on the way to the office, she saw more signs planted in yards with SOLD on them. Georgie had been made privy to his plans soon after she moved onto the street. She was minding her own business in a back booth at Fisher's Cafe, trying to eat a turkey sandwich while reading a brief before going downtown to meet with a potential client, when Handler sauntered up to her table and sat down across from her without being invited.

She had seen him around but hadn't been introduced to him. Her office manager, Gwen Jenkins, lived in the neighborhood and knew practically everything that went down in the community. Whenever Percy Handler passed their office, whose picture window faced the street, Gwen would announce, "There goes the neighborhood!" Or she would proclaim the latest statistics from the Handler tally: "He got the Evans house yesterday! Got his eye on the Johnson house next. Mr. Johnson died a month ago, and now Mrs. Johnson's afraid to live in the neighborhood alone. She ought to be an easy target for him."

"Hello, pretty lady," he said to Georgie in the cafe, with the practiced charm of a man who was confident of his effect on women. In his mid-thirties, Percy was five-eleven and trim. Georgie glanced down at his manicured nails. They had been buffed to a shine instead of covered with a clear gloss, but she knew manicured nails when she saw them. The ring on the middle finger of his right hand had a large white diamond in it. He wore a gold watch, the band at least an inch and a half in width. When his lips parted in a smile, she expected to see gold there, too, but no, they were perfectly normal teeth.

"Do I know you?" she asked him, none too friendly. She leisurely wiped the corner of her mouth with a napkin and met his eyes. Next, her eyebrows arched in an askance expression. "Is 'hey, pretty lady' your entire repertoire?"

Percy simply smiled at her rudeness. "You're the lawyer who just moved in. I'm Percy Handler of—"

"Handler Realty. Yeah, yeah . . . how do you do? Excuse me if I don't shake hands. I'm in the middle of a rushed lunch, and after that, it'll be a rushed meeting."

Percy rolled his shoulders and pointedly glanced at his expensive watch. "Time is money. So I won't waste yours, or mine." His light brown eyes bore into hers. "You and me, tonight. At Chauncy's. Eight o'clock?"

Georgie held up her left hand so that he got an unobstructed view of her engagement ring *and* her wedding ring. She thought that said it all.

She was mistaken.

"That's only a hindrance if you let it be," he told her with a rakish grin.

Georgie pushed her plate aside and gave him a look that could freeze hell. "Exactly what are your balls made of, mister? Titanium-enforced steel? Must be if you're risking getting them crushed by a ballbuster like myself! What hidden qualifications do you possess that would make you think I'd cheat on my husband with the likes of you?"

"Baby, when I'm finished with this neighborhood, you aren't going to recognize it. I have investors who're just waiting to move in and convert this place into a Yuppie paradise. We've already started buying up homes from these fine folks. In a few years' time, the old will be replaced by the new, and you can be a part of it." His hungry eyes roamed over her smooth, dark brown skin and the bountiful hair that fell nearly to her waist. "I like you. I like what you stand for. You're the new black woman. You know what you want and you know how to get it. You're not like some of these other tired sisters who ain't about nothin'! All they want is someone to take care of them while they sit on their butts and look pretty. Hell, I'm tired of that crap! Give me a woman who's out there doing her own thing!"

Rising, Georgie hastily put the file back into her briefcase. After snapping it closed, she grasped the handle in her left hand and placed her purse on her shoulder. Peering down at Percy Handler, she said, "Well, on behalf of sisters everywhere, have a cup of coffee on us!" With that, she adeptly slid the three-quarters-full cup of black coffee across the table. Percy saw it coming but didn't possess the physical adeptness he needed in order to be able to move out of the way quickly enough. The still-hot liquid spilled down the front of his trousers. He let out a screech, and all eyes in the cafe were on him as he leapt up from the table and beat the front of his trousers with both hands in an effort to cool off the area where the coffee had landed. "I'll sue you for everything you're worth!" Looking around the cafe, into the eyes that were trained on him, he said, "You all saw what she did. You're all my witnesses!"

"Saw what?" asked an older gentleman, who sat at the booth right next to the one Georgie had just abandoned. "All I saw was you spill coffee on yourself. You can't blame someone else for your own clumsiness, Percy."

"Liar!" Percy shouted. The coffee had cooled now, and he looked as though he had just peed his pants. It was the embarrassment that kept him raging. "You all hate me because I'm trying to bring about change in the neighborhood. But did I hold a knife to the throats of those people who sold out? No! I offered them a fair price, and they jumped at the opportunity."

"It was more likely *you* jumped at the opportunity!" a woman said from the back of the cafe. Laughter was immediate. "Daphne, come over here and refill my coffee cup. I've had enough for today, but I've discovered another use for it."

"Yeah, Daphne," an elderly woman sitting at the counter cried, holding her mug toward the stout Daphne, who held a carafe of coffee aloft. Daphne's ample belly was shaking with laughter. "You had better get on out of here, Percy Handler, before I start refilling all the cups in this place. . . ."

"You're all going to be sorry!" Percy ineffectively threatened as he hurried out the door, shaking his right leg as he did so in a futile attempt to keep the cold clothing from sticking to his warm skin.

Georgie stood in the middle of the room after he had left and just looked at the denizens of Fisher's Cafe with amazement and gratitude. "Thank you," she said softly.

"Naw," the gentleman who had spoken up first told her. "Thank *you*, Mrs. Georgette Shaw-Knight. Thank you for being a stand-up type who knows how to put a sleaze in his place." He rose and came toward her, his hand out. "I knew your husband, Clayton, when he was a kid. Good kid. I hear he grew up to become an even better man."

Georgie pumped his hand. He was a small man. No more than five-six, with a gentle smile. His dark skin had the suppleness of a forty-year-old man's, but Georgie knew he had to be pushing seventy. "Isaiah Whitaker. Welcome to the neighborhood."

From that moment on, Georgie felt like she was a part of them.

* * *

Gwen stuck her head in the office now. "I'm going to lunch. Are you going out, or would you like me to bring you back something?"

Georgie thought for a moment. The way her stomach felt, she shouldn't eat anything for a while. "Nothing for me, thanks. You go and enjoy yourself."

"I'll lock the door behind me, then," replied Gwen, a petite African-American woman in her late forties with twinkling black eyes. Georgie's staff consisted of two assistants, one a single mother attending law school and the other a paralegal. Gwen was the secretary, the gofer, and, in Georgie's opinion, the only indispensable member of the staff. Gwen insisted on locking the door when there was only one person in the office.

"Okay, Gwen. I'm just going to finish these depositions and think happy thoughts."

"Your stomach still bothering you?" Gwen asked, concerned. "Georgie, you ought to see a doctor. You could have an ulcer. They're nothing to play with!"

"If it doesn't let up soon, I'll make an appointment. I promise," Georgie said. She was beginning to think she had hired another Alma, the woman who was Clay's office manager and surrogate mother.

"Okay. . . ." Gwen drew out the word, her voice doubtful. Turning away, she said, "I'll bring you back some saltines and skim milk. That'll help soothe your troubled tummy."

She was gone before Georgie could tell her of her suspicion that dairy products were behind the recurring problem. She returned to her reading.

A few minutes later, from the direction of the street, she heard voices raised in argument, generously colored by violent expletives. Quickly rising, she grabbed her coat from the rack and ran toward the front door of the office. With both sides of the coat flapping, she rushed through the door. She was greeted by the tableau unfolding on the sidewalk directly in front of the law office: a young kid, fifteen, maybe sixteen years old, was trying his best to beat the face of another kid to a pulp. He was on top of his prey, grunting and swearing with the effort, his fists pounding into the flesh of the downed kid again and again.

Georgie didn't think. She simply acted. She threw her body onto the youth's who was on top, and the two of them rolled onto the sidewalk. She was taller than he was by about two or three inches, but he outweighed her by at least twenty pounds. "What the—" She had caught him by surprise. "Get offa me! Are you crazy, woman?"

"I'm not the one trying to kill somebody on a city street."

He struggled beneath her. "Dude got my little sister pregnant and now don't want nothin' to do with her. The son of a bitch deserves to die!"

By that time, several patrons had spilled out onto the sidewalk from Fisher's Cafe. Among them was Gwen, who came to Georgie's assistance by grabbing the kid by the legs and holding on while Georgie straddled him and held his arms down.

Mrs. Fisher was kneeling next to the victim. She touched his face. "Hey, baby. Can you hear me?" He was bleeding from his nose and his mouth, but he was conscious. "Mama," he whispered, his eyes rolling around in his head like those of a terrified animal. Mrs. Fisher, a grandmother, shook her head in sympathy. She knew this boy. Had known him since he was a baby. His mother was a God-fearing woman who had lost control of him somewhere around his thirteenth year of life. He was a gang banger. Had no respect for authority. No respect for his mother. Now he was calling for his mama. "We're gonna get you some help, baby. Just be still. Be still."

Soon, the sound of approaching sirens split the air.

Two men had stepped up to take the outraged kid off Georgie's and Gwen's hands.

Gwen pulled Georgie aside to berate her. "Have you lost your mind, jumping on that kid like that? What if he'd had a gun or a knife? What if he'd hauled off and coldcocked your behind?"

Georgie didn't defend herself because it had become difficult to hear anything. She felt woozy all of a sudden, and her balance was off. Gwen's pretty face swam before her eyes, and why was the sidewalk coming up to meet her? The last coherent thought she had was, *Clay isn't going to be happy about this.*

Gwen stepped forward and wrapped her arms around Georgie's waist. At five-two, and a hundred and ten pounds, she hadn't a chance of being able to prevent the five-eight, one-hundred-forty-pound Georgie from falling. So the both of them sank, unharmed, to the sidewalk.

The police were first on the scene. After they had carted the assailant away, still hyper and uttering curses at the boy who had impregnated his kid sister, things settled down somewhat. The paramedics arrived shortly afterward and took the boy who had been beaten senseless to the nearest hospital, the V.A. Medical Center.

When Georgie came to, she was lying on the sofa in her office, and Gwen was pressing a cold cloth to her forehead. She sighed. "How long was I out?"

Frowning, Gwen answered, "Five minutes, maybe. I phoned Clay while Bill and Cedric brought you inside."

Georgie went to sit up and found she was still a bit woozy. "Oh, no. Why did you do that? He'll worry unnecessarily. . . ."

"He's your husband, that's his job," Gwen deadpanned. "Lie back down. Knowing him, he'll be here soon. I'll not have you make me out a liar by looking hale and hearty when he arrives."

Georgie had no choice. The room had begun to spin again. She lay down.

"And another thing," Gwen continued, now that she had Georgie's attention. "I think you ought to face the facts, young lady. You're pregnant. It isn't lactose intolerance, although that's part of the symptoms. You're pregnant. Now, the first thing you need to do is make an appointment with your doctor. Who is he? Dr. Leibermann's a good obstetrician. He's old, but solid. Besides, you don't want some inexperienced kid taking care of you and the baby. A baby!" She sounded excited enough for the both of them.

Georgie loved Gwen, but she wished the woman would shut up. She couldn't think! Pregnant? Why hadn't that occurred to her? Especially since she had been praying for Clay's child since they were married. Was she that dense? Dense? No. Just inexperienced. She hadn't gotten around to buying the pregnancy books, or the pick-your-baby's-name books. She was aware of some of the symptoms of pregnancy: morning sickness, a missed period and unexplained weight gain. However, what with the Manfred Jones case, she hadn't been paying close enough attention to the important things in life. When *was* her last period anyway? She used to mark it on the calendar on her bedroom wall each month. And she had been experiencing nausea even if it hadn't been limited to the morning hours. She felt it throughout the day. The term morning sickness was definitely a misnomer!

Her mind went back to Clay, and she looked up at Gwen, who was still rambling; but for the last few minutes, Georgie hadn't heard a word she had said. "What did you tell him over the phone?"

"I told him you had fainted outside and we'd brought you inside to rest," Gwen said. "Don't worry, I didn't tell him you tackled that kid. I'll leave that bit of news for you to deliver." She picked up the cloth that had fallen from Georgie's forehead when Georgie had sat up, then placed it on the coffee table nearby. Picking up a glass of iced water, she sat next to Georgie and brought the glass to her lips. "Drink."

Georgie obediently took a few sips. "Thanks, Gwen."

Before Gwen could reply, the sound of Clay's truck pulling up outside made both women jump. Georgie could tell by the sound of the tires screeching to a halt against the blacktop that he had been speeding. And he was probably double-parked.

Gwen put the glass down and hastily rose. "I'll just make myself scarce," she said, and began walking in the direction of the ladies' room toward the back of the building.

Clay came through the door, his black duster settling around muscular, jeans-clad legs. His hazel eyes sought Georgie's from across the room, and she gave him a weak smile. Covering the distance between them in a few long strides, he gathered Georgie in his arms without saying a word. His voice was soft when he murmured, "What's wrong, baby girl? What happened?"

Georgie held his face between her hands and peered into those eyes that she loved so much. "You've got to promise me you won't get angry when I tell you what I did. . . ."

Clay closed his eyes a moment as he tried to calm down enough to listen. But his heart was still playing a staccato rhythm, even though he was holding her safely in his arms.

Georgie waited. She knew him so well. He was going to be livid when he heard what she had done. But she didn't even consider not telling him the truth. That was not how they did things.

After a minute or so Clay sighed, sat down, and said, "All right, I'm ready now."

He looked her straight in the eyes as she related what had gone down less than half an hour ago. When she got to the point where she had collapsed, she paused. Tears had formed in her dark eyes. "Oh, sweetie, I've been so preoccupied lately. I haven't been keeping track of my periods. I've been having bouts of nausea—"

"You didn't tell me that!"

"I didn't want you to worry."

"Well, I'm worried now!" he cried. He let go of her and rose to his full height. Striding over to Gwen's desk, he riffled through the Rolodex and found Georgie's gynecologist's number.

When he began dialing the number, Georgie asked, "Hey, what are you doing?"

"I'm phoning Dr. Michael's office. You're going to the doctor . . . today!"

Georgie petulantly chewed on her bottom lip. She hated it when he just came in and took control like this. She could make her own appointment. It was just like him to see a problem and immediately get to work on solving it. It was the thing that irked her most about him. She simmered while he spoke into the handset.

Clay hung up the phone after about five minutes. "Come on. If we can get there in the next fifteen minutes, Dr. Michael can work us into her schedule."

Georgie rose. She was feeling much better. Eyeing him, she defiantly said, "And what if I can't make that appointment? You just waltz in here and start giving orders. I'm not sick, I'm pregnant!"

"You're not even sure about that!" Clay shouted, eyes narrowed in anger. "You're too damned stubborn for your own good, Georgette." He reached out and clasped her upper arm between strong fingers. "What if that kid had hurt you? What if you'd hit your head on the sidewalk when you fainted?"

"But I didn't!"

Clay let go of her to take a step back from her. Shaking his head, he expressed air between full lips. "How do you think it made me feel when you told me what you'd done? How you'd stupidly risked your life to break up a neighborhood fistfight?" His voice was hard. Harder than Georgie had ever heard it. There was a bitter edge to it. But she knew why he was angry. And she hated herself for causing him unnecessary pain. But if she gave in now, what would their lives be like a few months from now when she was big with their child? He wouldn't want to let her out of his sight. If she went to the supermarket, he would be there to protect her. Always the vigilant bodyguard. Hovering like a mother hen. Making her life a living hell and adding to his obsession about losing her to violence, the way he had lost Josie.

Tears continued to roll down her cheeks and into her trembling mouth as she told him, "Clay, you can't always protect me. You have to trust that in your absence, I can take care of myself. Otherwise, it'll drive you crazy!"

Clay came close. "Can we discuss this on the way to the doctor's office?"

Georgie threw up her arms in resignation and marched to her office to grab her shoulder bag and her briefcase. Returning to the outer office, she looked up at Clay. "Oh, I almost forgot about Gwen. I'll ask her to lock up and tell her she can go home for the day."

"Gwen!" Georgie called as she hurried down the hallway toward the ladies' room.

Gwen came out of the ladies' room looking around. "How'd it go?"

"We're on the way to Dr. Michael's office," Georgie

told her, coming close enough to Gwen to whisper, "He's mad enough to spit bullets!"

"Mmm-huh. Knew he would be," Gwen said.

"Would you lock up for me? Take the rest of the day off."

"I've got some typing to do first," Gwen told her, conscientious worker that she was. "Then I'll head on home." She gave Georgie a serious perusal. "Don't be too hard on him. He loves you. Hope you know how lucky you are to have a man like that!"

Georgie gave Gwen a brief parting hug. "I do."

Clay held the door for Georgie, then trotted ahead to unlock the car door and hand her in. Georgie leaned over and unlocked the driver's side door. As he was climbing in, the key at the ready, she got up on her knees and threw her arms around his neck, hugging him tightly, thereby preventing him from starting the SUV. "I'm sorry for scaring you, baby."

Clay laughed softly, flashing white teeth in his dark brown face. He pressed his lips to her forehead in a tender kiss. "I know you, Georgette. You didn't even think before jumping into the fray. . . ."

Georgie raised her head to peer up into his eyes. "You're right. I didn't think about it. I just saw someone getting beaten, and the only thing I thought about was stopping it," she said regrettably. "But, believe me, if I'd put two and two together and guessed that all my symptoms added up to pregnancy, I wouldn't have done what I did."

Clay smiled, crinkles appearing at the corners of his hazel eyes. "You should have thought twice even if you didn't have a child to consider. It's a dangerous world. You had no way of knowing whether the kid was carrying a piece. He could have shot you, and left you to die on a cold street." *Just like that bastard did with Josie,* he thought, but wouldn't have dreamed of saying aloud. He didn't have to. Georgie knew what he was thinking.

She lay her head on his chest. "I'm hereby hanging up my cape. No more superheroine antics for yours truly. If I see a mugging, I'm calling the cops. A kid beating the crap out of another kid? Nine-one-one!"

She felt Clay's breath on her face as he sighed. "If only I could believe that, Georgette. But you've got Toni Shaw's blood coursing through your veins. There's no way you're going to stop getting involved." He tipped her chin up with a finger as his eyes bored into hers. "But I will hold you to your word. No more street brawls." Then he bent his head and kissed her.

Seven

Jack Cairns' face was covered with red and purple bruises. Solange winced when she moved around the hospital bed to peer down at him. "It looks worse than it is," Jack said in his gravelly voice, startling her. His eyes were so swollen, she couldn't tell whether they were open or closed. She had assumed he was sleeping.

She smiled at him. "Hello, Jack. How do you feel?"

He actually cracked a smile. "I ain't feelin' no pain," he told her, implying that the painkillers he was on were highly effective.

Solange gently took one of his hands in hers and gave it a reassuring squeeze. "Well, good. Is there anything I can do for you, Jack? Maybe there's something you'd like to eat that the hospital isn't providing for you?"

"Nah, Dr. DuPree. I don't need anything," Jack said. He shifted in the bed so that he could get a better look at her. "Did you hear? The guys who beat me got out on bail."

Solange was so shocked, she felt as if her heart had fallen to the pit of her stomach. "What? I can't believe any judge in his right mind would allow such a thing!"

"That's what's wrong with the system today," Jack said. "Everybody's too busy protecting the rights of the criminal, and nobody cares about the victims. . . ."

Solange's mind was preoccupied. She was remembering what her mysterious visitor had told her last night. *If you can keep the goddess out of his hands for the next few days, the situation will diffuse itself.* What if the two men, no, *three* men—James Bond's darker brother had mentioned a third man—came after her again? How long would it take them to get the location of the goddess out of her? She didn't have a high threshold for pain.

"I can see you didn't know they were out," Jack was saying. "Detective Montez should have phoned you."

Solange realized her emotions must have been showing on her face. She forced a smile. "If you were in their shoes, what would your first priority be, following a dead end—after all, they didn't find what they were looking for at the office or at my home—or getting out of the country as soon as possible?"

Jack grunted. "I wouldn't know, Doc. It'd depend on how desperate I was."

Solange released his hand and gently patted it. "Listen, Jack, don't you worry about me. You just concentrate on getting better. I'll drop by police headquarters later and ask Detective Montez why no one saw fit to inform me about their release."

"Give him hell," Jack encouraged her.

"I intend to," Solange assured him. "Now, tell me, when are you getting out of here?"

Yusef walked the corridors of his home, thinking. Attired in a flowing white robe and loose-fit slacks and sandals, all in white, his progress was followed by state-of-the-art cameras stationed throughout the edifice. The marble floor upon which he walked was polished to such a high sheen that it appeared as if he glided across the placid surface of an alpine lake. The floor reflected the colors of the mural on the wall, which depicted the history of his family, from the first merchant who was reputed to have organized caravans that took Arabian treasures throughout ancient Asia and Africa, to stately portraits of his mother and father, who were still alive and residing in Riyadh. The ten-thousand-square-foot structure was composed of sandstone and rose four stories up from the desert like a monolith in an otherwise flat landscape.

Turning the corner, he arrived at his destination, Mubara's quarters.

He knocked because, even though it was his house, he never failed to show respect for his guests' privacy. No cameras recorded their actions while in their bedrooms; however, once they stepped out of their rooms, their every movement was recorded for security purposes.

The door creaked open as if by itself, and Yusef walked into the large, airy room. Airy when occupied by anyone else. Now the room felt strangely constricting. The smell of incense, a combination of fragrances, assailed his nostrils, and the room was in shadows. Candles were placed about the room, some lit, some not. He had trouble focusing. Squinting, he said, "Mubara?" His deep voice held a warning. He had grown impatient with all the spiritualistic trappings Mubara enjoyed flaunting. "Show yourself. There have been several unexpected changes in my plans."

The door closed, and standing next to it was Mubara. Clothed in layers of silk in varying pastel shades, she was a tiny wisp of a woman. Swarthy skin, slanting dark eyes, black hair, and a face that defied aging. Yusef had stopped guessing at how old she actually was, even though he had the feeling she was ancient. Her race? Asian. But whether she was Japanese, Chinese, Korean or Vietnamese, or hailed from any number of other Asian countries, he had no way of knowing. His people had tried, but hadn't been able to glean any information on her. She had a commanding voice: deep and imperious, lacking the warmth he had come to expect from women's voices. Indeed, at times he had the distinct feeling that when she spoke directly to him, she was implanting directives into his brain. As if she were hypnotizing him for nefarious reasons.

"I have been here all the while," she said, her tone brooking no opposing opinions. For the life of him, he couldn't place her accent.

"My people have failed to get the final statue," Yusef told her.

She turned and walked to the French doors, the silken layers of her robes rustling. "Then, we'd just as well call off the ceremony. I cannot guarantee success without the squatting goddess. She is the most powerful. Without her, the others are incomplete." Yusef followed her to the French doors and opened them. The indigo night sky was sprinkled with stars. Yusef found the world outside infinitely more pleasant than being in this woman's presence.

"In that case, I suppose I'll have to get it. I was hoping that it wouldn't come to this. But, I'll have to resort to—"

Mubara held up a cautionary hand. "I don't wish to know the details." Her obsidianlike eyes hardened even more. "I assume Dr. DuPree is still in possession of the statue. I suggest you convince her to hand it over. There is little time remaining. The window of opportunity presents itself at exactly 6:01 P.M. on October twenty-seventh."

Normally, Yusef would not allow anyone to speak to him with such lack of respect. He was committed to seeing his plans come to fruition, though, and would stomach Mubara's attitude until after the ceremony was complete. Who knew? If the ceremony was a success, he might be induced to buy her her own psychic network!

Turning away from the tiny woman, smirking because

of his little joke, he said, "Good night, then. Don't let the bedbugs bite. Or would they have the temerity to try that with a witch?"

Mubara ignored his remark. "You may leave," she said, as if giving permission to a small boy to go to the bathroom.

Yusef firmly closed the door behind him. He breathed in great gulps of incense-free air as he stepped into the corridor. The sooner that woman was out of his house, the better. Striding purposefully toward his own private suite of rooms, he wondered what Salah was doing at this moment.

"Mmm . . ." Toni moaned as she bit into the ripe, succulent strawberry Chuck held to her mouth. Chuck popped the rest of the strawberry into his mouth, then leaned forward and pulled her closer to him on the bed. They were sitting facing each other, both naked as the day they had been born; however, Toni had the corner of the sheet draped across her torso, and Chuck had a pillow strategically placed in front of him.

"You're a romantic fool, feeding me strawberries in bed for breakfast! How're you going to top this?" Toni lightly accused him as she swung one long leg up and around and settled her foot in his lap. Chuck immediately began massaging her foot with strong fingers. He loved her feet, the even toes, the nails cut short and painted seashell pink. The tops of her feet were tanned. She enjoyed going barefoot in the summertime. Finished kneading the muscles of her left foot, he ran his hands up her leg.

Toni giggled. "What do you think you're doing?"

Chuck gave her a frankly sensual look. "We should work off some of those calories."

Toni placed her right foot against his chest. "You forgot this one."

Chuck grasped the foot in both his hands, bent his head and kissed the top of it. He then gave it as much attention as he had the left one. His eyes were on her, though, enjoying the delightful vision she made lying on the bed with the sheet running up over her torso and between her legs, which were held open. He wanted to move the sheet aside so he could see what it was hiding.

"You get better at this all the time," Toni complimented him. She moistened her lips with the tip of her tongue. Her brows shot up suddenly. "Your pillow just moved."

She bent forward and snatched the pillow from in front of him, and sure enough his manhood had doubled in size and was still growing. "Chuck, you know we're supposed to meet Solange at her bank in less than an hour." But her tone was speculative and lacked conviction.

Chuck knew she, too, was wondering what pleasures they could partake of in thirty minutes or less. He reached down, grasped her by both ankles and pulled her toward him on the bed with her legs spread-eagled. "We're wasting time talking."

Toni laughed delightedly. She felt wanton when she was with Chuck, like a woman who had spent her life as a spinster and then along came the one man who could awaken the Jezebel in her. Chuck sat between her legs, his erect penis on her belly. Toni peered up at him. "Aren't you going to put a cap on that bad boy?"

"We're out of condoms."

"Liar."

"What are you afraid of, Toni? We're both healthy. We're soon to be married. . . ."

"That's the point, Chuck. Your boys are undoubtedly

strong swimmers, and I'm strong and healthy. Menopause is a few years away for me. I can get pregnant."

Chuck massaged her breasts. "Would that be so bad?"

Toni smiled at him. "Spoken like a man in the throes of sexual excitement." She rolled over and pushed him off her. Getting to her feet, she went to the nightstand and retrieved a foil-wrapped condom from the top drawer and tore it open. Returning to the bed, she lovingly gazed down at him. "I love you, Chuck. But we need to discuss having a child." He was sitting on the edge of the bed. She came close, knelt and grasped his penis in her hand. Still holding Chuck's gaze, she said, "Our discussion should be long and hard." She ran her hand along the length of him. "You'll need to persuade me that bringing another child into this world is the right thing to do." Then she slowly rolled the condom onto his now engorged member.

Chuck drew her to him and kissed her forehead. Toni ran her hands through his hair. He pulled her to her feet. Brushing her short hair away from her face, he said, "I want everything with you, Toni. Everything we missed because of my stupidity. But if you think it's too late for us to have another child, I'll understand. Because my first priority is, and always will be, your happiness. I don't need another son to validate me. I've got two wonderful daughters. If I can just have the next fifty years with you, I'll be a deliriously happy man."

Chuck was only two inches taller than she was, but Toni found she liked the way she fit in his arms. They were strong arms. Warm and reassuring. Solid. She grinned roguishly. "See? Now you're going to make me want to have your child. You and your unselfish ways!"

Chuck laughed, grabbed her buttocks with both hands and pressed her firmly against him. "Listen, *we* are eager to dance with Miss Antoinette. Do you think she'd welcome a slow waltz?" He always referred to her feminine center as Miss Antoinette.

Toni brought his head down and kissed his mouth. "I think she's more in the mood for a hot tango between the sheets."

In spite of the time constrictions, their movements were slow and deliberate as Toni backed toward the bed and fell onto it, Chuck on top of her. He kissed her mouth, parting her lips and tasting the strawberry she had eaten on her tongue. Toni opened her legs and welcomed him inside of her as she raised her hips to facilitate a deeper penetration. As his tongue plundered her mouth, their urgent thrusts rose and dipped to the same primeval rhythm. He knew where she was most sensitive. His hands found those spots, from her firm, round bottom to the hollow in the small of her back as she arched to meet his passion with needs just as strong. Breaking off the kiss, Chuck said, "You're panting, baby."

Toni took a deep breath and released it. "Don't make me laugh, Chuck. This is feeling too good." He would often make her laugh right in the middle of lovemaking, and although she knew his purpose behind it, a longer period of time during which he could hold an erection, she found the habit distracting. Sometimes, she simply wanted to come fast and furious, whereas Chuck liked to make love all night long or, at least, the better part of it. She enjoyed those times, too. Right now, however, she felt a whopper of an orgasm coming on, and he was pulling her back from it. Still, she knew how to turn the tables on him. "Remember our first time together at the cabin?"

Chuck groaned. Toni thrust upward. He pushed deeper still. "Oh God, oh God, oh God. . . ." He squeezed his eyes shut, and when he did, he couldn't hold on to his control any longer. He came with a shout, and Toni reached her peak a few seconds later. She held on to him until they both stopped shivering.

Chuck briefly kissed her mouth, then peered down into her eyes. "That was unfair, reminding me of that weekend." He playfully tweaked her nose.

"You know I don't fight fair, Chuck," was all Toni said. Their skin was covered with a thin layer of perspiration. The hair on his chest was slightly matted. She put her hand there and felt the thud of his heart against her palm. She hoped he would awaken her in this manner from now on.

"Who paid their bail?" Solange asked Detective Montez as she sat across from him in his office. If you could call it an office. Actually, it was only a space within a larger room, partitioned off by a room divider. Seeing the conditions under which the police worked made her wonder where her tax dollars were actually being spent. On Caribbean vacations for city officials? It certainly wasn't being spent on serviceable equipment for the police department.

Detective Montez gave her an apologetic half smile. "All I know is, a lawyer in an expensive suit arrived, said he would be representing them, and less than two hours later, both men were walking out of here." His brown eyes were red-rimmed, and there was a half-eaten tuna sandwich growing mold on his desktop.

"Is this what they mean by 'Justice is blind'?"

"And deaf and dumb," the beleaguered detective added, sounding weary.

Solange sighed and got to her feet. "Jack Cairns identified them as the men who beat him to within an inch of his life, and they still walked! Amazing."

"I don't know what to tell you, Dr. DuPree. We arrest them, book them, and cage them, and a few hours later, the judge releases them. It isn't right, but until we get a better legal system, we have to live with it."

"Or die with it," Solange said, realizing she was on her soapbox now but unable to quit. "What if they come back?" She looked around them. "Maybe you've got an extra gun in your desk I can borrow."

Rising, Detective Montez walked around his desk and took her by the shoulders. "A black-and-white will be patrolling your neighborhood for the next two days. Take normal precautions. Lock your doors and windows. Pay attention to what's going on around you when you're walking to and from your car."

Solange nodded. She was grateful for his advice, but frustrated that she still had to be constantly watching her back. The measures he had suggested were things she did as a matter of course. What woman living in this day and age didn't worry about her safety? "Okay."

He let go of her and she turned away.

"Thank you, Detective." But the words nearly stuck in her throat. She had never felt more vulnerable. And she couldn't depend on the police to adequately protect her.

Raul Montez looked after Solange until she turned the corner. He sympathized. He had often felt as if his hands were tied while trying to perform his job. He supposed that was why he had an ulcer and drank Mylanta as if it were a tasty milk shake.

Solange left the police station as swiftly as her legs could take her. As she stepped outside into the balmy air, she tried to shake the tightness gathering around her shoulders and neck. Stress. She walked past a group of recruits in their spiffy blue uniforms. They were laughing about something or other. She wondered how long the excitement of being a cop would stay with them. Detective Montez had the eyes of a man who knew he was whipped.

She pulled out of the parking lot in her black Mustang convertible with a mind to just keep driving south until she wound up in Key West. Lara and Cameron Maxwell, her best friend's parents, lived there, and she could use a hug right about now. When she was growing up, they were the ones who made her feel that she was always welcome in their home. That she mattered and that she was loved. Her own mother lived right here in Miami, but Etienne DuPree had never made it a secret that her daughter was more of a burden than a blessing. Once Solange graduated from high school, she had never gone back home to stay. Not even for a prolonged visit. Would she and her mother ever have a normal relationship? She had stopped allowing the situation to color her present or her future. So what if her mother didn't love her? It didn't prevent her from loving others or hoping with all her heart that she would one day be blessed with a child. At least she had a perfect example of how *not* to raise a child.

Chiding herself for momentarily wallowing in self-pity, Solange pointed the car west.

Toni and Chuck would soon be arriving at the bank. She had promised Toni a look at the goddess before she and Chuck had to catch a flight to San Francisco.

Salah Makonnen sat in Dr. David Song's waiting room reading a Dean Koontz novel. In it the heroine was also waiting in a doctor's waiting room; however, her doctor was a mind-controlling sociopath. Dr. David Song was a saint.

A middle-aged woman sat down next to her. "I read that," she couldn't help saying. "It was wonderful!" She had a thick Brooklyn accent.

Salah smiled politely, but she wasn't interested in conversation. She was giddy with happiness. Dr. Song had phoned her at her hotel this morning and told her the X rays of her uterus looked promising. It seemed the scarring in her Fallopian tubes had been minimized with the aid of her last surgery, and maybe, just maybe, that meant pregnancy was viable. She hadn't phoned Yusef yet because she wanted to make certain the good doctor wasn't giving her false hopes. But she was elated nonetheless. It was the first glimmer of hope that she had had in ten years.

"Yes," she said, looking into the woman's green eyes. "It's delightfully frightening."

"What a lovely accent you have," the woman said, in the mood for a chat. "British?"

"Sudanese," Salah told her.

"I know who you remind me of now, that model. What's her name? She's married to David Bowie. I love his music. She's breathtaking. And you have her exact bone structure. I know good bone structure. My son's a plastic surgeon. Not that you need his help." She riffled in her bag until she came out with a business card. Handing it to Salah, she said, "Pass it on to a friend. He has a Manhattan office. He's done some of New York's most famous faces."

Salah accepted the card and slipped it inside her purse. "I'll do that."

"Mrs. Makonnen?" a fresh-faced nurse called from an open doorway. She had a clipboard in her hand and an expectant expression on her brown face.

Rising, Salah looked down at the green-eyed woman. "That's me."

"It was a pleasure," the woman assured her.

Salah followed the nurse down the hallway to the second examining room on the right, where the nurse placed her clipboard on the counter that had a stainless-steel sink in the middle of it and medical supplies in glass jars lined atop it. The jars contained tongue depressors, long cotton swabs, individually wrapped bandages, and other items Salah didn't know the uses for. She read the nurse's name badge: Kylie King.

Kylie smiled warmly at her. "If you'll just step up there and have a seat, Mrs. Makonnen, I'll check your blood pressure and heart rate."

Salah placed her book and her purse on a nearby chair and climbed onto the padded examining table. "How are you today?" Kylie asked as she wrapped the upper part of Salah's arm with the cuff on the blood pressure machine and secured the Velcro fastening. She then pressed a button, and the machine automatically inflated, tightening around Salah's arm until it was uncomfortably tight but not painful. The air was then released, and Kylie waited for the digital readout. She smiled. "I can see you're taking good care of yourself. Excellent numbers."

Salah found Kylie's cheerfulness a little grating, but she was willing to walk over hot coals if it got her closer to good news about her condition.

Kylie then grasped Salah's left wrist and, with an eye on the second hand of her watch, counted Salah's heartbeats. Again, she pronounced the results to be excellent.

Going over to the counter to record her findings in Salah's chart, Kylie said, "Dr. Song will be in shortly. He's running a bit late this morning, I'm afraid, because he had to perform surgery before coming to the office."

"Does he ever rest?" Salah joked.

"I think he sleeps at his desk," Kylie said on her way out.

Alone, Salah paced the small room. Her Ferragamo pumps made crisp clicks on the tile floor. She was five-ten in her stocking feet, slim but not to the point of emaciation. After a childhood of deprivation, she was not willing to go without today. It amazed her that even when she was a model, she didn't survive on saltines and water as some of the other girls seemed to. Of course, denial to a model who avoided food in order to stay slim was different from the sort she knew first-hand. She was surprisingly devoid of eating disorders. When she lived in New York City, a friend of hers convinced her to see a therapist and discuss her childhood. Toward the close of their sessions, the therapist admitted she was in awe of Salah's strength, considering everything she had been through: losing her parents to tribal war, becoming a scavenger on the streets, spending most of her formative years in an orphanage run by Catholic nuns where she slept in a room with twenty other children. What the therapist didn't understand was that all these things only strengthened Salah's resolve to create her own happiness, which was why she didn't shy away from Yusef Makonnen when he started to pursue her. Some women might have been intimidated by his good looks, his wealth or his apparent need to possess them. Salah, on the other hand, looked past the obvious and saw the man underneath, a man who was in desperate need of someone to love him for himself.

Her love shocked him and thrilled him simultaneously. He couldn't believe that his money had no influence on her. She told him to keep looking if he expected her to kowtow to him simply because he had a bigger purse. They would come together as equals, or not at all. Yusef was not used to a strong woman. He had formerly wasted his time on simpering girls who fell over themselves to remain in his favor. He had thought he wielded the ultimate form of power, that of masculine control. But what he was doing was getting nowhere fast. He would tire of one and move on to the next. When he met Salah, she would not jump when he called. He had to see her when it was convenient for her. And when it came to intimate relations, she told him she was a practicing Muslim, a religion she had ironically discovered while modeling in New York City, and there would be no sex before marriage. He was on his knees proposing marriage within six months of their meeting. Salah agreed to wed him, and they had spent nine wonderful years together—years marred only by their inability to produce a child.

"Good afternoon, Salah," Dr. David Song said pleasantly as he entered the room. The door closed with a soft swish, as if the room would soon be vacuum-sealed. Salah turned to smile warmly at the small man. Dr. Song was a Chinese-American in his late fifties. His brown hair was graying, and he was bald on top. He didn't, however, employ the comb-over, which rather endeared him to Salah.

"Stop wearing a hole in my floor," Dr. Song said lightly, his brown eyes twinkling behind thick glasses. "I have good news today. I'm sending you home, Salah. Go home to your husband and engage in conjugal bliss. Doctor's orders."

Salah could have kissed him, but figured it would embarrass the doctor too much. Instead, she listened intently as he told her the scarring on her Fallopian tubes was practically nonexistent and, for all intents and purposes, she had just as good a chance of conceiving as any other healthy, thirty-something woman.

Salah practically floated out of his office that afternoon.

The bank's assistant manager was a tall black gentleman in his early forties. He was attired in the customary dark suit, and the tops of his dress shoes were glossy enough to reflect one's face in them. As he led Solange, Toni and Chuck down the corridor to the bank's storage vault where the safety-deposit boxes were housed, he chatted amiably. "Dr. DuPree, I told my daughter Shana about you. She's interested in majoring in anthropology next semester when she begins school at the University of Miami. She was thrilled to find out there's a black woman anthropology professor on the faculty."

Solange smiled at him. "There are a few of us."

Actually, Solange had two Ph.D.s, one in anthropology and another in archaeology. She had no trouble marrying the two disciplines. Anthropology was the study of present-day mankind. How they developed as a people, their physical and mental characteristics. Why they behave the way they do. Archaeology also dealt with mankind, but with the detritus of mankind. What they left behind. It was the scientific study of ancient people. Solange could sometimes look at a modern culture and see the direction it was going, just by knowing the way an ancient civilization had already gone.

Soon, they were in the vault, and the assistant manager and Solange each had to insert and turn a key in the box in tandem in order to open the lock on the safety-deposit box in which she had left the goddess. With his part performed, the assistant manager prepared to take his leave. "It was a pleasure meeting you," he said to Toni and Chuck. "Dr. DuPree, when you've finished, simply close the box. It automatically locks."

"Thank you," Solange said with a warm smile. "And tell Shana to come visit me before she registers. We should talk about the courses she'll need to take her first year."

His dark eyes lit up at this offer. "I will. Thank you!" Then he left them alone.

Solange went to the wall safe and pulled the metal box from it. She, Toni, and Chuck moved over to a nearby rectangular-shaped table where she placed the box with the goddess in it flat on the tabletop. As Toni and Chuck looked on, she pried open the wooden lid that had been made to fit snugly. Once the lid was off, she moved aside so that Toni could get a better look at the wooden statue.

Toni moved closer and touched the box with—and she hated to admit it—slightly trembling fingers. She wasn't a superstitious person. At least she didn't think she was. But after everything she had heard about the goddess, a bit of reverential fear had crept into her and settled.

"You can pick it up if you like," Solange said.

Toni saw the smirk on Chuck's face and knew what he was thinking after their conversation about babies that morning.

Even though the small, red-brown statue seemed to beckon her, she wouldn't touch it. "I'd rather not," she said with a smile in Solange's direction. "Just in case."

Solange laughed softly. "I understand."

"I don't believe the intrepid Toni Shaw is actually afraid of picking up a fertility goddess," Chuck joked. He reached into the box and picked up the goddess. It was heavier than it appeared. The wood was polished to a smooth finish. Turning it over, he observed it from all angles. "It's actually beautifully crafted. The artist was very talented." He moved closer to Toni, turning the goddess in his hands so that she would have a clearer view. "Look at the expression on her face. She almost looks as if she's alive."

Toni reached out to touch it. However, her hand remained suspended above the goddess. "She is lovely." She expressed a regretful sigh. "Put her back in the box."

She looked up at Solange, who had been watching her interaction with Chuck. They were in love. Solange instinctively knew this. When this thought occurred to her, something else important came to mind. She hadn't told them about the warning James Bond's darker brother had given her to pass on to them.

"I had another visit from our mysterious rescuer last night," she said without preamble. "Yesterday, after he left us, he looked around the area to make sure the two men he had handcuffed were alone. Well, he found the lens cap from a camera, and from this he deduced that a third man had been outside as a lookout. And while he was concealed, he took photos of us."

Toni and Chuck exchanged worried glances.

Toni suddenly felt vulnerable. What if her curiosity had brought her and her loved ones to the attention of the person behind the thefts? And since she already knew he would stop at nothing to get what he wanted, the fact that he was now in possession of photographs of her and Chuck didn't sit well with her.

"Did he say why he felt a need to warn us about this third man?" Toni asked, her eyes meeting Solange's. She didn't think Solange was holding anything back. However, life had taught her that things were rarely as they seemed. "Did he give any clues as to the identity of the person behind the thefts?"

Solange hesitated a moment. "He did have this to say about the man behind the thefts: if he can use the photos against us in any way, he'll do it." Chuck had placed the goddess back into the cloth-lined box. Solange secured the lid in place, carried the box back to the safety-deposit box and slid it inside before adding, "Oh, he also said that time is running out. If I can keep the goddess out of the culprit's hands a few more days, the situation will diffuse itself."

"Well, I hope so anyway," Toni said. She tried to shrug off the chill she had felt upon hearing that she and Chuck had inadvertently been drawn into the intrigue because of her insatiable curiosity. But she couldn't.

Chuck went to her and took her by the shoulders. "Come on now, I know what you're thinking. But just because they took photos of us, it doesn't mean they're going to come after us or anyone else we know."

Solange came around the table after shutting the safety-deposit box and putting the key in her shoulder bag. She gently placed a reassuring hand on Toni's arm. "Mr. Waters is right. I'm sure all of this is going to blow over soon."

Toni brightened. Why borrow trouble? As of this moment, all was well. She would cling to that thought for as long as she could. But as soon as she got out of this vault and she and Chuck were in the car on the way to the airport, she would phone Mere, Georgie and Bree to see how they were doing. Paranoia? Maybe. But better safe than sorry.

Solange saw them off at the Lincoln Town Car. Toni firmly hugged her. Peering down into Solange's up-turned face, she playfully said, "Dr. DuPree, it's been a treat getting to know you. Don't be a stranger. And speaking of strangers, if the mysterious stranger turns up again, tell him I said he should stay around long enough to take you to dinner."

Chuck shook Solange's hand, stiff Bostonian that he was. "Don't mind her. She's an inveterate matchmaker. It's been a pleasure, Solange."

"Oh, the pleasure was all mine," Solange said, grinning at the both of them.

She took a step back as they got into the Lincoln Town Car and waved as the car sped off. Then she trudged across the parking lot to her Mustang and headed home. She was going home to change into work clothes. She still had to tackle the mess at her office on campus. Though the custodial staff had cleaned up the bulk of the debris, she needed to sort through her personal papers and books herself.

* * *

Georgie sat on the floor in the living room, the cordless phone in her hand. Clay sat on the sofa right behind her. While she placed a few calls, he was rubbing her shoulders. She looked back at him and smiled. He hadn't left her side since they got the news this morning. If he wasn't bringing her something, he was touching her in any way he could: playing with her braids, getting close to nuzzle the side of her neck, giving her feet massages to die for. The phone was ringing. "Pick up," Georgie impatiently urged.

She had always promised herself that when she got pregnant, her mom would be the second person she told. The first person was busy kissing her nape. And the second person wasn't picking up. . . .

"Hello," Toni's voice anxiously said.

"Mom. . . ."

"Georgie. I was just going to phone you. I need your opinion. I'm researching this story and I may have gotten in too deep." Her mother sounded worried. It was Georgie's initial instinct to listen to what her mother had to say before giving her the news. But Clay had other ideas. He took the receiver from her and said with a huge grin on his handsome face, "Mom, this is the happiest day of my life . . . next to the day I married Georgette, of course!"

"What's up?" Georgie heard her mother scream as she snatched the phone back from Clay. "Oh, my God! Are you pregnant, Georgie? Chuck! Our daughter's expecting!"

Her father came on the line. Georgie could hear her mother having a screamfest in the background. "Calm down, Toni, you'll scare the driver," her father said. Then, to her, "Sweetheart, is it true? You're going to have a baby?"

"Yes, Daddy," Georgie said quietly. There were enough

GET YOUR
FREE ISSUE!

Smart, Stylish & Sexy.

Your Guide to Staying Ahead of the Latest Trends.

YES! Please send my FREE issue of HONEY right away and enter my one-year subscription. My special price for 9 more issues (10 in all) is only $9.95. I'll save 69% off the newsstand price. And if I decide HONEY is not for me, I'll write "cancel" on the invoice, return it, and owe nothing. The FREE issue will be mine to keep.

5AR3

Name	(please print)

Address	Apt. #

City/State/Zip

e-mail address

Please allow 6-8 weeks for receipt of first issue. In Canada: CDN $19.95 (includes GST). Payment in U.S. currency must accompany all Canadian orders. Basic subscription rate: 1 year (10 issues) $18.00.

VISIT WWW.HONEYMAG.COM

BUSINESS REPLY MAIL
FIRST-CLASS MAIL   PERMIT NO 1389   BOULDER CO

POSTAGE WILL BE PAID BY ADDRESSEE

honey

P.O. BOX 52067
BOULDER CO 80321-2067

excited people around her. Someone had to maintain a sense of decorum.

"Oh, baby . . . ," her father said, his voice catching. She could have sworn he sniffed.

"I'm back, sweetie," her mother said in a calmer voice. "Your father's crying."

Eight

Solange climbed the three steps to her front porch. As she placed her feet on the welcome mat, she glanced down and saw what looked like the corner of a manila envelope protruding from underneath. She bent and pulled the eight-by-eleven envelope free. Printed on it in bold black script was *Solange*. Turning about, peering all around her, she checked out the area. At a little before noon, her street was quiet. Kids were in school. Many of her neighbors were at work. She did see elderly Mr. Wychowski walking his dog, Jimbo. "Hi, Solange," he called as he passed her house. "Good morning, Mr. Wychowski," she returned, trying to appear calm. She was anything but.

He paused a moment. "Is anything wrong, dear?"

Jimbo was champing at the bit, eager to get on with his walk. Mr. Wychowski, a tall, gaunt man with wisps of white hair bordering his head, pulled firmly on the leash. "In a minute, Jimbo."

Solange smiled at him. "Oh, everything's fine! Thanks for asking."

"All right. It's just that you seemed to be looking behind you. I thought somebody might be following you. You can't be too careful these days."

"No, no," she insisted as she held up the envelope. "I found this under my mat and was looking around just in case whoever left it was still in the area." She walked down the steps and stood on the lawn so she didn't have to raise her voice in order to be heard by him. "You haven't see any strangers on the street this morning, have you?"

Mr. Wychowski shook his head. "Just the regulars. Mrs. Brennermann, taking her morning constitutional. Kids off to school. Parents off to work. The postman delivering the mail." His eyes clamped on the envelope. "Hand delivered, huh?"

"Yes," Solange confirmed for him. She smiled. "Well, I won't hold you any longer. Thanks. And have a nice day!"

"You, too, dear," Mr. Wychowski returned the sentiments. He didn't seem in any rush to go, however. "If you need me, just holler."

"I will," Solange promised and turned to head back up the steps.

"Now, Jimbo," Mr. Wychowski scolded the Jack Russell Terrier. Jimbo had gotten comfortable on Solange's lawn. Mr. Wychowski jerked on the leash. "Don't be contrary. Or there will be no 'Frasier' for you tonight."

Jimbo immediately sprang to his feet and took off at a leisurely pace.

Solange laughed softly and went on in the house. Imagine a dog being hooked on a sitcom. The four-legged charmer did help to dispel a modicum of her nervous energy, though. In the house she locked the door behind her and went to sit on the sofa, depositing her shoulder bag and car keys on the coffee table in front of her. Examining the flap on the envelope, she discovered it wasn't sealed; the metal clasp was simply closed. "Here goes," she said, as she undid the clasp and ballooned the envelope so she could look down inside the belly of it. Photos. She poured them onto the tabletop and spread them across the surface. There was also a slip of white paper, folded over once. She picked it up and read, "Turnabout is fair play. The three fellows you see boarding the plane are well on their way out of the country. Thought this would give you peace of mind. And maybe earn me a few brownie points. Yours, Rupert."

Solange laughed aloud. Not a soft twitter, but a big, healthy laugh of pure delight. She laughed for a solid minute, and by the time she had composed herself, tears sat in her eyes. Rupert? She loved it! Her strong, hand-some, daring, exciting—to say nothing of being a great kisser—hero's name was Rupert!

While this sank in, she picked up the three snapshots. Yes, indeed, she recognized two of the henchmen climb-ing the steps of a 737. The third was a man of apparent African descent. He was smaller than his companions. Perhaps that was why they used him as a lookout, while the hulks invaded her home.

She silently thanked Rupert for this comforting piece of evidence. Now, perhaps, she could go to bed tonight with the assurance that she wouldn't be awakened in the middle of her slumber by the sound of someone walking about in her house.

Sliding the photographs back into the envelope, she picked up the note and read it once more. "Will I ever see you again, Rupert?"

Dominic rolled over in bed, his sleepy mind expecting to feel Bree's warm body next to him. When he didn't find her there, he assumed she had gone to the bath-room, so he rolled back onto his side of the bed, his eyes closing. They had shot the last scenes of *Queen of Sheba* only hours ago, and he had spent more than six hours going over the rushes while the rest of the cast and crew went off to the wrap party, the end-of-the-shoot celebration that was being held at their hotel. Bree had attended the party. However, when Dominic returned from the tech trailer, exhausted and bleary-eyed from going over the film they had shot that day, she was in his hotel room waiting for him. She had insisted he have some dinner, and then she had coaxed him into the bath. Afterward, they had made slow, sweet love, and he had gone down for the count.

Bree had been asleep, too, until the time she got up to go to the bathroom. On her way back from the bathroom, she encountered a whining Pierre in the hallway. It occurred to her that she hadn't taken him for his nightly walk. Thinking it might ruin years of training and conditioning if she allowed him to go on newspaper there in the hotel room, she slipped on a purple fleece jogging suit and a pair of worn white Nikes in preparation for taking him out. Just before she left the room, she remembered her coat. The temperature fell dramatically when the sun went down in Addis. After clipping the leash to Pierre's collar, slipping her hotel key into her coat pocket, and getting the requisite little blue bag that would be used to dispose of Pierre's offering, she was set. She looked back at Dominic, sleeping peacefully, and thought how lucky she was to have him in her life.

The hallway was abandoned at two in the morning. Pierre was straining at the leash, heading toward the back exit that led to the garden he liked to romp in. Bree picked up her pace. She didn't want him to have an accident in the hotel hallway.

A chilling wind swept in as she pushed open the door. She glanced down at the locking mechanism, wondering if she would be locked out if she didn't prop something in the door to prevent it from completely closing. On her way to the outside door, she had passed an empty food service tray left in the hall for room service personnel to retrieve. She retraced her steps to borrow the tray and use it to prop the door open. This done, she and Pierre left the relative warmth of the building for the garden.

"Okay," she warned Pierre, "I'm taking the leash off. It's late, so don't be difficult. If you run when I come after you, I'm liable to leave you outside all night instead of searching the grounds in the dark for you."

Pierre licked her hand. As soon as Bree removed the leash, he took off at a sprint in the direction of a frangipani bush he was fond of. Bree hoped the plant would continue to fare well in spite of the extra "water" Pierre left at the base of it.

She had never been out this late here in Addis before. When the crew had first arrived, they had been warned to look out for pickpockets when they visited the street marts, but she hadn't had any trouble whatsoever. Rather, she was surprised by the amount of animals in the streets. Sometimes at night when she took Pierre for his walk, she heard dogs barking nearby. Not just a couple of dogs, but scores of them. And donkeys. Even in the main thoroughfares, many times her driver had been forced to brake suddenly to avoid hitting them. Goats, kept for their milk and for their meat, grazed everywhere they could find patches of grass. Birds were also prevalent in the area: the largest crows she had ever seen, and others she hadn't seen but had heard singing beautifully in predawn. Addis was cool, too. Though the air was a bit warmer during the day, at night it got extremely cold, about ten degrees. And since they had been there, it had rained only once. The sky was almost always blue.

The people were, for the most part, polite but standoffish. Bree could understand their reticence. They had lived under the terror of the Mengistu regime for nearly twenty years, during which they learned that having an opinion could get you killed.

Addis was a city of contrasts: a mixture of the modern and the ancient. The hotel they were staying in had all the amenities, but when you stepped outside onto the street, you were sometimes greeted by locals dressed in traditional garb, and leading a train of ten to twenty goats down the middle of the street.

Bree yawned and ran a hand through her short locks. Since the film was in the can, so to speak, she no longer needed the extensions. The hairdresser had removed them shortly after Dominic had yelled, "Cut! That's a wrap, ladies and gentlemen. Thank you all for a once-in-a-lifetime experience!" Now her hair was back to its normal chin-length, layered style.

While she had been ruminating on her stay in Addis, she had kept her eyes on Pierre as he placed more liquid fertilizer at the base of the frangipani. She hoped he finished his business soon; it was cold out. She was rubbing her arms and marching in place when she thought she heard a twig snap to her left. She turned her head in that direction and saw two males, one a behemoth of a man, the other, shorter and slimmer, rushing toward her. Not exactly running, but moving entirely too fast to classify their approach as friendly. Bree had lived in major cities all her life. Therefore her senses, by natural evolution, were attuned to threats to her person. She sensed these men were up to no good. However, just as she pushed off on the balls of her feet, preparing to run like the wind, she ran smack into a hard body. The appearance of the first two men to her left had been designed to throw her into a panic and make her run right into the arms of their waiting partner.

Bree's scream was cut off by a huge mitt that nearly covered her entire face. The assailant held her against his body with an arm that felt as firm as a tree branch. She couldn't move her upper body at all. She tried stomping on his foot, but found out the hard way that he was wearing boots with steel-reinforced toes. A sharp pain traveled all the way up her leg to her back. She continued to squirm. Soon, the other two men joined their partner, and while he held her, one of them came forward and slapped duct tape over her mouth, rapidly winding it around her head. She was effectively silenced. Bree struggled even harder. She had heard about kidnappings like this. If they got her off the property, she was a goner for sure. But if she could get out of their clutches before they bound her hands and feet, she had a chance. She knew she could do no damage to the man who was holding her, but the one who was wrapping the tape around her head was vulnerable. She kneed him in the groin. He muttered a curse in Amharic, doubled over in pain and grabbed his wounded privates. The smaller man who had been standing to the side suddenly kicked her legs out from under her. She and the man who was holding her were knocked off balance. They fell, and Bree could almost envision their descent in slow motion as his two-hundred-plus pounds propelled them both to the ground. She fell on top of him and actually heard the wind shooting from his lungs. The smaller man was trying to grasp her legs, but she was furiously kicking at him. In the meanwhile, the one she had kicked in the groin was slowly getting to his feet.

"It's a good thing he wants you alive," he said menacingly. "Otherwise I'd slit your pretty throat right now."

He had earlier spoken in Amharic. Bree now knew she wasn't dealing with local thugs. This was, as one of them had said, a job with a purpose. Someone wanted her brought before him. The question was, once he had her, what did he plan to do with her? She didn't want to go out as just another Hollywood statistic. Actress kidnapped and killed by crazed fan. These days bodyguards were as essential to actors as a cutthroat agent.

Bree put up a good fight, but she was outnumbered. The one she had kneed grabbed her by the legs and held on, and this time he wasn't going to be caught unaware. The smaller man wrapped the duct tape around her legs at the ankles. Then, as one of the bulkier men held her arms behind her back, he wrapped the tape around her wrists as well.

It was at this point that Pierre, growling ferociously, burst from behind the frangipani shrub and sank his sharp teeth into the exposed ankle of the very man who had already sustained an injury that night. Not too happy with the tiny barracuda attached to his leg, the man reached down, grasped Pierre around the middle and jerked him off his ankle. He swung around and flung the black toy poodle away from him as if he were an Olympic shot-putter. Bree's eyes stretched in horror at the sight of her beloved companion flying through the night air. There was a sickening thud as Pierre's body hit the ground, and one pitiful yelp. After that, silence.

"Grab her and let's get the hell out of here," ordered the smaller man, obviously the brains of the outfit.

Tears of frustration rolled down Bree's cheeks as one of the larger men threw her, with as much regard as he would give a sack of potatoes, across his shoulder and marched off with her. As she was carried deeper into the darkness, she desperately searched the grounds for Pierre, strained to hear any sign that he was still alive. Nothing.

The men had parked an expensive all-terrain vehicle on the other side of the wall separating the hotel from the street. The small man climbed behind the wheel and started the car while the hulks scrambled to get Bree situated on the backseat between them.

The overhead light allowed her to see her assailants well for the first time. Two of the men were black. The third looked Norwegian, he was so blond and pale-skinned. He was sitting on her right and he actually smiled at her. "I've seen all your movies. I loved you in *Dark Universe*. I told them you were awesome and should be approached with more caution. But they thought that just because you're an actress, you're defenseless."

The black man to her left shot daggers at his blond partner. Apparently he was the one Bree had kneed. "Shut up," he said. "You talk too damn much."

"And I'm surprised you can talk at all," the blond returned with a snicker.

"Both of you, shut up!" the smaller man snapped. He put the car in gear and pulled away from the curb. Then he began speaking to Bree in calm, reassuring tones. "Miss Shaw, we were instructed to take you to our employer. He means you no harm. He simply wants to speak with you. Nod your head in the affirmative if you understand me."

Bree nodded as he had instructed.

"Good. We're going on a journey. The outcome of this journey depends upon you and how you behave. If you cooperate, you'll get out of this unscathed. However, if you persist in your present behavior, we've been given permission to rough you up until you feel more amenable to behaving yourself. Same instructions as before. Do you understand?" He had a lilting British accent tinged with an African dialect she couldn't place. Bree nodded in the affirmative.

"Excellent. We have a forty-five-minute drive out of town, then another hour by helicopter. Sit back and try to gather your wits about you. I do apologize for the rough handling. I rather dislike the tactics my simple-minded brethren sometimes employ."

The blond looked across Bree at his companion. "Simple-minded. Is that some kind of an insult?"

They rode in silence for the next few minutes; then

the blond, sounding for all the world like a bored child on a road trip, asked, "Can we have some music?"

"No," said the driver.

"Why not?"

"Because I hate rap music, and I happen to know that since you were responsible for prepping the car for this trip, those are the only kinds of CDs you packed."

"Well, then let me take the tape from her mouth and then she and I can talk about Hollywood and the movies. I'll never get this chance again. Nobody can hear her if she screams. Please?" he whined.

"Oh, all right," the driver said with an exasperated sigh. If he didn't placate the big baby, he would never get any peace.

The blond reached into his pocket and produced a multipurpose tool that had as one of its features a pair of scissors. "Hold still," he told Bree as he carefully began cutting the tape at a downward angle, close to her right cheek. Once the tape was cut all the way through, he gently peeled it from her mouth.

"Thank you," Bree said.

"I'm afraid it's stuck to your hair," he went on. "I'll have to slowly pull it loose." He glared at his companion on the backseat. "Why'd you have to wrap it all the way around her head like that? She's going to lose some hair."

"She injured the goods, and her dog bit me. I don't care if all her hair comes out," his comrade in arms belligerently said. An evil grin spread across his dark face. "And why are you being so nice to her? It isn't as if you aren't going to be punished to the full extent of the law along with the rest of us if we get caught for kidnapping. Do you think she's going to speak up for you simply because you're smitten with her?"

The blond's cheeks were faintly tinged with red as he said, "Don't pay any attention to him, Miss Shaw. He's still sore where you kneed him."

Bree turned her head to look the dark-skinned fellow straight in the eyes. "If you've permanently injured or killed my dog, I swear, I'm going to hire someone to drop you from an airplane over a flagpole factory."

The blond guffawed. However, the man she had insulted angrily drew back a fist at her. "Don't bruise the merchandise," the driver warned sharply, watching his partner via the rearview mirror. Bree continued to look him in the eyes. Even though she was trembling inside, she wouldn't give him the satisfaction of seeing her flinch. The man wanted to hit her so badly, his jaws were clenched and his muscles quivered.

"I bet you beat up on women and children all the time, big man!" Bree swallowed her fear and said, "Now you can add tiny dogs to your list of helpless victims."

"Miss Shaw, shall I instruct one of my friends to tape your mouth shut again? Because I won't hesitate if you persist in provoking Mr. Omoro. He doesn't have a particularly high threshold for insults, I'm afraid. I once saw him shove a man's head through a wall. You wouldn't want your pretty head to be put through a window, would you?"

"Where are you taking me?" Bree asked. She thought it wise to let the matter drop.

Omoro seemed to be rapidly approaching his boiling point.

"Oh, I can't tell you that," the driver said, managing to sound regretful. "If you don't know where you're going, once you're returned to your loved ones, you won't know where you've been."

Sighing as the blond giant gingerly removed the tape from her hair, Bree said, "Well, that makes perfect sense."

Dominic was awakened by the strident ringing of the telephone. "Baby, would you get that?" he mumbled.

The phone continued to ring. He reached over and succeeded in knocking the receiver off its base. Then he had to open his eyes to see where it had landed on the floor. Having found it, he yawned and said gruffly, "Yeah?"

"Dominic, is Bree with you?"

Dominic cocked an eye at the clock on the nightstand. 6:12 A.M. Then he looked around the room. No Bree. "Bree? Baby, are you back there?" He put the phone down and trudged to the bathroom. The door was open. He could see there was no one in the room from six feet away. The next thing he noticed was Pierre's absence. His initial confusion dissipated somewhat. She had obviously gone to take Pierre for a walk.

He returned to the phone. "Hey, Margery, she must have taken Pierre for a walk. They're both gone."

"Well, all right," Margery said. He could hear the anxiety in her voice. "It's just that both Toni and Georgie have phoned me this morning. And they each said she wasn't answering her phone. Georgie and Clay just found out they're going to have a baby. . . ."

Dominic laughed shortly, genuinely pleased for Georgie and Clay, whom he liked a great deal. "I'm happy for them."

Margery's voice softened. "That could be you and Bree a year from now. . . ."

"Now, Auntie Margery, don't lay it on me first thing this morning."

"I don't have to go into it. You know how I feel about you and Bree. You're perfect together. But, all right, I'll let you off the hook this time. Just tell Bree to phone Georgie when she gets in. I'm going to start packing for my flight." The actors and support crew were going home today. However, Dominic and the technical crew were expected to stay on another day or so. Bree was staying behind with Dominic. "I'll drop by and say good-bye to you and Bree before I head for the airport."

"It's a plan," Dominic told her, and they rang off.

Fully awake now, he went to the bathroom and relieved himself and then took a shower. When Bree still hadn't returned by the time he came out of the shower, he quickly dressed and went downstairs to the garden he knew Bree and Pierre frequented. It was cold, and he felt it as soon as he stepped outside without his hat. Hairless, the heat escaped more rapidly than it would if he didn't shave his head. About thirty yards from the back door of the hotel, on a grassy incline, he found Pierre. At first he thought the small dog was dead. He lay so still on the cold ground, and Dominic couldn't detect any sign of breathing just by observation. But when he went to touch the dog's head, he felt air on his fingers. Pierre was hanging on by a slender thread. And his hind legs were twisted at such an angle that it was apparent the pooch had sustained a broken hip. Dominic was amazed at the level of distress he felt at seeing the animal in pain. He had never particularly cared for Pierre. Pierre was very protective of Bree and jealous of any attention she bestowed on anyone besides himself. Dominic had learned to tolerate him. Now he felt his stomach twist in sympathy.

Bree!

Rising, Dominic frantically scanned the surrounding grounds. There was no way Bree would leave Pierre outside all night. She was too conscientious. Too softhearted. And Pierre's injuries. How had he gotten them? By trying to protect his mistress perhaps?

Dominic glanced down at Pierre. He knew he shouldn't attempt to move the dog. "I'll be back, boy. I'll get a vet here as soon as possible. Hold on. Hold on for Bree." He felt a little foolish saying all that to the animal. After all, Pierre probably didn't understand a word he had uttered. But in Bree's absence he was overcome by a sense of responsibility for the dog.

Running back to the hotel because, by now, he knew in his gut that something was terribly wrong, Dominic still silently prayed that he would encounter Bree once he was inside again. He didn't stop running until he was at the front desk. A gentleman with horn-rimmed glasses looked up from a computer screen. "Mr. Solomon. What can I do for you?"

"Have you seen my . . . Miss Shaw this morning?" Dominic knew he must look like a madman because the desk clerk's eyes widened in distress. "No, no sir. I haven't seen Miss Shaw. But I've only been on duty since five o'clock."

"Okay. Listen carefully. I need someone to help me search the grounds. Miss Shaw is missing, and her pet is lying out back probably dying from injuries I have no way of knowing how he got. Get a vet over here as fast as you can."

"A vet?" The man was confused.

"A veterinarian. An animal doctor!"

"Oh, yes, yes. Of course, Mr. Solomon. I'll do that right away."

A white-jacketed hotel worker walked past the desk. "You!" called the desk clerk.

The young man paused in his tracks and pointed to his chest. "Me, sir?"

"Yes, you!" the clerk said. "We have an emergency here. Go round up as many men as you can. Miss Shaw, the actress, is lost, maybe injured somewhere on the grounds. We have to find her as soon as possible. Go, go!"

The worker ran past the bank of elevators and down the corridor to the employee lounge where he knew he was assured of finding at least two or three others who could help him search for the lovely actress who had always had a smile for them, and a generous tip, too.

The desk clerk regarded Dominic and solemnly said, "We should telephone the police, Mr. Solomon. Things being the way they are, Miss Shaw could have been spirited away by thugs. Kidnappings aren't unheard of in the area."

"Yes, yes, do it!" Dominic cried as panic clutched his heart and mind. If anything ever happened to Bree, he didn't know what he would do.

At that juncture, the white-jacketed hotel employee returned with three other men and a woman in tow. All their brown faces reflected their concern.

Dominic beckoned to them as he began walking in the direction he had come. They followed at a trot. He left the desk clerk with the parting words, "Phone Margery Devlin-Lincoln, she's in room 710, and tell her what's going on. We'll be searching the grounds."

Bree had never ridden in a helicopter before. And once she was back on the ground, she swore, if it was within her power, she never would again. The moment the contraption climbed straight up in the air, her stomach seemed to plummet. Nausea set in, and it took a great deal of willpower not to retch all over her captors, which she would have gleefully done if it could guarantee her release.

Once again, she was sandwiched between Hyde and Omoro. She had learned Hyde's name when Omoro had cursed him in fluent French. Bree recalled enough of her high school French to translate. All three spoke several languages. But, she supposed, if you worked as a mercenary all over the world, it was advantageous to be able to communicate in various dialects. They were equal-opportunity criminals.

As the helicopter, capable of holding six adults, ascended, the noise from the blades deafening, Hyde had taken her small hands, which were still taped together, between his paws and said in soothing tones, "Don't be frightened, Miss Shaw. It's sort of like riding a roller coaster; you dip, you go forward real fast and you'll puke if you're not used to it."

Bree looked into his light blue eyes and wondered how he managed to reconcile the fact that he was a kidnapper with his seemingly kind side. She wouldn't allow him to win her over. He was the bad guy. She had heard of the Patty Hearst syndrome, where the captive suddenly identified with her captors, sometimes even joining them in their cause. That wasn't for her. At the first opportunity, she would knee Blondie as quickly as she had kneed Omoro and make her escape.

She gave him an appreciative smile. She could play the game with the best of them. "Thanks," she said weakly. Hyde smiled back. He was enjoying getting to know a famous actress. She was so warm and friendly. He wished they had met under more normal circumstances. They could have been friends, pals, maybe more. . . .

On her left, Omoro looked out the window as they sped through the night sky. He hadn't said a thing to her in some time. And when he glanced at her, he had murder in his dark depths. Now that she knew he couldn't harm her without incurring the wrath of their employer, she intended to make him suffer further for hurting Pierre. "Just wanted you to know that Pierre hasn't had his rabies shot. You could contract hydrophobia. You should know the symptoms, just in case: You'll dread drinking water. Eventually, you'll go stark raving mad. They'll have to shoot you down like the animal you are. . . ."

"Shut up!" Omoro shouted. "Or, I swear, I'll toss you out the door."

"Do I have to separate you two?" the smaller man—

Bree hadn't yet heard his name—cried from his seat next to the pilot.

Margery stayed with Pierre while Dr. Joseph Amlak, the veterinarian, a soft-spoken middle-aged gentleman with prematurely gray hair, examined the toy poodle. Wrapped in a down coat, Margery exuded star quality no matter what situation she found herself in. The doctor sincerely tried to give his undivided attention to his patient, but Margery's presence distracted him mightily. "There is no bleeding, which is a good sign," he said, as he peeled one of Pierre's eyelids back to examine an eye. "It means he hasn't any internal injuries. Those kinds of injuries are among the most difficult to survive for small animals such as—"

"Pierre." Margery provided the name as she gently brushed the fur on top of Pierre's head. "My niece has had him since he was a puppy. She'll be heartbroken if he doesn't survive."

The doctor worked slowly, transferring Pierre to a padded basket for transport to his animal hospital. "Don't fear," he said, his golden-brown eyes sympathetic. "I'll do everything in my power to help this little fellow." He rose, the basket in his arms. "Would you be so kind as to help me to my car?" He indicated his black bag sitting on the ground with a glance. Margery immediately picked up the bag and followed him across the deep lawn.

On the way to the car, they passed a group of the people, now numbering nearly twenty, who were searching for Bree on the extensive grounds. The police had arrived, and they were asking Dominic questions about the last time he had seen her.

Margery didn't think she had ever seen Dominic look so worried.

"When you awakened and found Miss Shaw missing," an inspector, who appeared to be too young to have any experience, asked Dominic as the two men stood beneath an acacia tree, "you weren't unduly concerned?" He inquired as though he didn't believe what Dominic had told him three times already.

"This isn't getting us anywhere!" Dominic said, frustrated. Next to the inspector, he looked like a bald NBA player. "Are you going to investigate or not? Round up the usual suspects? Don't tell me you've never investigated a kidnapping before! I want to see some action here!"

"Mr. Solomon," the investigator patiently reiterated, "we already have people searching the neighboring area for Miss Shaw. If she is in the area, we'll find her."

"And what if she isn't in the area? What if she's across the border, in another country by now? It's been hours. She could be hundreds of miles away depending on the mode of transportation." Dominic stalked away. "This is an international incident. I'll have to contact the U.S. embassy. Maybe they can help me get some answers!"

It was still dark when the helicopter landed atop a helipad in the middle of nowhere. For the majority of the ride, all Bree saw out the window, aside from a small village with very few lights on, was blackness. She would have had a darkness-induced panic attack if not for the helicopter's headlights and Hyde's voice in her ear rambling on about science fiction films. *"Dark Universe,"* he informed her, "is right up there with the *Star Wars* trilogy and *Alien,* one and two. They could have stopped that series after the second one. Ripley just never dies, does she? Very unrealistic. Now, your character, Romalia, was fierce! She was one part Ripley, one part Xena and one part Joan of Arc. A mighty woman. A true heroine. Why didn't you do the sequel—which was a flop by the way? The actress they chose for Romalia was all wrong. She didn't even look right in the breastplate and could barely raise a sword let alone wield one. It was pitiful!''

Bree had to admit he had that much of his Hollywood trivia correct. The sequel to *Dark Universe* was a bomb. But then, in her opinion, it was exceedingly difficult to produce a sequel that was as good as the original film. That was why she had shied away from the film. When Arieanna Sanchez, her agent, had presented her with the script to the project, she had read it, hated it and put Ari off for weeks before admitting she wouldn't touch the project with a ten-foot pole. Dominic wasn't directing. They had gotten a well-known European director whom she respected. But she still felt unsure about doing it. Luckily, she got the role in *Now and Again,* an action-adventure in which she had portrayed a detective who had to rescue the child she had given up for adoption years ago, from the clutches of terrorists who had kidnapped the child and were holding her for ransom. The role won her a People's Choice Award for Best Actress in a drama. She hadn't been nominated for an Oscar, but she was positive that honor was in her future.

After cutting the tape from around her ankles the thugs ushered her out of the helicopter, forcing her to stay well below the blades. Bree marveled at her ability to think of anything other than Pierre's fate and her own safety. It was amazing the lengths to which the human mind would go in order to protect itself from breaking down completely. She was definitely in panic mode. But somewhere deep inside, mechanisms were being thrown into place to prepare her for the long haul. She thought of her mother and her sister, and when she thought of Georgie, she couldn't help recalling Clay's quiet strength. She concentrated on her father and her *gran mere.* Her paw paw. Her auntie, Margery. She saved Dominic for last. Dominic, who was the only man she had ever considered spending the rest of her life with. Would she ever see him again?

From the roof of a tall building where the helipad was located, they went through a door and to an adjacent elevator designed to hold perhaps eight people, tops. Ultra-modern, but not for public use. Bree guessed they were at someone's private estate. Some super-rich mogul with too much time on his hands? Bored? Why not kidnap an actress for entertainment? She just hoped he wasn't some kind of freak. But then that hope was in vain. He had already had her brought here against her will. What did he have left to lose? If Bree wasn't mistaken, kidnapping was a capital offense in many African countries. They hadn't been in the air that long. She assumed they were still on the continent of Africa.

When the doors of the elevator slid open, Bree was led through another door, and they were once more in the elements. The wind howled, and she felt the sting of sand on her face. Squinting to keep the sand out of her eyes, she hastened, with the three men, to a waiting luxury car. Once inside, the sound of the wind receded, but its power was still evident as it gently rocked the automobile. The car's driver started the engine, and they rode in silence for perhaps five minutes. Bree saw nothing outside except the desert. And then they passed through a tunnel of palm trees. Shortly after that the car stopped on the circular paved drive of a palatial home. Golden lights illuminated the sandstone structure, which reminded Bree of pictures she had seen of the Taj Mahal.

"We're here," the leader announced unnecessarily.

Bree was helped from the car by Hyde. He made sure she didn't bump her head while exiting. Once again, they rushed her toward the double doors of the abode. The leader actually pressed the doorbell. They stood there several minutes before the door was opened by—

and you could have knocked Bree over with a feather—Yusef Makonnen.

Dressed in casual clothing of off-white cotton slacks and shirt and loafers, he still managed to look resplendent in his garb. Smiling and bowing slightly, he said, "Welcome to my humble home, Miss Shaw. So glad you could come."

"I felt compelled to," Bree returned as she stepped inside.

He laughed at her sarcasm. Glancing at the leader, totally disregarding the presence of the other two men, he said, "Congratulations, you pulled it off. You three may partake of refreshments in the kitchen and then retire for the evening."

"Don't you mean morning?" Bree said as she walked farther into the foyer. The soles of her Nikes made squeaking sounds on the flagstone floor. She moved to the left, observing a painting by a well-known contemporary artist. "The original, I suppose?"

"Of course," Yusef said with a note of pride.

The three men made themselves scarce. Hyde took several backward glances at Bree as if he were concerned she wouldn't be safe out of his presence. But then they turned the corner and were out of sight.

Bree rounded on Yusef Makonnen, her dark eyes flashing angrily. "What is the meaning of this? Are you some kind of pervert? You get your jollies by scaring women? One of your men badly injured my pet. If he dies, I swear, I'll make you pay!"

Yusef allowed her to vent. She was within her rights. Then he bent his well-shaped head toward her and quietly said, "Your stay here will be brief as long as your parents cooperate with me."

Bree couldn't believe her ears. "My parents? What have my parents got to do with this? I thought you were filthy rich. What do you need with a ransom?"

Yusef chuckled. "What I need from your parents isn't money. It's a certain object I want. I believe they can get it for me. Now, if you'll follow me, we'll get this show on the road. That is the correct saying, isn't it?"

"I'm not here to correct your English," Bree said, not moving an inch. She glanced back at the door.

"Don't even think about it," Yusef told her. "There is nothing but desert for at least fifty miles in every direction. None of the cars have any more than two gallons of gas in their tanks. Unless you can fly a helicopter, there is no means of escape at your disposal."

He held out his hand. "Come, my dear."

Refusing to take his hand, Bree followed him down the corridor. Any other time, she would have been impressed by the splendor that surrounded her: marble floors, furnishings inspired, undoubtedly, by the Ottoman Empire, modern but reminiscent of the majesty of harems of olden times. There was definitely a Middle Eastern flavor to the decor. In spite of the richness of the setting, the place was homey. How the decorator had accomplished that task was a sign of a genius at work.

Going to an intricately carved desk of blond wood, Yusef picked up a cordless phone and offered it to Bree. "I want you to phone your mother. Don't worry, the call cannot be traced, so you can chat longer than a minute." Don't worry? Bree stared up at him, certain he was quite mad. "You are to tell her that I want the goddess. She'll know to what I'm referring. Tell her she is to have the goddess in Addis Ababa by the morning of the twenty-sixth of this month. No later. Once she's in Addis, she is to go to Giorgis Cathedral, where she is to leave the goddess on the second pew from the back. The right side of the cathedral."

Bree shocked him by saying, "No!"

Yusef went to her, grabbed her by the arms and shook her. "You'd defy me? Are you so sure of my motivations that you'd risk your life by refusing to do as I ask?" He regarded her through narrowed slits. "You don't realize what I've been through to get this far. I will *not* be thwarted now!"

Bree just stared at him, unmoved. She glanced at the phone in his hand. "Obviously your plans hinge on my making that call. I won't do it now. Maybe in the morning." She turned away. "Be a nice host and show me to my room. Let me sleep on it. It's very tiring being kidnapped and hauled across the desert." She genuinely yawned, daintily covering her mouth with a hand. Meeting his eyes again, she added, "And another thing, if my dog dies, I'll personally have your ass in a sling."

Yusef could barely contain his anger. However, he knew what she was doing. She was testing her worth to him. The tactic was used in business all the time. Cross a boundary and check your opponent's reaction to your temerity. He almost admired her chutzpah. He would allow her this victory.

Going to stand next to her, he gallantly offered her his arm. "I believe you've already issued that warning, Miss Shaw."

"Well, I just want to make sure you heard it," Bree said, taking his arm and stifling a yawn. She peered up at him. "Can a girl get a cup of tea before bed around here?"

"But, of course," Yusef said, smiling. They walked through the doorway of the library and turned right. "The kitchen is this way. I let the servants take a few days off. . . ."

"Yes, you couldn't have witnesses around who might report your extracurricular activities," Bree returned knowingly.

"Indeed. Therefore it's self-serve, I'm afraid."

"What a horrible host you are, making a guest prepare her own food."

"Believe me," Yusef said, "you wouldn't want to consume anything I prepared."

"What of your wife? Does she cook?"

"Beautifully," Yusef replied before he caught himself. He had planned to leave Salah out of this. What she didn't know couldn't harm her in a court of law. He didn't want her becoming an accessory to his crimes. The cat was out of the bag now, however, so he tried to play it down. "How about Dominic Solomon? Does he prepare meals for you?"

They were still walking after several minutes, and Bree remarked on the size of his home. "Wow, you should have golf carts around here for those of us who're too lazy to actually walk to the kitchen. And, yes, Dominic can cook when the mood strikes."

Yusef laughed. "Believe it or not, my wife expressed the same sentiments upon seeing the plans for the house. She wanted something a bit more intimate."

"It's a good thing you're a wealthy man and she doesn't have to clean this baby," Bree said with a grin. She was on now. Whatever it took to buy her time, she would do it. Her decision to call his bluff and refuse to make the call tonight had been designed to delay his plans for as long as she could. Did she actually trust that once he got what he wanted, he would let her go? From the beginning she had noticed one breach of conduct among her abductors: they hadn't blindfolded her. She had seen all their faces. If they intended to set her free when they got what they wanted, they would have taken precautions to conceal their identities from her. Their total disregard for this one small point spoke volumes.

The large kitchen was a cook's dream. Two restaurant-size, top quality gas ranges with double ovens stood beside a gargantuan refrigerator and a walk-in freezer. Bree strolled around the room admiring the decorator's handiwork. All the while, Yusef Makonnen watched her.

She was peering in the refrigerator when he commented, "Are you always this cool and collected when you've been abducted?"

Bree had hold of a can of Diet Pepsi when she turned to face him. She walked over to the sink and rinsed the can's top, then flipped the tab. She drank a few swallows before bothering to reply to his query. "Funny you should ask. The last time something like this happened, no, I wasn't so calm. In fact, if not for the timely interference of my family, I would've probably been a goner. That time, it was my poor judgment that got me in the fix I was in. This time I did nothing to place myself in this predicament except be who I am. I suppose I can, at least, feel good about that."

Yusef looked confused. "I was being facetious. I had no idea you'd been in this sort of situation before. But, as a celebrity you are probably the target of all kinds of nuts."

"Are you including yourself in that category?"

Yusef laughed and went to stand in front of her with his arms akimbo. "Aren't you afraid you're going to eventually say something that will set me off? Your tongue is sharper than a double-edged sword."

Bree set the soda on the nearby countertop and placed her hands on her hips. Circling him, looking him up and down, she said, "What have I got to lose? We both know that until you get that statue from my mother, I'm worth gold to you." Pausing, she added, "Why don't you tell me why the statue is so important to you, and maybe I'll consider making that call sooner rather than later."

Yusef pursed his lips, thinking. She was nothing like the image he had seen of her up on the silver screen. But then she was only an actress portraying a character. He had to remember that she was paid to deceive people, to make them believe she was someone she actually wasn't. He was certain she could express any emotion just through minute nuances in her limpid brown eyes. Males of their species were undoubtedly mesmerized when she parted those luscious lips to speak. And it wouldn't matter what sort of words issued forth from them. From her they would be pure poetry. Of course, he was entirely immune to her charms. His heart belonged to Salah.

He gestured to the semicircular kitchen nook. It was large enough to accommodate eight stools. "Why not?" he said, surprising her. "I'll tell you a story, and perhaps you'll understand my urgency."

Bree collected her can of soda and followed him to the nook, where they sat facing each other. Her captor met her eyes, and got comfortable on the cushioned stool before beginning. "Tell me, Miss Shaw—"

"Oh, please, whenever anyone has me kidnapped, he earns the right to call me Bree."

"How far would you go to make someone you adore happy, Bree?"

Nine

The morning after their return from Miami, Toni was on her knees scrubbing the tub in the master bedroom of her San Francisco condo when Chuck entered the room. "Not that you don't make a fetching sight from this angle, but why are you doing that? The tub is perfectly clean."

Toni paused in her scrubbing to turn and frown at him. "My eldest is pregnant; my youngest isn't answering her phone. I'm worried about them, okay?"

Chuck laughed shortly and went and took the green, oversize sponge from her hand and dropped it into the tub. Pulling her up, he wrapped his arms around her jeans-and-T-shirt-clad body. "Am I going to have to live with an obsessive-compulsive who cleans the house instead of talking to me when something's on her mind?"

Toni stuck her bottom lip out. "Maybe!"

"Uh-uh, baby," Chuck admonished as he kissed the side of her neck. "Get used to talking to me." He kissed the tip of her nose. "Now, tell me why you're worried about Georgie. I understand your concerns about Bree. But when you phoned Margery, she promised to tell Bree to call you. We just have to wait until she does." He hugged her tighter. "Come on, speak!"

"My child couldn't even read her symptoms," Toni began. "Behind the joy, I could hear the fear in her voice.

She wants this child with all her heart, but she's afraid she's going to make mistakes. . . ."

"You've just described every new parent," Chuck said quietly, peering lovingly in her eyes. "Don't worry about Georgie. She always manages to take care of herself. And she has Clay. The most solid, dependable, loving man I've ever known aside from your father." He smiled. "Did you know I envy you your relationship with your dad? My father and I didn't really have a relationship. He believed being a good father meant providing for me. But that was it. No baseball games, no fishing trips or any other kind of an outing. I was a responsibility to him. Not a person. Not an individual with a mind of my own. Social responsibility meant more to him than family. I don't think he knew the importance of love within the family unit."

Toni pressed her cheek to his. "Didn't he love your mother?"

"He chose her because she was suitable. But love? I don't believe she loved him either. He was a good catch. I know you'll never forget that day at Greenbriar when Mother pounced on you and you defended yourself by saying you weren't like those women whose only reason for attending college was to find a rich husband. Well, you hit the nail on the head with her when you said that."

"I sensed as much," Toni said softly. She turned her head to plant a kiss on his chin. "I wish I hadn't allowed her to rile me that day. But when she started in on my parents, I lost the tenuous grasp I had on my self-control."

"She deserved it," Chuck told her. "From the moment she set eyes on you, she was determined to prove that you weren't good enough. I should have defended you better than I did. But I was too busy enjoying how uncomfortable you made them."

"Evil wretch!" Toni half joked, pushing out of his embrace. Pointing a finger accusingly at him, she added, "Using me to declare your independence from your stifling parents. That was childish and selfish of you, Chuck!"

"Now, Toni, you said you had forgiven me for that. I was young and stupid. I didn't know what I was giving up when I allowed you to walk out that door the next day."

"Let's get this clear, Charles Edward Waters. I may have forgiven everything, but that doesn't mean I'll ever forget it all. Sometimes, I may have the occasional flashback and suddenly start hitting you in the middle of the night in my sleep. That's how imbedded the hurt is in me. Forgive? Yes, I can do that. *Have* done it. But I'm not perfect. I can never forget what happened between us. And there will probably always be a worrisome doubt in the back of my mind that will make me wonder if you've really changed, or if it's just guilt that's compelling you to love me and want us all to be one big, happy family!"

Chuck simply stood watching her, listening to what she had to say. This was what he had been trying to get her to talk about for months now. He knew they couldn't forget the past. They could, however, forgive it and move on, leave it behind them and look to the future they would build together. That was all he wanted her to understand. "I know I'm asking you to go on faith here, Toni," he said now as he took a step toward her. His light brown eyes narrowed. He reached out and clasped both her hands in his and pulled her into his embrace again. "But know this: I'm out on a limb, too. My heart is unguarded. You stand as good a chance of hurting me as I do of hurting you. I'm not that same callous boy who could allow you to leave me simply because you had wounded my pride. I have my priorities straight now: family first. That means you, Toni. You are my soul mate, whether you're ready to admit it or not. Did I love you back then? Possibly. In my own myopic way. I loved your fire. I loved the spirit that lived within you. But I was just a pretender to the throne then. I wanted what you could give me, but I wasn't strong enough to take it. I'm strong enough now, and I'm not going to take no for an answer anymore. I won't let you reason me right out of the picture. So what if you can never forgive me for certain things. The question is, can you love me in spite of them?"

Toni's head was tipped back. She smiled slowly. "I can, and I do. Besides, I've *got* to marry you now."

Chuck liked the sound of that. "Oh? Why is that?"

"Because we're going to be grandparents. We don't want to confuse the child, having to go to Boston to see Granddad and to San Francisco to see his *gran mere.*" She laughed suddenly when it dawned on her. "Oh, God. I'm going to be someone's *gran mere!*"

Chuck kissed her cheek. She smelled faintly of the cologne she had put on that morning and the disinfecting cleanser she had used to clean the tub. "I haven't given up on having another child with you, Gran Mere!"

Toni turned her face so that their mouths touched. "I said you had to convince me of that, remember?"

Chuck groaned and kissed her full on the lips. "Let's get married as soon as Bree returns from Ethiopia," he said when he raised his head.

"Oh, no you don't," Toni protested sharply, her eyes flashing. "Our wedding is not going to be a rushed affair. I've waited all my life to marry you. And I want the works! A beautiful wedding with all the trimmings, my father to give me away. . . ."

"He won't have a shotgun with him, will he?"

"An extended honeymoon," she continued, ignoring his joke. "I might not be a blushing bride-to-be, but this is my one and only wedding we're talking about, and I want it to be an occasion people will remember for a long, long time!"

"All right, all right," Chuck happily relented. "Whatever you want, you'll get, my love."

The phone rang, and Toni went into the adjacent bedroom to answer it. Chuck followed. Picking up the extension on the nightstand next to the queen-size bed, she said, "Toni."

"Miss Toni—"

"Dominic!" Toni's legs went weak, and she sank onto the bed. Dominic had never phoned her. Whenever she spoke to him over the phone, it was after Bree had initiated the call. She would phone her mother and hand the receiver to Dominic. "Here," she would say, "say hello to your future mother-in-law." Toni liked Dominic, but she got the feeling she intimidated him.

His voice didn't sound right now, as if he had something important to say but dreaded saying it. Toni knew that tone—had heard it too often through the years. Her mother's voice had held the same intonation when she had phoned to tell Toni her father had just suffered a stroke.

"Has Bree been in an accident?" she asked urgently.

Dominic hesitated too long.

"Dominic! What's happened to my child?" Toni screamed.

Margery came on the line. "Toni, I want you to sit down."

Toni's heart rate quickened. "I'm sitting, Margery."

"Is Chuck there?"

"Yes."

"Good."

"Margery, what's going on? Where is Bree? Is my baby . . . is my child d—"

"No!" Margery emphatically said. "No. There's no way

I'll believe that." Her voice got quieter. "But, Toni, she's missing. Early this morning, she took Pierre out and she didn't return. We found Pierre on the grounds. He had been badly injured. We suspect he tried to defend Bree, and whoever took her had to hurt him in order to get away with her."

Toni glanced up at Chuck, who had been hanging on her every word. "Baby, get on an extension. You should hear this. Our Bree has been abducted over there in Ethiopia." She willed herself not to panic. Panicking would only cloud her judgment and she needed her wits about her now. Bree was missing. And her mind was going a hundred miles an hour. She recalled the warning Solange had issued about the third man and the photographs. She had said the mystery man had told her whoever was behind the thefts would use those photos against them if the occasion arose. His men failing to locate the final statue obviously had forced his hand. That had to be it. Toni heard the distinctive click that indicated Chuck was on another extension. She then began asking Margery questions. "Was Dominic with Bree before she went missing?"

"Yes, and he blames himself for not getting up and going to look for her when he first noticed she was no longer next to him in bed. But he thought she had gone to the bathroom. He went back to sleep, and I woke him up four or five hours later. It was then that he realized Pierre was missing, too. He went to look for them, and that's when he found Pierre near death."

"Is he . . . ?"

"He's hanging on. We don't know if he's going to make it or not."

"The police?"

"They're investigating. But let me tell you what Dominic and I have been able to piece together on our own. Dominic says there's a local man who has shown interest in Bree lately. He has no proof whatsoever against this man—it's just his gut talking—but he believes Yusef Makonnen might have taken Bree."

"Why?"

"He's enamored with her?" Margery said. She sounded exhausted. Toni tried to count the hours since that morning in Addis Ababa. There was a five-hour difference between San Francisco and Addis. That meant it was the early-morning hours in Addis. Around 3:00 A.M. Margery and Dominic had gone all day long worrying about Bree. Searching for her. Trying to decide when would be the best time to notify Toni and Chuck. Hoping against hope that the longer they put it off, there was the possibility of having the good news that they had found her to relate when they did call. Toni could feel their pain and frustration across the miles. It was now hers.

"Chuck?" Toni spoke into the receiver.

"Margery," Chuck said, "we'll be there as soon as we can. Toni, I think you know what we have to do."

"We've got to locate the mystery man," Toni said. "He's the only one who knows the identity of the person behind the thefts. If the culprit and Yusef Makonnen are one and the same, we've got our man."

"What?" Margery asked, confused.

"We'll fill you in later, sweetie," Toni promised. "We've got to get things rolling on this end right now. You and Dominic hang tight. We'll be in touch soon."

Hyde turned out to be a culinary wizard. The first morning of Bree's captivity, she went into the kitchen, expecting to have to scrounge up something to eat. Instead, the big blond was whisking eggs in a stainless-steel bowl, crepes were bubbling on a griddle atop the gas range and the smell of coffee permeated the air. Wearing the same purple fleece outfit she had worn the night before, Bree entered the room and headed straight for the coffeemaker.

"Good morning, Miss Shaw," said Hyde as he poured the whipped eggs into a large nonstick skillet. "Did you sleep well?" He appeared not to have missed a wink. Blue eyes bright and expectant. Bree had taken a shower and brushed her teeth with the brand-new toothbrush and toothpaste her captor had stocked his guest bathroom with. She felt grungy even though she had had the foresight to wash out her bra and panties and hang them to dry before crashing last night. She had slept surprisingly well, resting soundly less than ten minutes after her head hit the pillow.

Hyde had set out several mugs on a tray next to the coffeemaker along with teaspoons, napkins and containers of sugar and cream. Bree poured herself a cup of coffee and took a sip before answering him. "What do you think?" She tried to keep her tone light.

"Still sore at us, huh?" Smiling, he continued turning the eggs in the skillet until the consistency was light and fluffy. He then transferred the eggs to a warm platter he had set aside for that purpose. "I promise you nothing is going to happen to you, Miss Shaw."

Bree was glad no one else had risen yet. She wanted to be able to speak with Hyde in private. "How can you make that promise, Hyde?"

"Hyde isn't really my name; that's just what I'm known by," he informed her as he went to the oven and removed a pan of link sausages. The aroma made Bree's mouth water. She was ravenous. "I don't want to know your real name," she said, just in case he was getting ready to reveal it to her. "It's safer if I don't."

"We know that, that's why we all use false names."

"Except Mr. Makonnen."

"He doesn't need to. No one can touch him."

"He's that powerful?"

"No. He's that smart."

Omoro entered coughing. Bree moved aside as Omoro walked toward the counter with the coffeemaker on it. She had decided to give him a wide berth. It could have been that comment about his putting an enemy's head through a wall that helped make up her mind.

"Morning," Hyde said pleasantly to Omoro. Omoro grunted and cut a malevolent look at Bree.

Bree went to stand on the other side of Hyde. "I'd just as well make myself useful. Need any help?"

Hyde's eyes brightened at her offer. "You can put the food on the table," he said, glad she was willing to cooperate. Everything would run that much smoother if she went along with the program. They would acquire the last statue. Makonnen would be happy; and he, Omoro and Ishi could get out of here and on to the next job.

A few minutes later Bree was sitting at the large kitchen table with five males: Makonnen, the three who had brought her there, and the helicopter pilot, a young Brit with gray eyes and curly light brown hair who introduced himself as Harris. The chatter was constant while they consumed the crepes with strawberry sauce and scrambled eggs and sausages, all cooked to perfection. Bree went around the table refilling coffee cups. When she got to Omoro, he held his cup away from his body. Bree assumed he was afraid she was going to purposely spill hot coffee on him. She carefully refilled his cup and met his dark eyes. "Shall we call a truce? I won't bother you if you won't bother me."

Omoro nodded his big head.

Bree returned the coffee carafe to its base. She knew all the eyes in the room were on her. It wasn't that she was devastatingly attractive in her rumpled clothing; it was simply because she was more pleasant to look at than their male companions.

She sat down between Hyde and Makonnen. "Thank you," she said to Hyde. "That meal was delicious."

He appeared genuinely pleased she had enjoyed his cooking. "It was an honor to cook for you, Miss Shaw."

"Under different circumstances, I'd say you can cook for me anytime."

Dropping his napkin onto his plate, Yusef rose and looked down at Bree. "I'd like a word with you, please."

Bree took a long sip from her coffee and got to her feet. "Of course." Yusef took her by the elbow and directed her toward the doorway. Once in the corridor, he said, "You've slept on it. Are you ready to make that call now?"

Bree stopped in her tracks to look up at him. Although dressed in his usual expensive loungewear, he had bags under his eyes, which told her he wasn't sleeping well at night. She wondered what he had to worry about.

"I'll make the call," she said, "if you allow me to phone Dominic first. He must be going out of his mind with worry."

Yusef shook his head in amazement. "Still negotiating, I see." He sighed. "The answer is no. You can't phone Dominic Solomon. You'll try to give him a hint as to my identity, and we can't have that." In a moment of self-chastisement, he said, "Why did I send that bottle of champagne to your table?"

Last night when he had told Bree his story, the reason behind her abduction, he had confessed that their two previous meetings were purely coincidental. No, he hadn't been stalking her, nor was he an amorous fan. He had been as astounded by the news of her connection to the intrigue as anyone else.

"All right," Bree conceded. "I probably would try to

give Dominic a clue to your identity since I know he'd remember you." She smiled at him. "It was worth a try."

"Shall we?" Yusef inquired softly. They continued their trek down the long corridor.

"What I don't understand," Bree said, referring to their conversation of the previous evening, "is why a man as modern and forward-thinking as you are would believe in a myth about fertility gods."

Yusef shrugged his broad shoulders. "When you've been through what Salah and I have been through in order to conceive a child, you can get a little crazy."

"Why not adopt? There are plenty of brown babies who need good homes."

"I think in Salah's case it's connected to her belief that she isn't a good wife unless she can give me a child. I would be happy to adopt. I've tried to talk her into it time and time again. She promised that when she turned forty, she'd give up on conceiving, but until then, she'll keep trying. She's only thirty-four. Six more years of watching her desperation would have driven me crazier than I already am. So . . ."

"You came up with this scheme," Bree finished for him. "But you didn't tell her about it, did you?"

Yusef's facial expressions couldn't conceal the perturbed emotions she had elicited in him when she made that statement. Frowning, he stared down into her upturned face for several seconds before saying, "Salah has nothing to do with this. That way, she remains free of culpability."

"Oh, yeah!" Bree cried, laughing shortly. "Let's assume the fertility god mumbo jumbo really does work, and Salah becomes pregnant. However, you get caught and sent to prison. I'm sure she'd appreciate going through a pregnancy without her husband at her side. Oh, and don't forget the actual pain-wracking delivery! She'd really enjoy hours and hours of labor—again, without you there by her side. Before it was over, she would be cursing the day she ever met your sorry butt!"

"I'm beginning to understand why Omoro wanted to cut your tongue out," Yusef told her frankly.

"Oh, him," Bree said in dismissive tones. "I'm not finished with him yet. If my Pierre isn't all right, Omoro will be sorry he ever laid eyes on me."

"I believe you," Yusef said.

They arrived at the room Bree had come to think of as the library. It was beautifully decorated with low-backed sofas and chairs in off-white. Two walls were lined with filled-to-capacity bookshelves, and in one corner state-of-the-art computer equipment sat on a teakwood workstation.

She went to the phone on the desk next to the computer and picked up the receiver. Glancing up at Yusef, she joked, "Hope you have a good long-distance carrier."

"Just make the call," Yusef said, smiling.

He opened the drawer of the desk, and inside was another telephone, the base of which was built into the custom-made desk drawer itself. He put the receiver to his ear. "In case you try anything," he said.

Bree narrowed her eyes at him and dialed her mother's number in San Francisco.

It was around 10:00 A.M. there in Djibouti; therefore it would be 5:00 A.M. in San Francisco, or thereabouts. She hoped her mother was asleep and not lying awake worrying about her. She knew Dominic had to have phoned her parents with the news that she was missing by now.

It was her father who answered the phone.

"Hello."

Bree thought he sounded weary. "Daddy, it's me."

"Bree, baby!" She heard him calling to her mother, "Toni, Toni, wake up. Bree's on the phone."

"Baby, where are you? We've been worried sick here!

Dominic phoned to tell us you were missing, broke down and Margery had to take over for him," her father said.

"Bree, are you safe?" were the first words from her mother.

"I'm all right, Mom," Bree said.

Yusef placed his hand over his receiver and whispered to Bree, "Just tell her what I instructed you to say. Now!"

"Mom, the bozo who had me snatched wants me to give you this message: you are to bring the goddess, and he says you'll know which one, to Addis—"

"What bozo? Is he listening in? Is that why you sound so cryptic?"

"Yes, the bozo's listening in," Bree said regrettably.

Yusef was sending daggers at her with his eyes.

"Okay, sweetie. Follow instructions. Don't do anything foolish," her mother advised.

"Wise woman, your mother," Yusef said under his breath.

"You are to have the goddess in Addis by the twenty-sixth, Mom. That's in three days I believe. . . ."

"Today's the twenty-third so, yes, that would be three days from now."

Bree knew her mother was already one step ahead of Yusef Makonnen. What her mother's involvement in all of this was, she didn't know. And Yusef Makonnen wasn't going to stand there and let her question her mother about it. She would just have to have faith that her family would get her out of this, just like they had gotten her out of the last predicament she had been in.

"This is just like old times, huh, Mom?" she joked, her voice catching.

"Listen to me, baby. None of this is your fault. I'm the one who stuck her nose where it didn't belong. And now look what's happened!" her mother said. "Don't you lose your focus, baby. You are going to be all right. I promise you. Your father and I are coming to get you. I know exactly what the bozo wants. I'm sure once I explain to Dr. DuPree why I need the statue, she'll hand it over." Her voice became hard now. "And you"—she spoke directly to Bree's captor—"you don't know me. You don't know our family, so this promise may fall on deaf ears. But know this, if you harm our child in any way whatsoever, there will be no safe place for you on this earth."

Once again, Yusef placed his hand over his receiver and issued an order to Bree. "Just give her the rest of the instructions."

"Mom, you are to bring the goddess to Giorgis Cathedral. Leave it on the second pew from the back. The right side of the cathedral."

"Tell her you'll phone her back with the location where they can find you, after we've authenticated the goddess."

"You—"

"I heard him, baby. No need to repeat it," her mother told her. "Stay strong for me and your father. . . ."

Yusef reached over and manually severed the connection. "That's enough," he said, taking the receiver from Bree and placing it back on its base. He hung up his phone as well. Meeting her eyes, he told her, "Now we wait."

Salah decided not to phone Yusef with the good news. She wanted to see the look on his face when she told him. So, she spent Monday, October 23, doing a bit of power shopping in the Union Square Area, hitting her favorite stores: I Magnin, Sak's Fifth Avenue and Neiman-Marcus. She was in Sak's Fifth Avenue, in the lingerie department fingering a silky peignoir set, when, out of the corner of her eye, she noticed a tall black man standing nearby watching her. It wasn't the first time she had seen him that day. He had been in a nearby coffee shop a couple of hours ago when she had taken a cappucino break. She wasn't naive. Men found her attractive. They had from the moment she started developing. She would watch him, and if he actually got up the nerve to say something to her—many men just liked to look—she would set him straight. Otherwise, it was a free country, and if he wanted to watch her from a distance, it didn't bother her.

She held the material of the peignoir set against her reddish-brown skin. It was champagne-colored. Making up her mind to try it on, she placed it across her arm and moved on to the next garment. She had to remember to phone Yusef later and tell him she was coming home a day early. He would have Harris meet her in Addis and fly her on to their home in Djibouti. Salah didn't understand Yusef's attachment to the house in Djibouti. It was so remote, they never saw anyone unless they had specifically invited them for a visit. If not for the fact that they also had homes in New York City, Paris and here in San Francisco, she would put her foot down and refuse to ever return to Djibouti. But she loved him and allowed him this strange desire for isolation. At the compound, it was as if he were the king of his very own kingdom. He treated her like a queen, so why should she complain? Still, the only thing that drew her back to Djibouti was her husband.

When she had three garments hanging across her arm, she began looking around for the dressing rooms. A tall brunette approached her. "May I help you with anything?" she asked politely, smiling.

"I'd like to try these on," Salah told her.

"Right this way," the woman said, turning to lead Salah to the back of the room. Salah saw the sign then, and thanked the woman. In the dressing room, she removed the navy blue designer pantsuit she had on, being careful not to catch the material on her gold necklace. After slipping on a skimpy black gown with spaghetti straps, she observed her five-foot, ten-inch body in the mirror. Her perfect body. A body that had served her well in many ways. It had earned her a reputation as a top model. It hadn't given out when she was a child and rarely got enough to eat. And it had captured Yusef's attention. He had admitted that he had noticed her long, shapely legs before anything else when he had first laid eyes on her. Yes, her body significantly figured into her enjoyment of life. It had only let her down in one area. . . . She placed her hand over her flat stomach. And suddenly she was sobbing. They were tears of thankfulness. Tears of joy. Tears of relief. Now, after so many years of praying and hoping, there was the promise of a child. Yusef's son, or daughter. She didn't care which sex the child was as long as it was healthy. As long as she was the one to feed and bathe the baby, stay up nights when the child had the sniffles. As long as she was the one the baby called to when his or her little voice filled with fright, after awakening from a nightmare. *Just let me be a mother,* she thought prayerfully.

When she emerged from the dressing room, her tears had dried, and she had reapplied her lipstick. The same woman who had shown her where the dressing rooms were was at the register when she went to pay for her choices. Placing all three garments on the counter, she smiled, presented her Visa Gold card and said, "I'll take all three."

The woman beamed her pleasure. She no doubt earned a commission on sales. She glanced at the card. "Very well, Mrs. Makonnen."

Later, pulling her coat closed against the chill of the late San Francisco afternoon, Salah hurried along the street, hoping to get a cab without much difficulty.

She stood on the walk in front of Sak's, unsuccessfully trying to flag down one of the fast-moving vehicles. She remembered what one of her friends had told her about big city cabdrivers, "Unless they're hard up for a fare, they speed right past blacks. No matter how affluent you might look."

Salah tried not to be pessimistic, but after several minutes of standing in the cold, she was beginning to think her friend had a point.

"Allow me," a deep, British-accented voice came out of nowhere. Salah peered up at the man. Yes, he was the beautifully attired man who had been watching her earlier.

Not waiting for her permission, he stepped off the curb when he saw a cab approaching, raised his right arm in the air, placed two fingers of his left hand between his lips and let rip a shrill whistle. The cab came to a halt in front of them. Salah smiled her thanks. "You're a godsend," she said. "Thank you."

"It was nothing," he said with a gentle smile. He handed her in and firmly shut the door. Salah watched as his figure receded in the distance. A perfect gentleman. In this day and age!

"I'm sorry, Toni," Solange said sincerely. "But I don't know how to contact Rupert."

Toni laughed in spite of herself "Rupert?"

Solange laughed nervously, too. She knew Toni was under pressure after finding out her daughter had been abducted. A good laugh probably served as a stress reliever. "However, you can take the goddess. I had a feeling when Rupert told me about the photographs that he was trying to warn me that something like this might happen. I'm very sorry it happened to your family, Toni."

"We'll find Bree," Toni strongly stated. "I can't let myself think any other way. Thank you for cooperating, Solange. I'll come collect the goddess as soon as—"

"Toni, there's no need for you to come back here for the goddess, I—"

"I couldn't trust an overnight service to deliver it, Solange. It's too important that I get it into the hands of that maniac!"

"No," Solange said. "That isn't what I was going to suggest. I'd like to go to Ethiopia with you, Toni. Give me your flight plans and I'll come to San Francisco, and we'll fly together."

"We're not leaving out of San Francisco," Toni told her. "My daughter and her husband are going, too. We're all leaving from a private airfield near Boston on the morning of the twenty-fifth. Can you be in Boston by then? You can come with us on the company's jet."

"Yes," Solange said, sounding definite. "We'll be there." Meaning herself and the goddess.

"I can't take this waiting around," Dominic said. He was sitting on the sofa in his suite, his head in his hands. Margery was seated on the chair across from him. She was exhausted. Perhaps that was why the stress of the moment got the better of her.

She looked at Dominic, and suddenly all the bitter feelings she had kept pent up came spilling out. "Why couldn't she let Pierre go on newspaper? Why did she have to go outside in the middle of the night? At the very least, she should have gotten you to go with her. She's much too independent. Just like her sister, just like her mother."

"And just like you," Dominic told her as he came to her and wrapped his arms around her. "Just like you, Auntie Margery."

Margery burst into tears. "Oh, if anything happens to that child, I don't know what I'll do. I was there when she was born." She sniffed and pushed out of Dominic's arms to walk around the room, gesturing with her hands. "She came into this world wailing her head off, and she hasn't shut up since then."

When Bree returned to her bedroom to get ready for bed the second night of her incarceration, there were boxes on the canopied bed. She pulled the lid from the largest. Inside were two pairs of casual leggings, one black pair, one royal blue, and two oversize tops, also, one black, one royal blue. Fresh clothing. In the other boxes were underwear—whoever had guessed her sizes had assumed her bra size was larger than it actually was— and a couple of nightgowns. She selected one of the nightgowns and went into the bathroom to shower.

Two hours later, though in bed for more than an hour, she was wide awake. Her stomach growled, and she thought a snack might hit the spot. Climbing from the bed, she put on the Nikes—they were the only shoes she had with her—and, in lieu of a robe, slipped on her coat. The house was too cool anyway. Yusef Makonnen must be part polar bear. He had to have the thermostat set at sixty degrees or lower!

Her Nikes made squeaking noises on the marble floor from her bedroom to the kitchen, but once she stepped onto the tile floor of the kitchen, the sound receded. There was recessed lighting high on the walls throughout the huge house, so she had no difficulty finding her way.

In the large kitchen, she went to the refrigerator and stood there perusing all the food inside: fresh fruits and vegetables, several kinds of cheeses, roast beef left over from Hyde's dinner that night, eggs, milk, soda pop. Yogurt. She reached in and picked up a cup of Dannon Yogurt with peach preserves on the bottom. Popping the lid, she dropped it in the nearby trash receptacle and went to the drawer where she knew the silverware was kept. When she opened it and selected a teaspoon, she thought she heard a noise behind her. Quickly turning in the direction she had heard the sound, like that of a stealthy footstep, she saw a small figure in the shadows— too small to be any of the five men who were sharing the house with her. The figure was quickly moving away. Bree hurriedly abandoned the cup of yogurt and the spoon on the countertop and took off after the figure. What if Yusef Makonnen had been hiding his wife in the house all this time? Keeping her locked away in the daytime and letting her out only at night? The novel *Jane Eyre* by Charlotte Bronte came to mind. Was Yusef Makonnen another Mr. Rochester? Realizing that the person was getting too far ahead of her, Bree took advantage of the Nikes she was wearing and began sprinting. As she turned the corner and entered the straightaway, which was the long corridor that led to the bedrooms, she saw the figure about ten yards ahead of her. The person was slipping and sliding on the slick marble floor. Apparently she or he didn't have on shoes with rubber soles. Bree's legs were pumping now. And she knew if her prey kept sliding around like that, she would catch up with whomever it was before long. Then what? The question gave her pause. Exactly what would she do when she caught the person? Say, "Hey, your husband is holding me hostage, can't you talk him into letting me go?" Nah. If indeed the figure she was in pursuit of was Salah Makonnen, wouldn't she know what her husband was up to? Yes, indeed. Breathing hard now, Bree slowed and finally stopped. Sometimes it was best to play it safe. She would wait until daylight and look around then. Makonnen hadn't forbidden her from exploring. Of course, it hadn't occurred to her until now. He might put his foot down if she suddenly went poking her nose in all the rooms. In which case, she had to make certain she didn't get caught doing it.

Turning and retracing her steps, she went back to the kitchen, retrieved her cup of yogurt and returned to her bedroom. She made certain her door was locked and then propped a chair under the knob for added peace of mind.

In the morning, she showered and put on the black leggings and oversize shirt with her Nikes. Entering the kitchen, Hyde issued his usual cheerful, "Good morning, Miss Shaw!"

"Good morning, You!" Bree said. Ever since he had confessed to her that his name really wasn't Hyde, she referred to him as You whenever they were alone. In the presence of others, she was careful to call him Hyde.

"Today's the twenty-fifth!" he said, excited. "Tomorrow, you're out of here! We're all out of here." His square-chinned, clean-shaven face broke into a grin. "I have to tell you, I didn't want to take this job. But Ishi said it paid well and there would be no wet work involved."

After several long conversations with him, she now knew that wet work involved jobs in which blood was spilled. No wet work meant he had been advised that he wouldn't have to kill anyone. That was good news to Bree's ears. But, really, could she trust the word of a mercenary? She simply kept her mind focused on getting out of here. And on the fact that these people didn't know her family. They had no idea how tenacious they could be. If anyone could find her, her family would. Between her mother, her father, Georgie and Clay, she was confident that she would be getting out of this compound without any wet work being done on her.

She pretended to go along with his way of thinking, though. "I'll be happy to be back home. For one thing, my hair could use some professional care."

"I'm sorry about that," Hyde said, his eyes regretful. He was flipping pancakes. A large platter with two side-by-side stacks on it was already sitting on the stovetop. "But you're still the most beautiful actress in Hollywood with or without makeup."

Bree smiled at him, but his compliments and his incessant cheerful attitude were beginning to grate on her nerves. She admitted that the setup was preferable to being shackled in a dark room and fed bread and water, but she still found his hypocrisy reprehensible. She knew that if Yusef Makonnen ordered it, Hyde, or whatever the hell his name was, would gladly silence her forever.

Yusef Makonnen entered the kitchen as Bree was pouring herself a cup of coffee.

"Pour me one while you're at it," he told her from across the room. He then joined her at the counter. "I see the clothes fit. Good."

"Yes. I appreciate the change. I was beginning to feel like a prisoner."

"I see your tongue's wide awake."

As was her routine by now, Bree set the platters Hyde had filled on the kitchen table. Yusef followed her around. There was obviously something on his mind. Just as she placed the platter of scrambled eggs on the table, he came out with it. "Were you up raiding the refrigerator last night?"

Bree met his eyes. "Guilty as charged." The person she had seen last night must have told him about the incident. There was no use lying about it. She was found out. She would wait and see what he had to say next, though. "I was hungry so I came in here and got a cup of yogurt from the refrigerator."

"That's all?"

"Yeah, that's all. I didn't think a side of beef would sit well that late at night."

Hyde chuckled. Yusef cut his eyes at his hired strongman. Hyde clamped his mouth shut. "I believe you know that isn't what I'm talking about!" Yusef forced out. "You saw someone when you were in here last night."

There goes my plan for a bit of snooping, Bree thought. She smiled at Yusef and told him, "It's true. I did see someone last night. And when I tried to catch up with him, he took off like a scared rabbit. After a minute or so, I stopped chasing him. See, I didn't know if I actually wanted to catch someone who I had no way of knowing whether they were dangerous or not."

"Smart girl," Hyde commented.

Yusef shot him another sharp look.

"Anyway," Bree continued, "I just came back here, got my yogurt and went back to my bedroom."

Yusef's features softened. He seemed satisfied with her explanation. He did, after all, have it all on tape. His surveillance cameras had caught everything. She had not lied about the incident. Bree cocked her head and continued to watch him. "Is there anything you want to tell me? You don't have a mistress tucked away in one of those many bedrooms you have back there, do you? Tsk tsk, Mr. Makonnen. You're not being a bad boy while the wife's away?"

"Why don't you sit down and put some food in your mouth and give that tongue of yours a rest," Yusef suggested with a smirk. "Or I'll sic Omoro on you."

Bree went mute at the mention of Omoro. Yusef smiled his satisfaction.

"Come on, let's eat," Hyde said, trying to lighten the mood.

Bree showed Yusef her back and returned to her task of piling the table with Hyde's culinary treats. So, there was someone else in the house. He had neglected to mention another player in his twisted game when he had supposedly told her the whole sob story.

Yusef took his place at the table and began filling his plate with pancakes and eggs. He didn't eat pork. Didn't usually allow it in the house. Where Hyde had gotten it from, he didn't know. But then several of his servants weren't Muslims. They could have had their stash of bacon hidden in the freezer and Hyde had found it.

His mind was on Mubara. He wondered why she wanted her presence here kept a secret. The secret was out now, though. The nosy Bree had seen her. She would never be able to put two and two together and come up with the mystery person's ID, though. Not in a million years.

As he ate his pancakes, he thought back to his chance encounter with the mystic.

He was sitting alone at a sidewalk cafe in Manhattan. Salah was away at one of her interminable visits with Dr. Song in San Francisco. Most of his business concerns were centrally located in New York City. The headquarters of Makonnen Enterprises was in a building on Fifth Avenue. Sometimes he liked to get out of the office and watch the people walk past. He was enjoying his cafe au lait and a big New York bagel when a tiny woman came up to his table. She was attired in a multicolored sari which, surprisingly enough, wasn't unusual for Manhattan. He had seen a few other women walk past similarly dressed. She had eyes that looked right through to his soul, this woman. Dark eyes that didn't, at first, seem to have irises. Liquid and mesmerizing. "Good afternoon, Mr. Makonnen," she said. She had his attention from the first syllable. "My name is Mubara, and I've been led here in order to lend you assistance."

Yusef intended to send her on her way, as he would anyone disturbing his peace. But there was something about her eyes, and her tone of voice, her very aura, that negated those plans. And before he knew it, he was inviting her to sit with him.

Mubara briefly glanced up at the blue sky on that April day, then back at him. "Thank you. You're very kind."

She sat down and placed her voluminous bag underneath the table close to her feet. The smell wafting off her petite body reminded him of the air in the desert when the cactus flower was in full bloom. Her features were sharply drawn. Almond-shaped eyes, small nose with a little indentation at the tip. Funny how genetics had done that, he thought at the time. A thin-lipped mouth. She wore no makeup. And her long, dark hair was partially concealed by the material of her sari. The short-sleeve blouse she wore underneath the sari was peach-colored, which set off her mocha skin. Though she was dressed like an Indian woman, Yusef guessed she was Asian. It was the eyes more than anything else that brought him to this conclusion.

"You know my name," he said tentatively.

"More than that, I know your malady. A child, Mr. Makonnen. You and your lovely wife badly want a child. And I can help you reach that goal."

"Are you a fertility specialist?" Yusef had learned a long time ago not to judge women by their appearance. As fragile as Salah sometimes appeared to him, she had a backbone made of steel. "Because if you are, we've already been to all the specialists. They tell us the same thing over and over: adopt."

"I'm not a medical doctor. My science isn't even recognized as a true science." Her gaze had him in her thrall. "I'm a witch, Mr. Makonnen. A sorceress, if you will. I've been a student of the mystic arts all my life. And I'm here to tell you that with my help you and your wife will conceive a child. But not just any child, a special child. . . ."

Chewing his eggs thoughtfully now, Yusef couldn't figure out why he hadn't asked her to leave at that point. A witch? Nonsense. Ah well, he was in too deep now to start having doubts. As Sherlock Holmes would say, *The game is afoot!*

Ten

The wheels were turning in Toni's mind. While Chuck slept next to her on their flight to Boston, she sat and ran all the facts of this case around and around on those wheels. Rupert had told Solange he knew the identity of the statue thief. That meant Rupert must be some kind of an investigator. From what country or agency, she had no way of knowing, but his accent would point to Britain. Then again, the world had become one big global community. Just because he had a British accent didn't mean he was from Britain. And where he was from wasn't as important as what he did for a living. If she only knew that, she had a feeling quite a few pieces of the puzzle would fall conveniently into place. She could hazard a guess. The statues had been stolen from museums and art galleries in London, Cairo, New York City, Boston, Orlando, and Addis Ababa. Could he work for one of those museums? For some reason, she best recalled the story about the theft of the Orlando statue. The museum was Ripley's Believe It or Not! Ripley's boasted an unmatched collection of the strange and the unusual from all four corners of the earth. The ebony statue the thieves had taken was carved by the Baule tribe on West Africa's Ivory Coast. In the article, the Ripley's spokesman had said at least fourteen pregnancies were attributed to rubbing the four-foot-tall ebony statue. Several women were interviewed for the article, and they all testified that they had rubbed the statue. Some of them said they had been trying to get pregnant for years. A few had even been on fertility drugs with no positive results. A doctor interviewed in the article stated getting pregnant was sometimes tricky. She said some women simply needed to relax in order to get pregnant. Mind over matter?

Chuck stirred in his sleep. His hand fell into Toni's lap, and she grasped it in hers, holding on to it. He slept on. Toni relaxed in her seat and closed her eyes. If all went well, Solange, Georgie and Clay, possibly with reinforcements, would all be at Greenbriar later tonight. They would spend the night there and, in the morning, board the plane for Ethiopia.

Solange was hurrying through the air terminal in Atlanta, hoping to make her connecting flight to Boston, when her cellular phone, in the bottom of her shoulder bag, started ringing. She didn't miss a step as she shifted the carry-on bag from her right shoulder to her left and reached into the bag hanging from her right shoulder, retrieving the phone. Flipping it open, she breathlessly said, "Yeah?"

"I hope you're on the treadmill, Doc. I hate to think what else you could be doing that would make you sound like that."

Solange laughed into the receiver. "I'm rushing through an airport, that's what I'm doing. I'm glad you phoned. As my mother would say, the stuff has hit the fan! Toni Shaw and Charles Waters' daughter has been kidnapped in Addis. Well, she was taken from the grounds of her hotel in Addis. Heaven knows where she is now. Anyway, the kidnapper wants to exchange Briane for the statue."

Rupert sighed. "I was afraid of this. Where are you rushing off to?"

"I'm heading to Boston. I'm taking the goddess to Toni. I'll be going to Addis with them." She had come to the boarding desk of the carrier she was using. Going into her shoulder bag again, she retrieved her ticket and got in line behind about ten others. "Rupert, you've got to tell me who the man is behind the thefts. Knowing his identity may be the only means by which Toni and Charles can save their daughter. . . ."

"What are your plans once you get to Addis?" Rupert wanted to know. Solange was a bit irritated by the fact that he was still holding his cards close to his chest. Why wouldn't he simply answer her question? She told him about the drop-off at the cathedral, though. She didn't see any harm in it. After that, however, she once again asked him to tell her the identity of the culprit. "If you want to retain your status as my hero, you'll tell me the name now, Rupert."

"All roads lead to Yusef Makonnen," he said. "I'm presently in San Francisco keeping an eye on his wife, Salah. If I'm successful, we may have an ally in our quest to get the daughter safely back in the arms of her family."

"So, that's where you went, San Francisco."

"Mmm-huh. Miss me?"

"What do you think?"

"I think once this business is concluded, I deserve a vacation, and I hope to begin it in Addis with you, Doc."

"Will you show up in my hotel room, uninvited, in the middle of the night?"

"I'll climb through your window with a bottle of champagne and a rose between my teeth."

"Ouch! Watch out for thorns. And what if you drop the champagne? Huge mess. Just bring yourself. You're all I need. And knock on my door. Don't want you falling and breaking your leg before I can get my hands on you."

"Your hands, Doc? I was hoping to feel those beautiful lips of yours again."

"All over your body, Rupert. . . ."

"Say that again."

"All—"

"No, my name. You make it sound sexy."

"It is sexy, Rupert. It isn't the name that makes the man; it's the other way around."

"I've got to go, Solange. Something tells me I should have a nice chilly shower," Rupert said suggestively. "I'll see you in Addis. Where will you be camped?"

Solange told him where her party would be staying in Addis and then said, "Rupert, there's something I've been turning over in my mind. Once Makonnen gets the last statue, he's going to need someone to perform the ceremony that will entreat the gods to bless the couple to conceive. Have you gotten a lead on the identity of the person he's lined up for that honor?"

"Indeed, I have," Rupert said, sounding impressed that she had asked. "You aren't going to believe this one. . . ."

"I'm going with you, man," Alec O'Hara told Clay with conviction. "You'll need someone to watch your back."

When Clay had phoned his best friend, and partner in the agency, to tell him about Bree's kidnapping and the family's plans to fly to Addis Ababa in order to ransom her, Alec had immediately given the news to his wife, Dian. Twenty minutes after they hung up, both Alec and Dian were in Clay and Georgie's living room.

Dian and Georgie sat on the couch. Dian held on to one of Georgie's hands. The two women had become good friends since Georgie married Clay and moved to

Boston to be with him. Dian, thirty-five, was a black Irish lass, which meant she had very, very dark hair. Her large, beguiling eyes were dark blue. She and Alec had been married five years and had a three-year-old son who was lying in Georgie and Clay's bed right now, sleeping.

"Think positive, Georgie," Dian said. "Bree is strong, and smart. She'll make it through this; I know she will."

"I'm not going to think any other way," Georgie told her determinedly.

Dian impulsively hugged Georgie. "That's the spirit."

The two women's attention was suddenly drawn to a shouting match between their husbands. "You're not going, man," Clay told Alec. "You've got a family to think of now. It would be different if we were two blockheads just out of the corps or the academy, but you have Dian and Alec, Jr., to consider. If anything happened to you, I'd never be able to look Dian in the eyes again."

Dian and Georgie gave each other knowing looks and got to their feet to go stand between the two men. Dian placed a hand on her husband's broad chest. Alec, at five-eleven, was six inches taller than she was. But he immediately calmed down when she touched him. She had that kind of power over him. Georgie walked up to Clay and met his eyes. "Chill, baby."

"Clay," Dian said, "I think you know Alec and I consider you and Georgie family. If this mission is a family mission, then Alec should go along. We've discussed it. I've already told him he had better take every precaution."

"You know what a cautious fellow I am," Alec said to Clay in his defense.

Clay looked to Georgie.

"It has to be their decision, Clay. You can't decide what's best for everyone." That was a bone of contention between them, Clay's habit of always trying to protect the people he loved.

Frustrated, Clay blew air between full lips. "Okay, damn it!"

After Alec and Dian departed with Alec, Jr., wrapped securely in his father's arms, Georgie walked across the room and put *Supernatural* by Carlos Santana on low on the CD player. Seductive, enthralling music filled the air, and she closed her eyes and began to sway to it. Clay was sitting on the couch watching her walk toward him, realizing that she embodied everything that meant anything to him in this world. He got up and met her halfway. Georgie placed her hands flat against his chest and looked up at him. They were both wearing jeans and well-worn cotton shirts that had been laundered so often, the material was extremely soft to the touch.

Clay rubbed her back and pulled her fully into his embrace.

Georgie kicked off her leather clogs and shoved them to one side. "I'm going to tell you this once, Boston: if push comes to shove and you have to defend your life, I expect you to do whatever it takes. We know these people nearly killed a guard in Miami—"

Clay silenced her with a long kiss. Raising his head, he said, "You don't have to tell me that, my love. You know me. I'll go through whatever stands between me and my woman."

Georgie reached down and grabbed his taut bottom. "Just wanted to have my say."

"Well, I heard you. Now, tell me what I really want to hear."

"I love you."

"I can listen to that all night long."

God, please watch over Bree, Georgie thought. *And the men who're going to risk their lives to save her.*

With so much on her mind, Georgie thought making love was out of the question, but when her husband kissed her again, allowing his wonderfully pliant lips to pull away from her mouth and then move on to the hollow at her throat, she knew she wanted him. And then a thought, unbidden, sprang into her mind: what if this was the last time they made love? It wasn't inconceivable. Her best friend, Alana, had lost her first husband, a policeman, to violence. He had left for work one morning, and she never saw him alive again. Where Alana had gotten the strength to wed another cop, Georgie couldn't fathom.

Clay was looking at her intently, as if he were looking at her for the first time. She had never been able to resist his brown-green bedroom eyes. She began pulling the tail of the shirt from the waistband of his jeans. When she had succeeded in doing this, her hands ran up under the shirt until they were caressing his chest and stomach. Hard, warm skin. She had to kiss him there, so she bent and did just that. Clay was at once excited. Her mouth in that vicinity always excited him to a greater extent than he already was. But he was more interested in bringing her pleasure tonight because he wanted her to know how much he adored her. How happy he was that she was carrying his child. And, to him, that meant loving her in every imaginable way.

"Stand still," he told her.

Georgie stood up straight, her eyes on his. "What?"

"I want you to just stand there a moment, Georgette."

"All right," Georgie said, sounding a little doubtful, "but it won't be half as enjoyable if I don't join in."

"Oh, I don't know," Clay said cryptically. He bent and removed his black motorcycle boots. Georgie's impatience came to the fore when he took his time and walked them over to a corner of the room and set them down. Then he came back and slowly began to unbutton his shirt. He pulled it off and tossed it onto the nearby couch. The muscles in his arms, chest and stomach and even his back rippled with his every movement. Georgie called up all her restraint in order not to reach out and touch his dark brown body. Next, he removed the leather belt and undid the buttons on his button-fly jeans. Georgie was getting antsy. Slowly, he peeled the jeans past his hips, long sinewy legs and thighs until they were in a heap on the floor. Stepping from them, he circled her, looking at her from all angles and allowing her to get an eyeful. Georgie swallowed hard, wondering where this was going and if he could speed it up a bit.

"Now, take off your clothes," he ordered.

Georgie quickly began unbuttoning her jeans. Her nipples had grown tumescent, and her female center was throbbing almost painfully. She longed to feel his hands on her.

"Slowly," Clay said.

Tossing back her braids. Georgie narrowed her eyes. "How slowly? Because you know two can play this torturous game. . . ."

"Just humor me."

Georgie complied, going slower. She unbuttoned her blouse and allowed it to hang open, revealing the white, lacy bra underneath. But even though her movements were slower, her breathing was still rather erratic. Her chest heaved. The sight of Clay, standing a few feet away from her, totally nude except for a pair of those sexy boxer-briefs in white, the color a stark contrast to the blackness of his glowing skin—well, the anticipation was killing her.

"Pull your bra straps down off your shoulders, but keep your eyes here," Clay said, pointing to his own eyes. Georgie removed the shirt, allowing it to fall to the floor, and pulled first the left bra strap off her shoulder, then the right one. Her breasts seemed to swell, pushing against the fabric of the bra, making it appear suddenly too tight.

Clay came to stand in front of her. His eyes devoured

the ripe lushness of her body. And he wondered just how much more desirable she would be when she started showing. Already, her breasts seemed fuller, heavier. No longer able to stand it, he reached out and caressed her breasts through the bra. Then his body was pressed against hers, and Georgie moaned softly. "Good God, I thought I'd explode. . . ."

Clay, whose hands were used to adeptly undressing her, did not respond right away; he was too busy working the bra loose. This done, he took a breast in each of his hands. Georgie's nipples were hot and hard against his palms. He wanted to taste her and bent his head to run his tongue lightly across the left nipple. Georgie held his head there as his tongue continued to whip her into a state of delicious arousal.

Clay pulled away and moved on to the other breast. Her skin was fragrant with the aroma of honeysuckle. He knew the act made Georgie sound as if she were cooing, but he didn't think she knew he was as turned on by it as she was. The feel of her warm bud on his tongue increased his hunger for her. Georgie arched her back, feeling as if she were floating. "Clay, I'm ready now."

"I know you are, baby, but I'm not finished tasting every inch of you."

"You know you're driving me crazy. . . ."

"It'll be worth the trip."

His tongue flicked out again and claimed the bud between his lips as he suckled. Georgie's knees grew weak. Feeling the shift in her weight, Clay reluctantly pulled away, and while she stood there, dizzy from his ministrations, he undid the buttons on her jeans and pulled them down. Once they lay around her ankles, he lifted her off the floor and carried her to the couch and placed her on it. He buried his face between her breasts, then looked into her eyes. "Dr. Michaels says this is all right, huh?"

Georgie laughed. "Yes, baby. I hope you aren't going to start treating me like I'm the black Madonna. I'm still the lusty woman you married."

Clay kissed her from her breasts to her navel. "The night you seduced me was the luckiest night of my life."

"Mine too, baby, mine too," Georgie said, moving against his hardened member.

Clay rose up on his knees and grabbed her by the hips, pulled her to him and made short work of removing her panties. He tossed them behind him. Georgie's fingers were on the waistband of his briefs, pulling downward. Clay gently but firmly removed her hands. "Not yet."

"You like making me beg, Clayton Knight!"

Clay laughed shortly. "Nah, baby. I like to watch you when you're aroused. You're so beautiful."

Georgie thrust her breasts forward and sinuously wiggled her hips beneath him. His penis was fully erect within the confines of his briefs. She could feel it against the tops of her thighs. How he was managing to postpone the inevitable, she had no idea.

Clay spread her legs and bent his head to lick her soft inner thighs.

"What did the doctor have to say about this?" he asked as his tongue delved into her.

"Mmm," Georgie said, squirming slightly. "That's perfectly fine. . . ."

He had her panting now. His firm tongue, that versatile muscle, pierced her softness and then, when she was quivering, changed course and slowly brought her down only to take her soaring again once she had regained her normal breathing rhythm. He stayed there until he felt her body rock with an orgasm, and then he lingered awhile longer.

Finally lifting his head, he ran his tongue against her inner thigh again. "Was that good for you, too, baby girl?"

Georgie just sighed exultantly.

"I take that as a yes."

Clay gently kissed her forehead. "I love it when I can actually render you speechless."

Bree hoped she was either experiencing eye problems or going crazy, because if she wasn't mistaken, Omoro was smiling at her. It brought to mind what a cobra must look like if it could smile. But it was a smile nonetheless. She and the rest of the occupants of Makonnen's palace, aside from the mystery person, were having their evening meal. Hyde had pulled out all the stops seeing as how, in his words, it was their last night together.

Bree was dressed in the blue leggings and big shirt Makonnen had provided. She had helped Hyde prepare the grilled chicken and fixings that comprised what he called an American barbecue: potato salad, baked beans and coleslaw. She had even set the table. She should have known something was up with Omoro when he appeared in the kitchen while she and Hyde were cooking and stood around watching them as if they were the next best thing to high-definition TV. Makonnen took the opportunity to discuss their plans for tomorrow morning since all the participants were present. Bree was seated between him and Hyde. Omoro was directly across from her, eating his meal with practiced sensuality. If he licked his fingers one more time, she was going to grab a fork and stab him with it. His dark, smoldering eyes kept finding her. She knew it wasn't her imagination. And then, he smiled. She didn't think she had ever seen him smile before. Frankly, it was the most frightening thing she had seen in some time.

"Ishi," Makonnen was saying, "you and Hyde will go to the cathedral tomorrow and pick up the goddess while Omoro and I wait at the helicopter with Miss Shaw. When you return with the goddess, we'll drop Miss Shaw off just outside of town and come back here. If you are followed and can't shake the tail, you are to phone me, and I'll tell you where to go from there."

"Why can't we just take Miss Shaw with us and leave her at the cathedral once we collect the goddess?" Hyde asked.

Bree was genuinely taken aback when he suggested that. It made her believe he was genuinely looking out for her well-being. Perhaps she had misjudged Hyde, and he wasn't a complete sociopath, after all.

"Because, more than likely, someone will be watching the cathedral," Makonnen said with a disbelieving sigh. Hyde was a paid professional; he should know you didn't take your bargaining chip to the place where the exchange was to take place. Once you got what you had demanded, you left the ransomed object at a specific spot and then phoned to let the payee know where to pick it up. End of game. That was if all went according to plan. Makonnen was beginning to suspect he had hired the wrong man for the job.

"I appreciate the thought," Bree spoke up.

Omoro's face fell when she thanked Hyde for his apparent effort on her behalf. Next to him the pilot, Harris, must have sensed his mood and moved his chair over a bit. Omoro turned cold eyes on Hyde, and the muscles worked in his blunt jaw.

Hyde beamed at Bree. "Just trying to get you home safely."

"Look at him," Omoro cried, getting to his feet and throwing his napkin down hard on the tabletop. "He's become a security risk, the way he moons over her. We can no longer trust him. What if he goes to the authorities afterward?"

Bree instinctively knew it was jealousy talking. Too many days in close quarters, the testosterone was flying, and she was the only visible female for miles around. She turned to look at Makonnen, hoping he would put a stop to this right away. Makonnen simply smiled as if he was enjoying the action. She wanted to slap that smile off his smarmy face.

Hyde guffawed. "And implicate myself? Man, you're around the bend!"

"You've taken her side from the very beginning. If you'd done your job in the garden the night we snatched her, I wouldn't have gotten injured, and that rat of a dog wouldn't have bitten me," Omoro huffed.

"You're such a cry baby," Hyde said, his eyes filled with merriment. "As if you've never been wounded in the performance of a job!"

"Not on this kind of a job," Omoro spat out. "It should have gone smoothly. She's just one skinny woman. And if you had been paying attention to doing your job and not trying to slyly cop a feel while you were holding her, she wouldn't have kicked me, and that dog wouldn't have been able to come out of nowhere and catch me off guard."

"Has this been seething inside of you for three days?" Hyde asked, incredulous. "Man, you're nuts! It was all bad luck, not incompetence, that got your balls squashed and your ankle bitten." He glanced down at Bree momentarily. "Sorry about the balls comment."

"See what I mean?" Omoro exclaimed, sounding justified in his accusations. "He treats her with kid gloves. If she is a hostage, she should be treated like one. Throw her in a cell and give her gruel to eat and don't allow her bathroom privileges."

Ishi, realizing that their employer wasn't going to pull rank and put an end to this, rose and regarded Omoro with a silencing glare. "That's enough, Omoro. This is Mr. Makonnen's job. And if Mr. Makonnen doesn't specifically say Miss Shaw should be abused, then she is to be treated decently. You know the cardinal rule: whatever the employer says goes."

Omoro kicked his chair over, almost elbowing Harris in the face in the process, and stalked from the table mumbling curses under his breath.

"Ishi," Makonnen said. "I suggest you go after him and get him calmed down. He's a loose cannon. Can't have him messing up my plans."

"Yes, sir," Ishi said as he reluctantly rose. Hyde had done a good job on the meal tonight, and he had been enjoying it up until the moment Omoro erupted.

Makonnen met Bree's eyes. "Good going, causing dissention among the ranks. It won't do you any good, though. I'm paying these men handsomely to remain loyal to me. You'll get out of here when I say you'll get out of here. Not a second sooner." He then regarded Hyde. "And you! If you can't follow orders without questioning them, I'll have Ishi shoot you in the head and throw your body in the desert for the vermin to feed on. Understood?"

Hyde nodded. "Yes, I do. I was just trying to make a tense situation more pleasant."

"I know what you were trying to do," Makonnen told him. "And I know why." He cut a glance at Bree. "They don't pay Miss Shaw ten million dollars a picture because she's unattractive to the male sex."

Bree didn't think twice; she rose and threw her glass of spring water in his smug face. "You're a pig!" Backing away, she added, "What's more, you're a pig with too much time and money on your hands. Any normal person faced with your situation would've gone quietly through life suffering the pangs of disappointment at not being able to have a child, but he would have still had a fulfilling life. You go to the extreme and kidnap an innocent bystander expressly for your selfish purposes. Your life is pointless, Yusef Makonnen. With all your wealth, you can't find anything worthwhile to do with it? Pitiful!"

Never had a woman spoken to him with such disrespect. In his world, women stayed in their place. Salah was the only female he allowed to vent her anger or discontent on him. Breathing like an incensed bull, Makonnen rose and would have grabbed Bree around the throat if not for Hyde and Harris, who both quickly restrained him.

"Go!" Hyde ordered Bree.

Bree looked at Makonnen, his face dark with murderous intent, and decided the advice held merit. She fled.

"Good evening, sir, madam," Carson greeted Toni and Chuck at the door of Chuck's Beacon Hill mansion, otherwise known as Greenbriar. The house sat on twenty acres of manicured lawns, surrounded by maple trees. Chuck tried to keep the property as close to the way nature had intended as possible. There were wild roses growing along the perimeter. The house had been named after the wild roses that were so prevalent in the area when it was built more than sixty years ago.

Chuck set their bags down on the foyer floor. Carson would attend to them later. "Miss Toni. Always good to see you," Carson said now.

"Good evening, Carson," Toni replied, smiling at the tall, gaunt, dark-skinned elderly gentleman. Carson had been with the Waters family nigh on fifty-five years. He had come into service when he was twenty years old. Toni thought he still looked good in his dark butler's uniform with white cuffs at his thin wrists. Chuck would ask him to retire, but every time he tried, Carson looked sick at the notion of endless days during which he would be idle. So, Chuck had told him years ago to simply let him know when he was ready to retire.

The maid, Maggie, a red-haired young woman of Irish descent, took their coats and Chuck's hat. Warmly smiling at them, she said, "Welcome back, Mr. Waters, Miss Shaw." She hurried away to hang their coats.

As they moved farther into the foyer, Chuck said to Carson, "Would you ask Cook to fix us some sandwiches?" It was past 7:00 P.M., and Toni had told Chuck on the drive from Logan International Airport that she just wanted something light for dinner. They were expecting Georgie, Clay and whomever they might bring with them as backup anytime now. Toni was still waiting to hear from Solange. However, Solange had promised to be at Greenbriar by 9:00 P.M., so she wasn't particularly worried yet. After Carson disappeared around the corner, Chuck and Toni went into the nearby sitting room. The staff had a fire burning in the large room that was decorated in lovely Early American antique furnishings. On the walls were paintings from renowned African-American artists such as Romare Bearden, Robert S. Duncanson, Henry Ossawa Tanner and Ellis Wilson. Collecting art was one of Chuck's passions.

Trying to take Toni's mind off their present situation if only for a while, he joked, "When you marry me, I'll give you the Henry Ossawa Tanner painting as a wedding gift."

Toni had long coveted the beautiful painting of a black woman sitting on a porch that Tanner had painted in the 1920s. The talented African-American painter had emigrated to France in order to gain the freedom and acceptance he wasn't offered in the United States.

Toni loved to just stand in front of the painting and imagine she was that woman on the porch with sunlight bathing her face. She drew her eyes away from it now to purse her lips at Chuck. "I'll marry you without the bribe."

Chuck went to her and caressed her face with his right

hand, while placing his left arm about her waist. The last twenty-four hours had taken their toll on her. The lines were deeper around her dark eyes, and there was a sadness in their depths. He bent his head and tenderly kissed her forehead. "We're going to get our Bree back, my love. I swear it. If I have to call in every favor owed me by every powerful person on the planet, we *will* get her back!"

Just this morning he had made a phone call to Senator Brant Covington to enlist his aid in getting clearance to land the company jet in Addis Ababa. Covington, who was Chuck's nephew Benjamin's father, had come through for them. Now they didn't have to risk being shot out of the sky when they invaded Ethiopian air space.

"Have you been able to reach Benjamin and tell him what's going on?" Toni asked.

"I spoke with Cassie," Chuck said, brushing her hair back from her face. "Ben's up in Springfield making funeral arrangements for his grandmother. Cassie said he had gone to see Anne to tell her her mother was dead, but Anne wouldn't speak with him."

"Is that so surprising? She hasn't allowed him in to see her since she's been in prison, Chuck. After three years, she's still full of hate."

"According to Covington, who is still devoted to her after everything she put him through, she won't see Ben because he tried to get her declared insane. Now, as her only living relative, Ben just might get his wish."

"Do you think she should go to a hospital instead of remaining in prison?" Toni asked, tilting her chin up. She certainly didn't. Anne Ballentine deserved what she had gotten. Perhaps she had gone a little nuts when, at fourteen, she had discovered she was pregnant by rich boy Brant Covington. And then, though she had pleaded with her mother, her mother had forced her to put the

child up for adoption. Her son, Benjamin, had been
adopted by Chuck's brother and his wife. Years later, after
Benjamin's adoptive parents were both dead and he was
living at Greenbriar with his uncle, Anne Ballentine reen-
tered their lives under the guise of personal assistant to
Chuck. Five years after her arrival, Chuck's wife, Mariel,
and his son, Charles III, were killed in a car accident
when the brakes on Mariel's Volvo gave out. Come to
find out, Anne had tampered with the brakes. Two lives
destroyed because of her obsession with claiming Benjamin as her very own. By that time, however, she had
included Chuck in her sick scenario. She wanted the
three of them to be one happy family. To her chagrin,
Chuck began a search for the child he knew he had fathered with Toni. Because of his need for closure, he
brought Georgie and Bree to the attention of a homi-
cidal maniac. Anne found out about Toni and sent an
assassin after her eldest offspring, thinking this child
must have Chuck's blood coursing through her veins.
Once Chuck was left without an heir, Anne reasoned that
Chuck would leave his fortune to his nephew. And she
would offer him a loyal shoulder to cry on when his plans
fell through and he found out his longed-for daughter
was dead. In Anne he would find all the woman he would
ever need. Of course, nothing went according to plan.
Chuck hired Clayton Knight to locate his daughter by
Toni Shaw. Clay wasn't about to allow anything to happen
to anyone under his protection. Both Anne and her paid
assassin were arrested and incarcerated in the end. Anne
vowed to make them all pay for her downfall.

"No, absolutely not!" Chuck vehemently replied now.
"That woman's exactly where she belongs. Ben's just feeling guilty. He has this theory that if she'd been loved,
she wouldn't have turned out the way she did. I've tried
to tell him that Anne made her own choices. No one
forced her to kill. I hope she rots in prison!"

Toni took him in her arms and held on to him tightly. For years he had thought his dear wife and son had been killed in an accident. To find out that his trusted personal assistant had done the deed had reopened the wound.

Toni ran her hand over his close-cropped, wavy brown hair. "One good thing came out of this for Ben," she said. "Brant Covington has proved to be a surprisingly welcoming father to him. Imagine Covington giving an interview and admitting that he'd been in love with a black girl when he was a young man, had gotten her pregnant and she'd given birth to a son. And now he's reaching out to Ben at every turn."

"You know the state of things in Washington, DC, these days, my love," Chuck told her smiling down into her eyes. "They blab about the skeletons in their closets before the media gets wind of it. Then they're viewed as stand-up types and not as politicians trying to conceal their pasts."

"Oh, yeah," Toni said, laughing. "The I-Confess syndrome."

Eleven

Mrs. Adelaide Hughes, called Cook by everyone in the Greenbriar household, brought the tray of ham sandwiches, hot Colombian coffee and generous slices of her pound cake to the sitting room herself. When Toni saw her coming through the door, she sprang to her feet and went to meet her halfway. "Adelaide! It's so good to see you."

Adelaide placed the tray on the low, square coffee table and, rising, turned to exclaim, "Oh, Toni, when I heard what happened to that sweet child. . . ." She paused to fight back impending tears. "I can't stand the thought of her being afraid over there all by herself."

The two women embraced, and afterward Adelaide held Toni at arm's length to look into her face. She was a large woman at five-ten and more than two hundred and fifty pounds. But she carried it well. At sixty-two, she appeared younger and quite robust for a senior citizen. "The rest of the staff appointed me to come out here and express their concern. We all love Miss Bree. And we know everything's going to turn out just fine." Her voice held a note of prayerfulness when she said that. "Just fine!"

"Thank you, Adelaide," Toni said sincerely. But the sight of the dear cook's tears had started her own to flowing. Up until then, she had held them pretty much at bay.

Adelaide's dark brown face crinkled in a frown when she saw Toni's tears. "I didn't mean to come out here and reduce you to tears, sweetie." She wrapped Toni in her arms again. Looking over at Chuck, she said, "Good evening, Mr. Waters. I didn't see you standing there, sir."

Chuck was amazed by the level of warmth his staff bestowed upon his daughters and Toni, but when it came to him, he was regarded with respect and, sometimes, trepidation. Smiling, he said, "Hello, Cook. Thank you for bringing the sandwiches." He went and placed a comforting hand on Toni's back.

Adelaide put Toni away from her ample bosom. Looking down into her eyes, she said with determination, "You dry those tears now. You all are going to go over there and get my girl and bring her back home safe and sound. You hear me?"

Toni nodded in the affirmative, but she didn't trust herself to speak. For some reason, seeing the worry on Adelaide's face had brought home the severity of their situation. Adelaide let go of Toni, and Chuck put his arm around her shoulder. "Thanks for your concern, Cook," he said. "Tell everyone we'd appreciate their prayers for Bree's safe return." Toni turned into his shoulder, crying softly.

Backing out of the room, Adelaide said, "You can be certain you have them, Mr. Waters." With another quick glance at Toni, she left, her heart heavy.

Toni looked up at Chuck, her wet lashes sticking to her cheeks. "I don't know what came over me. I didn't cry this hard when I first heard about it."

"Let it out," Chuck encouraged her. "I'm glad Adelaide came in here with her fears written all over her face. It made you break down and release some of the stress that's been building up within you the last couple of days. You needed to do that, Toni."

Toni sniffed. "I'll save the crying for the relief I'll feel when we have her back. Right now, I need to be thinking of ways to accomplish that."

"We have top people working on it," Chuck told her. "Clay's whole staff is putting together a dossier on the man Dominic believes may be involved. We have clearance to land in Ethiopia. Things are progressing—"

The doorbell rang.

"It's Georgie and Clay," Toni said and headed toward the door. Chuck held on to her. "Let Carson do his job. You stay right here in my arms."

Toni gave him a wet smile and relaxed in his arms.

About three minutes later, Carson was coming through the door with Solange in tow.

"Sir, madam, a Dr. DuPree to see you."

Solange stood right behind him with a black tote in her right hand. Apparently she had left her luggage in the foyer. She moved around Carson. She was attired in jeans and a matching lined jacket. Underneath was a T-shirt with the message *Archaeologists do it in the dirt* emblazoned across the chest. She appeared a bit travel weary, but as far as Toni was concerned, she was a sight for sore eyes.

"Solange!" Toni went to her and threw her arms around her new friend's neck. "Thank you for coming!"

Solange hugged her back, and when they drew apart, she smiled at her and handed her the tote. "I made good time. Maybe the gods are on our side, huh?"

She smiled at Chuck. "Hello, Mr. Waters."

"Dr. DuPree," Chuck said, acknowledging her with a warm grin that set her heart aflutter. He had that effect on women.

Taking the bag and going over to the sofa to sit down and pull the wooden box from it, Toni told them both,

"Will you two stop being so formal? I think we know each other well enough now to drop the titles."

She pried the lid open and lovingly looked down at the wooden statue, the object that would ransom her daughter's life. Chuck and Solange flanked her on the sofa. Toni glanced up at Solange. "I really don't know how to thank you, Solange. Risking losing her to help someone you've just met. I'm in awe of you."

"You can't hold on to something that was never yours to begin with," Solange told her. "Besides, the goddess hasn't been legally registered with the university. If it turns up missing indefinitely, I'll fudge the paperwork."

"Oh, well now I feel doubly bad," Toni told her seriously. "Compromising your honesty. You don't think they'd fire you over this, do you?"

Solange's dark eyes took on a defiant look. "Let them try! It was my property, acquired on my time. I'll take them to court if they give me any grief!"

Toni liked Solange DuPree better by the second.

Toni reached out and placed a hand atop one of Solange's. "I won't forget this."

Feeling a bit embarrassed by all the attention, Solange looked around the room. "This is a lovely house, Mr. . . . Charles."

Both Toni and Chuck laughed.

Then Toni placed the box with the goddess in it on the corner of the coffee table and, gesturing to the food-laden tray Adelaide had brought in earlier, said, "We were just about to have a bite to eat. Won't you join us?"

"I could go for a sandwich. But first I have something very interesting to tell you."

"Oh, baby, I miss you, too," Margery told her husband, Daniel. "But I couldn't bear to leave until they find Bree safe and sound." Margery rolled over in bed and looked at the travel clock on her nightstand. It was a quarter past two in the morning. "If you're not back home in two days, I'm walking off the set," Daniel said, his voice emphatic. He was also an actor. Once, he had been at the top of his profession. As he grew older the parts started going to younger actors. He was still talented; however, now he was relegated to supporting roles instead of leading roles. It suited him well nowadays, because his first priority was his family, not his career. He and Margery had remarried after a ten-year separation. It had taken a divorce to get him to recognize his true feelings for her. "I'm not kidding, Margie. I should be there with you anyway."

"Oh, baby," Margery said, her voice filled with longing. "As much as I want you here, you can't just walk off the set. I will keep in touch. Toni and Chuck and the rest are going to be here soon. The kidnapper gave a deadline of the twenty-sixth. That's the day after tomorrow. As soon as we get Bree back, I promise you I'll be on the next plane to Los Angeles." They lived in San Francisco; however, Daniel was presently on location in Los Angeles. "Make sure you call Alana and Nico and tell them what's going on. And give our grandchildren smooches over the phone for me."

"I'll do that," Daniel promised, resigned for the moment. "But if you change your mind about my coming, phone me. I'll have my cell phone on me at all times."

"Okay," Margery said softly. "I had better try and get some sleep now, Daniel. I'm starting to see pink elephants. When Toni and the rest arrive I plan on being with them every step of the way from that point on."

"All right, sweetheart. I love you," her husband told her, sighing. He still wasn't satisfied with her decision, but he would go along with her. "Good night."

"I love you, too," Margery said. "Now go before I burst into tears again."

They rang off, and she lay there in the semidarkness, imagining Daniel in his hotel room half a world away doing the same thing. But when she started thinking about being alone in the dark, her thoughts turned to Bree and what she must be going through. Was she being treated fairly? *Please, God, don't let them hurt her!*

She was exhausted and fell asleep with those words playing over and over in her mind. As soon as she was firmly in Morpheus' arms, the phone rang again. Thinking it was Daniel, she reached over and mumbled, "I'm bushed, babe."

"Wake up, Margery, we've got some news for you and Dominic. I tried Dominic's number, but there was no answer."

"Dominic has started taking long walks at night. Seriously, Toni, the boy is losing it! He blames himself for not noticing Bree was missing soon enough to save her."

"Oh, that's ridiculous. He had no idea someone was stalking her!"

"I know that and you know that, but the boy is inconsolable."

"We'll talk when I get there," Toni said, sounding as though she was hyped. "Right now, you should know that the statue thief and Yusef Makonnen are one and the same. It's been confirmed by an investigator who was on the thieves' trail. We encountered him in Miami. Dr. Du-Pree, the archaeologist I told you about? Well, anyway, she brought us the good news, and she's going to be coming with us."

"Yusef Makonnen. Deceptively handsome. I saw him in the hotel restaurant one night when some of the cast and crew and I went to dinner. There are a lot of negative rumors floating around about him. They say he may have underworld connections. I hate the thought of Bree being in the hands of someone like that."

"Me, too," Toni said. "But Clay's people have collected

enough information on him to fill a book. The more information we have on him, the better. Oh, before I forget, how is Pierre? Any improvement at all?"

"He's still unconscious. But he's hanging on," Margery said sadly. "Dr. Amlak operated on his hip. He's in a cast. Dr. Amlak was worried that he might not awaken from the anesthesia, and he didn't. If anything happens to Pierre, it'll break Bree's heart. She treats that pooch like the child she craves."

Over the years Toni had not suffered the miniature French poodle gladly. She thought he was neurotic, the way he became jealous of anyone who got too close to Bree. However, she had to give him his props. This was the second time he had risked his life trying to save his mistress. "He's tough, he'll make it," she said with conviction. "Besides, he isn't done annoying me yet."

Margery laughed. "In his defense, it's been a long time since he left any 'gifts' in anyone's shoes."

"Listen, Margery, the pilot says we should be arriving some time after eleven, our time, the night of the twenty-fifth. We have a layover in London for refueling and to get a bit of rest. But we'll be there in plenty of time to have the goddess at the cathedral on the twenty-sixth. Makonnen hasn't allowed Bree to phone again. I hope nothing's wrong."

"Well, you told me he said they'd phone again after they authenticated the goddess," Margery reminded her. "So it isn't a bad sign that he hasn't phoned again."

"You're right," Toni said. "Okay, dear. I'm going. Tell Dominic we'll see you both tomorrow night. Good-bye."

In Chuck's office in Boston, after Toni hung up, Chuck went to her and pulled her in his arms from behind. They were alone in the room. Everyone else—Georgie, Clay, Alec and Solange—had retired for the night. He and Toni were headed upstairs soon.

"Why won't he let her phone, Chuck?" Toni asked worriedly. "If I could only hear her voice again!"

Bree stood on the second-floor ledge of Makonnen's palace, her back pressed against the wall. She was grateful there was practically no wind tonight; otherwise she would probably be splattered on the paved circular driveway below by now. The driveway was illuminated by rows of lights close to the ground, so she could see it with ease. She inched closer to the window to the left of her bedroom window. She didn't know if it was occupied. She had never heard any suspect noises from that side at night. Maybe it was empty. She peered at the base of the window, hoping to see some light spilling from the curtains. No such luck. She craned her neck to take a quick look at the window. Black. She scooted closer and tried to pull the window up. It was locked. She continued moving along the ledge. Now there were bushes below her. What type, she had no idea. This side of the house wasn't as well illuminated as the front. She thought of jumping onto the bushes, believing they would break her fall. But what if they had thorns? She might be cut up, or possibly impaled on a sharp branch. No. What she was hoping to do was find an unlocked window and climb through it to safety.

She cursed Makonnen. After she had given him a piece of her mind, she had gone to her bedroom and locked the door. A few minutes later, he came to her door. "You want to be treated like a prisoner, I'll treat you like one!" he shouted. Then she heard the sound of an electric drill. She rushed to the door and swung it open, but Omoro was there blocking her exit. He gave her a satisfied smirk. Finally, she was getting the treatment she deserved.

"What are you doing?" she spoke calmly to Makonnen.

Makonnen stood against the opposite wall, his arms folded across his chest. "We're locking you in, princess. I don't want you roaming the house tonight. Tomorrow morning, you will be where I expect you to be. Everything will go off without a hitch, or you die. You might say I'm saving your life."

"What if there's a fire? I'll be trapped!"

"If there's a fire," Omoro said, "we'll have barbecue two nights in a row."

At that moment he looked like a cannibal to Bree. She had never hated anyone so much in her life. However, she knew she couldn't prevent them from putting the padlock on her door. So while Harris continued attaching the screws, she simply stood in the doorway and helplessly watched.

The night was silent except for the sound of Makonnen's climate-control system. To Bree the temperature felt around sixty degrees tonight. And he had the air conditioner set at sixty-five. Why didn't he just open the windows? It was his electric bill. But, wait a minute, madmen who built fortresses in the desert didn't buy electricity. More than likely he had his own personal generating plant somewhere on the property. *Get a grip, girl. You're losing it!* She was approaching another window. This time she saw light coming from inside the room. Plenty of it. She peeped around and into the window. The curtains were wide open, and she could clearly see into the bedroom. The bed was still made. However, there was a bathrobe lying on it. The lamp on the nightstand was on. The window was closed. She reached down and tried it. It was, indeed, unlocked. She didn't immediately pull it open, though. What if the occupant of the room was just relieving himself in the bathroom? Clinging to hope, she waited. The problem with waiting was that if her theory was correct and he returned from the bathroom before she could get past his window, he would notice her if she tried to continue along the ledge. Another possibility occurred to her: what if no one was in the room now, and while she was hesitating out here on the ledge, he returned? Her best bet was to enter the room, enter it quickly, then get out again just as quickly.

She pulled the window open, pressed on the screen and found it came out easily. Too easily. It fell to the bedroom floor. It didn't make very much noise, not enough to be heard by someone in the bathroom with the water running, but enough to make Bree fearful she had been detected. She held her breath a moment, but she heard no sounds from the bathroom.

Hurrying to the bedroom door, she pulled it open and peeped in both directions before exiting the room and closing the door behind her. She thought about the screen lying on the floor only after she was running down the corridor, and she wasn't going to go back in order to correct her gaffe. If they found the screen and figured out how it had come to be on the floor, she hoped to be long gone by then. Makonnen had said all the cars had only a couple gallons of gas in them. Even if that were true, he had to have a way of refueling them, didn't he? Maybe she could find the gas pumps and refuel. He had said there was no town for fifty miles in any direction. Her years of scouting as a girl had left her with a good sense of direction. She knew they had passed a small village southwest of here. It wasn't exactly a bustling city, but maybe she could get help there. Perhaps make a phone call. The thing was, if she ran into trouble in the desert, she would need food and water to sustain her. That meant she had to make a detour by the kitchen.

It was after two in the morning. Would anyone still be up at this hour? Possibly. She observed the area before entering. Then, going to the pantry where she had noticed several cloth grocery bags hanging on a peg, she chose one and went back across the room to the refrigerator and began filling the bag with bottled water, fruit and vegetables. She didn't pick up anything that would spoil in a couple days if not refrigerated. Finished, a thought occurred to her: Where would Makonnen keep his car keys? In the cars themselves? Out here he probably had no fear of car thieves. Or perhaps he kept them somewhere in the garage. She had kept her eyes open for an opportunity such as this while being held here for the last two days. She hadn't noticed any keys hanging on the wall in the kitchen where some people kept their house keys and car keys. Makonnen wouldn't be that ordinary, would he? She would worry about that later. Now, to get out of the house.

He had a security system, no doubt about that. Fortunately for her he was rather lackadaisical about engaging it on a regular basis. The fact that he lived in the middle of the desert probably had something to do with that. Tonight, he thought he had her locked away in her bedroom. She was counting on his having been lazy about security. She paused in front of the display board near the entrance. The green light was on, denoting the system had not been engaged. She smiled to herself. Good old egotistical Makonnen. He was sure he had her exactly where he wanted her. Why worry about the security system?

Bree opened the door and stepped outside, closing the door behind her. Getting her bearings, she searched the area. He had allowed her the run of the house, but had not allowed her outside. She didn't know in which direction the garage might lie. There were no vehicles parked nearby, so there must be someplace where they sheltered them.

Going to the left of the front entrance, she walked perhaps thirty yards before she came upon a detached

building as large as the average American home. Flood-
lights were on at the top corners of the building. When
she got closer and saw triple garage doors, she knew she
had found the right building. But all three doors were
down. If they operated only by remote, she was up the
creek without a paddle. However, if they were the rolling
kind, luck was on her side. She leaned the grocery bag
against the wall and tried rolling up one of the doors.
It didn't budge. Biting her bottom lip in frustration, she
tried the next door, and it actually moved! She put her
back in it, and soon the door was open. She walked into
the dark space. Neat shelves were on all three walls.
There was only one thing that interested her, though, a
gleaming black Mercedes. She tried the driver's side door
and nervously laughed when it opened. Getting in, she
felt under the visor on the driver's side. No keys. Then
she tried the ashtray. Sometimes folks who didn't smoke
would leave a spare key in the ashtray. No key. Sighing,
she closed her eyes and laid her head on her folded
arms atop the steering wheel. Disgusted, close to giving
up, she opened her eyes, and that was when she saw
them. The keys were in the ignition.

Thinking her luck couldn't be that good, she turned
the key, figuring that at the very least, they had discon-
nected the cables. But, no, the motor turned over and
purred like a well-fed cat. She waited until the fuel indi-
cator came to a stop. The damned tank was full. Full!
Another Yusef Makonnen lie.

She switched on the lights, threw that slinky baby in
reverse and backed out of the garage. Stopping, she put
the car in park, got out and collected the grocery bag
of provisions. Getting back inside, she placed the bag on
the seat beside her and fastened her seat belt. It wasn't
a good idea to speed. If she drove out of here slowly,
not gunning the motor and bringing attention to herself,
perhaps she would reach the village she had spotted

southwest of Makonnen's compound long before anyone missed her.

"You're all packed, Mrs. Makonnen," Berta Lee said as she closed and locked the large suitcase sitting on Salah's bed. Salah was coming out of the bathroom, attired in her nightgown. She smiled at the middle-aged black woman who had taken such good care of their San Francisco home for them since they purchased it eight years ago. Berta was short and stout with a pretty round face and laughing black eyes. She seemed always to be in a good mood, even though Salah knew she had troubles of her own from time to time.

"Thank you, Berta. You're wonderful to me."

Berta picked up the suitcase, preparing to take it with her. "I'll have all your luggage downstairs in the foyer in the morning. That way, the cabdriver can easily collect it for you." It was their normal routine. Salah didn't have a chauffeur. She preferred driving or, when in a more adventurous mood, taking cabs or riding the famous San Francisco streetcars. However, when she was on the way out of town, she took a cab to the airport. It was less complicated.

"I'd appreciate that," Salah said, going to the vanity and sitting down to put a bit of moisturizer on her braids and cover them with a sleeping cap. She had recently had her natural hair rebraided. It was peculiar. She lived in Africa where the custom began eons ago, but she had found her favorite practitioners of the art right here in the United States. "Oh, Berta, I expect you to hire that house sitter we employed last year around this time. Then I want you and that nice husband of yours to take a two-week vacation on us. I left a check for you downstairs on my desk in the library. Just an expression of my gratitude." Berta placed the suitcase on the floor and went to hug Salah's neck. "Oh, Mrs. Makonnen, you're too good to me!"

Salah hugged her back. "You've earned it, Berta. And now that the doctor has given me the green light, it just may be that I'll have more work for you to do soon. So take a long vacation and just relax awhile. You and Nathaniel rarely do anything just for yourselves. You're always putting others first. This time, you come first."

Berta laughed. "Having a baby in the house will be a real pleasure." She and her husband, Nathaniel, were never blessed with children, although she had helped raise her sister's three children when her sister died of breast cancer fifteen years ago. They were all adults now and either attending college or out in the workaday world.

"I'm going to depend on you to give me a few pointers," Salah told her, holding her at arm's length. "Now, off with you. Go plan your trip with Nathaniel."

Berta went and picked up the suitcase and walked toward the door, but she had to turn once more before leaving and say, "You're going to make a good mother!" Kind and generous human beings always made good mothers.

Choked up, Salah watched Berta go. She decided at that moment that as soon as she conceived, she and Yusef would come to live in San Francisco. Yusef would have to go away, on occasion, to attend to his business concerns. But as for her, she would remain in the city and create a loving environment for their child. She wouldn't allow Yusef to talk her out of it. The thought of spending nine months of her pregnancy in his desert kingdom in Djibouti sent shivers down her spine. He had never denied her anything she truly wanted. He would not balk at this request.

Going over to the bed, which Berta had already turned down, she climbed in and laid her head on the hypoallergenic pillow. The sheets smelled of lavender. As her eyes slowly closed, she wondered what Yusef was doing. She hadn't phoned him yet. When she arrived in Addis, she would phone him then and surprise him. He would send his man with a car to collect her from Lideta Airport and drive her out to the heliport where Harris would be waiting.

When Harris returned from the helipad atop the tower where he had made an exhaustive check of the chopper, he was worn out. All he wanted to do was take a bath and fall into bed. However, when he walked into his bedroom, on the same floor as the Makonnens' suite of rooms since he was a trusted employee, he knew that wish would go unfulfilled. He spotted the screen, popped from the window frame, first. Walking to the middle of the room, he picked it up. Then his eyes went from the screen to the window, which was still up. A sharp pain actually pierced his gut. The actress had escaped. He envisioned the night ahead: searching the desert for a ditzy woman who had no idea what sort of hell was in store for her! Damn!

Blowing air through thin lips, he turned and marched down the corridor to Briane Shaw's bedroom. The padlock he had installed was intact. He had expected it to be because she had not exited that way. Oh, no, she had used her imagination and climbed out of her window, entered his and exited through *his* door. He knocked on the door anyway. "Miss Shaw? Miss Shaw? It's Harris. Sorry to wake you, but I need to speak with you about something." Sorry to wake her? He almost laughed. He would probably keel over from shock if she actually replied.

Just as he suspected, there was no answer from within. Turning, he trudged down the hallway to Yusef Makonnen's bedroom door. His knock got a nearly immediate response. "What the hell is it?"

"Sir," Harris said with understandable hesitancy, "I believe Miss Shaw has left the house."

Yusef wasted no time getting the door open. He stood there with disheveled hair and dressed in rumpled pajama bottoms. "Get the others," he bellowed. "And make sure they're supplied with a rope and chains this time. That little she-devil will be bound and gagged!"

Ten minutes later, all five men had piled into a Humvee, designed specifically for desert detail, and set off after the Mercedes with the Hollywood actress in it. Ishi drove. Makonnen sat in front with a pair of binoculars trained on the terrain. Omoro, Hyde and Harris sat on the backseat, each of them armed with various instruments with which to capture and restrain their prey. "You have to give it to her"—Hyde risked his life by saying—"it took guts to climb out of that window, and smarts to sneak out of the house and steal a car. She's still my heroine!"

"Silence!" Makonnen snapped. He had never been bested by a woman, and his record wasn't going to be broken tonight. Hyde didn't utter another word, but inside he was applauding Bree's daring. Next to him Omoro had a strangely sinister smile on his face.

"We may not find her," he said with satisfaction. "The desert has a way of swallowing up people who get lost in it. She and that German car may both be in the belly of the desert by now."

The muscles worked in Hyde's strong jaw. He knew Omoro was taunting him. He wouldn't rise to the bait, though. Looking straight ahead and seeing nothing but the beams of the Humvee, he hoped that Bree knew to stay in the flats of the desert and not to venture near the dunes. He assumed she was heading to the encampment nearby. It was the only settlement within a hundred miles. They had passed it on the way to Makonnen's desert domain. Luckily, they didn't have tracks to follow. Desert winds had eradicated any signs that the Mercedes had passed this way. "When we catch her, you now have my permission to rough her up a little. Teach her to behave herself," Makonnen announced. Omoro's smile got broader.

Bree drove at a steady pace of forty miles per hour. She was afraid to go any faster because the car's wheels had started wobbling. A fifty-thousand-dollar auto, and the wheels were shaking. Only slightly at first. She had noticed the movement after she had driven perhaps fifteen miles from Makonnen's compound. There was also the sound of sand hitting the undercarriage of the car. She assumed there was no harm in that. What damage could sand do to metal? Maybe over a hundred years or so, the constant beating of grains of sand against metal would cause a modicum of damage. She didn't plan on being out that long. If her calculations were correct, she should reach the village in about an hour and a half at the most.

The surrounding darkness unnerved her. A city girl, she wasn't used to this unrelenting blackness. Not a light along the road. To be honest, this wasn't exactly a road. After she had left Makonnen's property, the paved road gave out. Now there was nothing for miles but sand. She tried to stay on flat land as much as possible, but since there was no road, paved or otherwise, that was sometimes difficult to do. She would drive a long stretch on flat land, then suddenly come upon a dune, and she would have to back up and try another direction. If not for her knowledge of the stars in the sky, she would be hopelessly lost by now. But she kept her senses about her and continued heading in a southwest direction. It was so quiet she spent a moment looking for a CD to put in the CD player. She found Andrea Bocelli's *Romanza,* and it was playing now as she kept her eyes peeled for more of the dreaded dunes.

A few minutes into her trip she realized that the garage door that housed this luxury car was probably never locked for a reason. *What fool would take it into the desert?* She looked into the rearview mirror. "Only you," she said, the sound of her voice sounding peculiarly spooky to her. This Mercedes was probably used to transport Makonnen and his wife, Salah, back and forth from the helipad. He undoubtedly had sturdier vehicles for treks in the desert. And speaking of Salah, Bree wondered why she hadn't seen any photographs of her anywhere in the house. Makonnen being careful that the parties in his little game would not be able to recognize his beloved wife? He *had* said he wanted to keep her out of this and free of the possibility of prosecution. Bree still thought his reasoning was flawed. If he loved his wife so much, why risk going to prison and leaving her for a long stretch of time? Was that truly love? Or just his misguided desire to control everything around him? Bree wondered what his wife's reaction to his actions would be.

Andrea Bocelli was singing, "Con Te Partiro, I Will Go With You." Bree was more familiar with Donna Summer's version of the song, but she liked Bocelli's version as well.

She nearly panicked when she heard a phone ring. It sounded as if the ringing was coming from the car pocket, so she leaned over and pressed the button to the compartment. It couldn't be anyone but Makonnen. However, since he had inadvertently shown her where the phone was, she would use it to try to phone Dominic in Addis.

She brought the cordless phone to her ear and mouth. "Thank you. I didn't know I had a phone at my disposal."

"I suggest you turn around and come back to the compound, Bree. The desert can be unforgiving. Whereas I will forgive you your impetuous actions if you return."

"That's Miss Shaw to you," Bree replied and promptly hung up.

Having a facility with numbers, she recalled the number to the hotel in Addis with no trouble. She waited for the dial tone and then dialed the number. Nothing. Just a recurring dial tone. She tried again and got the same results.

The phone rang again.

"I get it!" she cried, irritated. "The phones only work between the vehicles."

Laughing, Makonnen said, "Exactly. Now, be a good girl and turn around like I told you. If you do this, I promise I won't let Omoro have his way with you. If you don't comply, I can't be held accountable for what he plans to do to you."

"You and Omoro can drop dead," Bree said and hung up the phone.

In the Humvee, Makonnen yelled at Ishi, "Can't you go any faster?"

"It isn't safe," Ishi told him. "Even in a vehicle built for this terrain, it's dangerous to be reckless. Do you want to be stranded in the desert?"

Makonnen fell silent.

They drove on, the deep rumble of the Humvee breaking the silence of the desert night surrounding them.

Several miles away, Bree was creeping along now. The engine light flashed red. She didn't know what was happening. The car's tires were making a *whup whup* sound as if sand had gotten into the rims. That would explain why they were wobbling. Stopping was out of the question. She didn't care if Makonnen's lovely Mercedes fell apart once she got to safety.

A few minutes later, though, nature intervened and

forced her to a halt. The steering wheel locked, and she ran into a small embankment, not nearly as high as some of the dunes she had avoided earlier. The nose of the Mercedes became embedded in the sand, and the engine stalled. It would not ignite when she turned the key. However, that was the least of her worries. The nose of the Mercedes began to slowly incline toward the floor of the desert. More accurately, it was sinking into the sand. Bree quickly undid her seat belt and tried the door, but the car had already sunk so far into the rapidly forming hole that the sand had effectively sealed the door shut. Thinking quickly, she found the button to the power windows, and the driver's side window automatically opened. She hoisted herself up and out of the window, falling to the ground below. Crawling on all fours toward higher ground, she got sand in her mouth. She groped with closed eyes, afraid to open them for fear the sand would blind her. She could feel the soft sand flowing into the hole as the Mercedes fell into it, much like a big fish caught in a net. And she was going to be dessert if she didn't gain purchase soon.

In the Humvee, Hyde suddenly screamed, "Back up!" Ishi put his foot on the brakes.

"I saw tail lights down there," Hyde told them, pointing behind them. He didn't wait for Ishi to put the Humvee in reverse. He opened his door and leaped from the vehicle and ran back to the spot where he had seen the tail lights glowing red in the darkness. Ishi backed the huge all-terrain vehicle, being careful not to run over his infatuated comrade.

"Bring the high-beam lamps, bring the rope," Hyde ordered excitedly. "It's the Mercedes caught in a sand trap. Hurry!"

"Stay back, fool," Makonnen said as he joined Hyde. "We don't want to have to rescue two idiots tonight."

Ishi came up with a flashlight. Hyde took it from him and began walking toward the area that now resembled a gaping black maw. The taillights had disappeared, but he spotted Bree still desperately clawing her way toward more solid ground. Omoro was coming around the Humvee with the rope, but he was taking his time. Makonnen went to him and snatched the thirty-foot hemp rope from his hands. "You're a real bastard, you know that?"

In spite of his threats, Makonnen wasn't a cold-blooded killer. To allow Bree to die, swallowing sand, fighting for her life, would be tantamount to putting a bullet in her head.

Hyde took the rope from Makonnen and tied it around his waist. "I'm going in," he told them. "You all will have to pull us both out."

Bree was huffing and puffing. Sand would get in her nose, and she would blow it back out, afraid she was going to drown in it. Tears came to her eyes, but she dared not blink. All the while she felt the relentless pull of the sinkhole, getting ever larger behind her. Her heart hammered in her chest, and her lungs burned with the effort.

Hyde had but to lie down at the edge and he was sliding fast toward her. What he needed to do was grab hold of Bree when he slid past her. He began picking up speed. Without goggles, he couldn't keep his eyes open; he had to depend on his sense of touch.

Bree felt a boot in her face. Instead of being offended, she grabbed for it with the last ounce of her strength. She clamped on to it so hard her fingers hurt. Hyde reached down and grabbed her around the waist with one powerful arm and yanked on the rope to give the men on solid ground the signal to pull them both up. Omoro—who had been threatened by Makonnen with firing if he didn't help—Makonnen, Ishi and Harris pulled backward on their end of the rope until Bree and Hyde were lying on solid ground.

Unmoving, Bree lay on top of Hyde. Hyde shook his head several times, dislodging most of the sand from his orifices. He rolled Bree onto her stomach so gravity would aid the sand in falling from her nose and mouth. She didn't stir. He straddled her from behind and firmly pushed on her back, up from the lower back all the way to the shoulder blades. "Come on! You're a fighter. Come on, Bree! Wake up!"

"She's dead," Omoro said.

"She's not dead," Hyde argued, continuing his ministrations.

Makonnen came to kneel next to Bree's prone body. "This has gone terribly wrong. I never intended this to happen. She would've been returned safely." He was bitterly remorseful. Still on his knees, he bowed his head as he had seen Salah do while saying her evening prayers. Holding his head in his hands, he wailed, "I've killed. My hands have blood on them."

While he was carrying on like a madman, Bree awakened and began coughing up sand. Hyde made sure she was turned to her side as she vomited, clearing all her breathing passages. After a while, her respiration was almost normal. Hyde bent and picked her up in his arms, not caring what Makonnen's orders might be. "You're going to be fine," he said. As he passed Omoro, he shot daggers at him. "You and I are finished. I will not cover your back any longer. We are not killers. We're soldiers. A soldier doesn't allow an innocent person to die. I knew you were over the top when you beat that security guard so badly in Miami. Stealing, okay. Blowing the bad guys away, okay. But I draw the line at beating helpless people and letting defenseless women die." He went on as he placed Bree on the backseat of the Humvee. "You hear me, Ishi? This partnership is dissolved."

Ishi nodded. He hated losing Hyde. Of his two partners, Hyde was the most reasonable. Omoro had a violent side that he could barely keep in check.

They all got into the Humvee and waited for their employer, who was still kneeling on the ground. Makonnen pulled himself together and climbed into the Humvee, slamming the door with more force than necessary. "Let's go," he said. "She may require medical care. We'll have to fly to Addis tonight."

Mubara stalked through Makonnen's palace. When he had told her the woman had escaped and he was heading into the desert to recapture her, she knew his plans had gone hopelessly awry. She had to think carefully. What if he didn't find the woman? Would he even go along with the program after that? If he didn't get the goddess to complete the seven, her con would collapse like a house of cards. She didn't know what to do next. So close to collecting a cool million. It would be her biggest take to date. Now, because that dumb little actress had escaped, she stood to come away from this game no richer than she had been upon its commencement. She couldn't have that. Months of laying the trap. Tracking the quarry. Weeks working to perfect her disguise and the Mubara persona. She had held Makonnen in the palm of her hand. All to see it go up in smoke?

Bree was practically held in Hyde's lap the entire trip back to the compound. She was so exhausted she hadn't said a word yet. Her thoughts were back in Addis with Dominic. What must he be going through? She knew she would be nearly out of her mind with worry if their situ-

ations were reversed. And poor Pierre. Was he living or
dead? He had the heart of a hero. Even in her weakened
state she could muster up venomous thoughts about
Omoro. First he had tried to kill her dog, and then, only
minutes ago, he had been willing to let her die back
there! She was certain he would die a death as horrifying
as he had meant for her. If not for Hyde, she would be
dead. She couldn't help feeling grateful to the big mercenary.

Should this come down to her testimony, she would
be compelled to speak in his behalf.

She hadn't been able to make out much of what went
on once they pulled her out of the sand trap, but she
sensed a subtle change in Makonnen. Could it be he was
thinking of letting her go and giving up on his crazy
plans?

She sighed, and Hyde pressed her closer to the side
of his bulky, warm body. Rubbing her upper arm, he
said, "Rest now. We're going to take you to the hospital
in Addis."

Seeing the lights of the compound ahead, Hyde said,
"We shouldn't waste any time. Let's go straight to the
tower."

"No," Makonnen spoke up. "You men should collect
your belongings. You won't be returning with me and
Harris."

"The job's over, then?" Ishi asked.

"Yes," Makonnen replied. "I'll pay you what I promised you, and you can depart from Addis."

Ishi pulled the Humvee in front of the house.

"Let's take Miss Shaw inside and get her cleaned up
as much as possible. And perhaps she can drink a bit of
water or some broth to help rebuild her strength," Makonnen suggested. "It's an hour's flight to Addis."

Harris held the door for Hyde while he carried Bree
over the threshold. The other men followed. Once inside

the foyer, Makonnen switched on the light. "Take her to the great room and lay her on the couch."

As they turned right from the foyer, heading in the direction of the great room, they were brought up short by the sight of a small woman with a big gun grasped competently in her hands. Omoro's eyes narrowed. That was *his* modified Uzi she was holding. Not thinking, he angrily stepped toward her, and she shot him without hesitation.

Bree cried out in shock and disbelief. Hyde turned her away from the gun-wielding woman. If she shot in their direction, she would shoot him in the back. Maybe Bree would be able to get away.

"Get in here, all of you!" the woman demanded, her tone brooking no disobedience.

They walked past the fallen Omoro, who was shot in the shoulder. He hitched his way to a sitting position and leaned against the wall, eyeing the woman with murderous intent.

"You too," she told him, not caring that he was losing blood. Harris paused to help Omoro to his feet and lent him a shoulder. The African leaned on the Brit as little as possible. He hated having to depend on anyone for anything.

Once they were in the well-lit great room, the woman told them, "Now sit down close together. I don't want you spread out. I want you together where I can see you all in one glance."

As they complied, muttering arose among them.

"Who the hell is she?" Ishi asked.

"Heck if I know," Hyde replied.

"She's a dead woman," Omoro said under his breath.

Bree was slowly regaining her strength. She knew who the woman was. She was the mystery woman she had chased through the corridors the other night. The woman was well over fifty. Of Chinese descent. Bree had grown up in San Francisco, and some of her closest friends were Chinese. She even spoke a bit of Cantonese. Makonnen had called her Mubara. Of course he knew her. He had simply kept her presence a secret from the rest of them.

Mubara paced back and forth, the gun waggling in her hand. Bree wished she would hold the Uzi with both hands. She had worked with one before in her role as Jody Freeman, private investigator, and she knew they had a hair trigger.

"Tell me," Mubara said to Makonnen. "And be truthful. Have you managed to ruin our plans? Will the ceremony still take place?"

"Well, I—"

Mubara shot a round into the ceiling. Her dark eyes found Makonnen's. "I told you not to lie!"

"No!" Makonnen said, tired of the whole mess. At this rate, Salah would find out about it all and divorce him anyway. She would be appalled at his behavior. His excuse of having done it all for her would fall on deaf ears. He had nothing else to lose. "It's all off. I want you out of my house, witch!"

Mubara laughed shortly. "I'm holding the gun. I'll give the orders." Walking in circles, she said, "I'll tell you what: if you give me the million you promised me, I'll gladly get out of your lurid palace." She wrinkled her nose at the decor. "Solomon's palace was probably no less garish."

"I don't have that kind of money just lying around," Makonnen tried to reason with her. "I'll have to have the funds transferred to an account. No bank in this area will give me that much in cash. I would have to go to New York or London or my bank in Munich for that kind of currency." He ran a dirty hand through his sweaty hair. "Surely you didn't expect me to pay you in cash?"

"All right," Mubara screeched, rethinking her position. "Your wife must have valuable jewelry stashed in a safe somewhere in this mausoleum. I want you to get it, but first . . . you," she said to Hyde. "Let go of the woman. See the ties on the draperies? Get all four pairs and come back here. And don't make any sudden movements, or the woman gets a bullet in her."

Hyde did as he was told. Returning, he offered her the sturdy ties, which were as thick as rope and undoubtedly as strong. Mubara glared at him. "Tie up the two blacks and the white boy, Blondie."

Twelve

They had been in the air nearly an hour before he approached her. Salah was engrossed in an Arabesque novel when she noticed a pair of male legs encased in tailored trousers pause next to her seat in first class, a large manila envelope in his left hand. She raised her eyes, and then they widened of their own accord. Smiling, she said, "We meet again."

The good-looking, dark-skinned man bent low to say, "Lucky for me. Are you on your way to London, too?"

Salah naturally removed her bag from the seat next to her. If the seat next to her was available, she usually booked it, too. She hated to get stuck with a seatmate who talked incessantly during long flights. "Please, join me," she said. She tucked her book into the side of her carry-on bag at her feet.

Smiling, he folded his long legs and sat. He was wearing a dark Armani suit with black Italian loafers. Since her days as a model, Salah had had an eye for recognizing the work of designers. "Actually, I'm on my way to Addis Ababa," she told him. His British accent was proper yet colored by some other dialect she couldn't place. Spanish, perhaps? Her eyes lowered to his hands. You could tell a lot about a man from his hands: was he a laborer or someone who hired others to labor for him? This man's hands were large and masculine. There were scars on his right one. He had either been in an accident or perhaps he had been a boxer in his youth. He definitely had the build for it: Tall with broad shoulders and slim hips. From what she could see through the suit, well-developed, powerful thigh muscles. Mid-thirties, she would guess. A wonderful example of black male pulchritude.

His eyes were on her wedding rings. "Been married long?"

"More than nine years. And you?"

"I've never been that fortunate."

"Oh? Your work keeping you from hooking up with someone?"

"Before we go any further, allow me to introduce myself." He offered her his hand. "Rupert Giles."

Salah took it and shook it firmly. None of that limp hand action. "Salah Makonnen."

"Yes," he said, answering her previous question. "I believe my job does keep me from establishing a lasting relationship. I travel a great deal, and my job can, on occasion, be hazardous to my health."

Salah's lovely brows arched with interest. "Oh? What exactly do you do?" She had been reading a lot of suspense novels recently. Could she be sitting next to a real spy? Or perhaps someone who worked for the CIA?

Rupert smiled, and dimples appeared in both cheeks. "I work for an international insurance firm. Out of London. We insure objects, people, anything if the price is right. However, like most insurance companies, when the time comes to pay a claim, we balk at it. Especially when there are millions involved. Therefore, I investigate high-profile cases. I'm presently on the trail of a thief who has robbed several major museums of very pricey artifacts."

Salah was intrigued. Turning on her seat to face him, she said, "Mmm, tell me more!"

Rupert picked up the envelope on his lap and opened the clasp. "I'll do more than that. I have photos of the man I think is behind the thefts. Would you like to see them?"

Salah hesitated. Yusef was always telling her to be careful of strangers. With their wealth and position, there was invariably someone out there looking to con them, or worse, threaten them with physical violence to get what they wanted. She looked into Rupert's eyes. "On second thought, I'm not sure I should get involved."

"You're already involved in this case, Mrs. Makonnen," Rupert told her, his tone serious. He pulled several eight-by-tens from the envelope.

Salah eyed him suspiciously. She looked around for a flight attendant. If he tried anything, she would scream bloody murder! "Just my luck, drawing the attention of a crazy man. I want you to get up and leave. Now." Instead, Rupert placed one of the photos on her lap. Salah couldn't help glancing down. It was of three men boarding a plane. She didn't recognize any of them. Reaching down, she picked up the photograph and perused it closer. "I don't know these men."

"Good," Rupert told her with a faint smile. "I didn't think you did." He placed a second photo in her hand. "Do you know that woman?"

Salah was reluctant to say. She regarded him with narrowed eyes. "How do I know you are who you say you are?"

Rupert was more than glad to show her his picture ID identifying him as a chief investigator for the prestigious insurance company that provided coverage for such diverse things as the Queen of England's jewels to a famous actress's gams.

Impressed, Salah handed it back to him. "Yes, I know this woman. I've only met her on one occasion, though. I was having lunch in a San Francisco restaurant when she walked into the room on the arm of my doctor. He introduced us."

It was dusk again in Djibouti. Mubara and Harris were long gone. Bree lay on one of the sofas in the great room, drifting in and out of consciousness. Omoro lay on another, burning up with fever. When Hyde had suggested he be allowed to remove the bullet, Mubara had said, "Let him die." Before absconding with Salah Makonnen's jewels, which totaled more than the million Mubara had initially bargained for, she had had Harris tie Hyde and Makonnen up.

"Miss Shaw!" Hyde called from across the room where he was sitting on the floor with his back against the wall. "Come on, you've got to stay awake. I'm sure help will be here soon. Think of your family. Think of your dog. Think of kicking Omoro for kicking your dog." He would try anything to get her to awaken.

Bree was weak from dehydration. Her tumble in the sand hadn't left her injured. But the struggle to free herself had left her debilitated for the moment. If she didn't get help soon, she might fall into a coma.

"She needs water," Makonnen said. He was sitting a few feet away from Hyde, his wrists and ankles tied together, too. "Blast Harris, did he have to tie us so damn tight?"

They had been trying to work their bonds loose for more than three hours now.

"The witch was standing there watching him with the gun trained on him. Of course he had to tie us up securely," Ishi said. Never again would he get involved in a kidnapping. He had learned his lesson. Hyde was talking about retiring from the mercenary game. Perhaps he would, too. With Hyde gone and Omoro possibly dead, where was the adventure, the fun?

He thought of something suddenly. That multipurpose tool Hyde kept on him . . . could he have it on him now? "Hyde! That gadget you carry. Is it in your pocket now?"

"Yes!" Hyde answered excitedly. That is, if he hadn't lost it when he was nearly sucked into that hellish sink-hole in the desert while trying to rescue Bree. "It was in my coat pocket." With his wrists tied together, he had to rub both arms across his chest in a back and forth motion in order to see if he could detect the telltale lump in his front coat pocket. He felt it! "It's in here," he said and began rolling on the floor, hoping that the gadget would fall from his pocket.

Makonnen scooted closer to Hyde. "Stop moving, you big idiot. Come close and let me see if I can remove the tool with my fingers." Although his hands were tied at the wrists, he still had movement in his fingers. Hyde quit rolling around on the floor and lay still while Makonnen scooted closer to the muscle-bound man and reached inside his coat pocket. Deeper. His fingers touched metal, and he got so excited, he lost his tenuous grip on it. He tried again, and this time, he had it. Pulling it out, he dropped it to the floor. Looking at Hyde, he said, "All right. How do we get it open?"

"Miss Shaw will have to open it; she's the only one not tied up," Hyde replied. "Miss Shaw! Miss Shaw, wake up!"

Bree was dreaming she was on the set of *Queen of Sheba*. Dominic was directing her in the scene in which Makeba, the Queen of Sheba, first met King Solomon. However, in the dream, Dominic was both the director and Solomon. Even in her dreams, she was editorializing, telling her dream self that the only reason she was comparing Dominic to King Solomon was that Dominic's last name was Solomon. Someone off to the side kept calling her name, "Miss Shaw, Miss Shaw. Wake up!"

On the sofa, Bree opened her eyes. She tried to focus
on the face below her. Pierre used to awaken her when
she slept on the sofa by licking her face. She tried to
focus now. The face below was tanned and handsome.
He didn't look a thing like her Pierre. He could talk,
too—something Pierre did only when he wanted a special
treat. He would hop on his hind legs and bark.

"Bree . . ." The voice was in agony now. "Please wake
up!"

Her eyes fluttered open. She knew who it was now:
Hyde. She would smile, but her lips were too cracked
and swollen from dehydration. He got on his knees and
nudged her face with his head. His straight hair irritated
her nose, and even if he didn't look like Pierre, he
smelled faintly like him. Bree said, "You stink."

"Well, you don't smell too good yourself," Hyde told
her, happy she had finally said something. "Now, wake
up. We can get out of here. I can give you some water
if you'll only wake up long enough to get my gadget
right down here next to my knee and open it and cut
the ropes on my wrists."

Bree wanted to wake up. It was scary drifting in and
out like this. What if she didn't awaken the next time
sleep drew her inexorably down into pitch blackness? She
would never see her family or Dominic again. Dominic.
"Love you, Dominic."

"Good!" Hyde shouted. He could work with that. "I'm
Dominic and I'm going to die if you can't pick up this
gadget and free me, Bree. Bree? Help Dominic. Help the
man you love . . . come on!"

Bree breathed in deeply. That seemed to help the oxy-
gen get to her sleepy brain. *Gotta save Dom.* When Hyde
saw her push up on her elbow, he shouted, "Yeah! Come
on, baby. Get the gadget and open it to the knife. Got
to keep your eyes open. Don't want you to cut yourself."

Bree reached down and felt around on the floor until

she touched the gadget. She had it. Stretching her eyes, trying her best to keep them open, she pulled out the scissors. "No!" Hyde said, "They won't cut through the ropes. The knife, Bree. Try again. Get the knife. You can do it."

Bree pulled out another section. It was a nail file. Its edge wouldn't cut anything except butter. She tried a third time, and up sprang the knife.

Hyde, Makonnen and Ishi all shouted with glee. The noise jolted Bree, and she came around long enough to cut the ropes on Hyde's wrists and free him. Once this was done, she fell back on the sofa and was out again.

Hyde hurriedly cut the ropes holding his ankles together, then freed Makonnen and gave the knife to Makonnen so that he could free Ishi.

Hyde had more important things to do. First, he ran to the kitchen and retrieved a bottle of water from the refrigerator. Returning to the great room, he took Bree into his arms and held the bottle to her lips. Bree felt the cold rim against her hot lips and leaned toward it. She gulped the water down.

"Take it easy," Hyde cautioned her. He pulled the bottle away. "More later." He laid her back down. Regarding Makonnen and Ishi, he said, "Who do we call for help in a case like this? Here we are kidnappers who've been bested by a little woman with an Uzi and a greed greater than our own. I suppose we could try to drive out of here in the Humvee if the witch didn't disable it first, which, I might add, would be the first thing I'd do if I were in her place." Looking at Makonnen alone, he asked, "Have you got any ideas, rich man?"

Rich men always had ideas. That was why they were rich men.

"I can hire another helicopter," Makonnen said, his confident gleam back in his eyes. "I only need to make a phone call."

* * *

The Waters Foods company jet landed on a private
airfield just outside of Addis close to ten at night. They
had made good time. Toni, Chuck and the rest all loaded
into a Range Rover Chuck had arranged to meet the
plane. Then they drove to the hotel in Addis where
Margery and Dominic were waiting.

In the meantime, at Lideta Airport, Rupert and Salah
were waiting in line to have their baggage checked. Impatient, Salah glared at the man who was fingering her
lingerie. "I assure you, there's nothing in there that isn't
perfectly legal."

He would not be moved. He meticulously searched
every nook and cranny of her bags, and then he did the
same thing to Rupert's which, thank God, consisted of
fewer pieces than she had.

"She tricked him," Salah kept insisting. "My Yusef is
a good, kind man. Wait until we speak with him. I'll
prove it!"

"He may well be a good and kind man," Rupert told
her. "But if I find the statues on him, he's going to
prison." Finally they were free to go. Salah pushed her
way through the crowd carrying two pieces of her luggage herself. Rupert had been kind enough to take the
heavier piece.

"What if he isn't in possession of the statues? Then
what? You'll take the woman into custody and leave us
be?"

"There's the question of the henchmen he hired. I
have photographs of them, and they have my fist print
on their jaws. Oh, he's guilty all right. And I'll prove it."

"If he did it, it was out of some misplaced loyalty to
me!" Salah cried. "If my Yusef is guilty of this crime you
accuse him of, I have to do something to help clear
him."

Tears had begun falling down Salah's cheeks. She had trouble seeing where she was going and ran into another woman. The woman was in a hurry and muttered an expletive under her breath. "Watch where you're going, fool!"

Salah peered into the woman's face, and her mouth fell open. Then she swung the heavier case up and around, hitting the other woman in the head with it. The woman fell to the slick floor, and the trench coat she wore facilitated a healthy slide across it.

"What the hell?" Rupert cried, looking at Salah and then at the woman who was knocked out cold.

Salah went to stand over the woman, a look of triumph on her face. "Got you, you deceitful wretch!"

Rupert stooped to feel for the woman's pulse, and that was when he got a good look at her face. She had a pulse. She would be okay. But she would probably have a powerful headache when she awakened. Laughing, he gazed up at Salah. "You're in the wrong line of business. How you identified her with this getup on, I'll never know."

"I was a model," Salah told him. "It was my job to become a different woman with each gig. I know makeup and a wig when I see it. And like I told you, I've seen her in the flesh before."

Airport security had been alerted. When four armed men in uniform arrived on the scene, Rupert explained everything to them, and they carried the woman into the security office to await the police and an ambulance. He and Salah were once again detained.

The phone rang in Dominic's suite. He was seated next to Margery on the couch, fighting his urge to hit something. Here it was the night of the twenty-fifth and Makonnen hadn't phoned with instructions on where to find

Bree once he had the goddess. So when the phone rang, he rushed to pick it up.

"Hello!"

"Dominic Solomon?"

"Yeah! What do you want? I'm expecting an important call."

"Listen carefully. . . ."

Margery and Dominic were racing out of the hotel and getting into a taxi when Toni spotted them from the front seat of the Range Rover pulling up to the hotel.

"That's Margery and Dominic," she exclaimed. "Where are they rushing off to like that?" Turning to the driver and pointing at the taxi, she cried, "Follow that car!" She almost struck Georgie, who was sitting between her and the driver, in the eye with her elbow, she was so upset by Margery and Dominic's mysterious actions.

"Maybe they've heard something about Bree," Georgie suggested.

Chuck, Clay, Alec and Solange were all sitting on the backseat. Chuck craned his neck, trying to see the car that Toni was referring to. "It must be something important. They wouldn't be tearing out of there otherwise. They're expecting us."

Addis' streets were like a labyrinth. They wound in and out of one another. Toni was happy they had a driver who was familiar with the city. From the National Hotel, they hit Bole Road. "This is the way to the airport," the driver said in French. Solange translated for her companions. "He said this is the way to the airport."

The driver's assumption was correct because the taxi pulled up in front of the entrance at the small airport, and Dominic and Margery fairly flew out and ran inside. The driver of the Range Rover parked directly behind the taxi, and his occupants also hurried inside the airport. Clay and Alec ran ahead, trying to catch up with Dominic and Margery, thinking if there was going to be trouble, they should be there to watch their backs. A few yards away, Dominic and Margery had been approached by a big blond guy who looked as if he had been dragged through the mud a couple of times.

The blond man looked up, alarmed, when he saw the two men approaching. He tried to say something, but Clay and Alec pounced on him before he could get a word out. The wind was knocked out of him, and he lay on the floor flopping like a fish out of water. Clay regarded Dominic and Margery, who were looking at him as if he had gone crazy.

"He has information about Bree!" Margery wailed.

Going down on one knee, Dominic grabbed the blond by the scruff of his neck. "Where is she?" he ground out. For days he had been a bundle of unexpressed rage. Now it threatened to be acted out upon this lone man.

"Helicopter," the man wheezed. His eyes rolled in the direction of the tarmac. Dominic let him go and slowly rose, his gaze on the double glass doors that led out to the landing area. He noticed an open space far behind the principal runway. A heliport.

His Nikes were about to see more action.

Clay and Alec each grabbed the felled man by an arm and hoisted him up. "Come on, buddy," said Clay. "Just want your friends to see we have you in case they try anything funny."

The blond laughed. His legs were a bit wobbly.

"What's so funny?" Alec asked gruffly. He hated hiredmen types, and this guy smelled to high heaven of the ilk.

"Man," the guy said. "If you knew what we've been through the last three days, you would have to laugh, too. Or go nuts."

Toni, Chuck, Georgie and Solange arrived, all trying to get their breath. "Who's he?" Toni asked, eyeing the stranger malevolently.

"We think he's one of the kidnappers," Clay spoke up.

"Can we discuss this later?" Margery asked anxiously. "Dominic is heading out to the helicopter alone. He doesn't know what he's walking into. He's mad as hell and he might not use common sense if he sees a gun in one of their hands."

Dominic tucked his head in and ran all out, skirting parked planes on the tarmac and, once he was on the grass, avoiding gopher holes. It took him three and a half minutes to cover the quarter mile the heliport sat aft the airport. His daily jogs stood him in good stead. He could see three men standing close by the helicopter. He didn't recognize the small, wiry, dark-skinned guy or the tall white guy pulling on a cigarette. The third, however, he knew. His legs pumped harder.

Yusef had been looking in another direction. He turned quickly when Ishi yelped, "Oh, hell, enraged boyfriend at three o'clock." After he said that, he took off at a sprint in the opposite direction. "Good working for you, Mr. Makonnen. Let's do it again sometime."

The helicopter pilot swallowed smoke and hightailed it right behind Ishi.

Yusef had a bemused expression on his face when Dominic crashed into him. "Wha—"

Dominic was on top of him, pounding his fists in his face. "Where is she, you son of a bitch?"

In the helicopter, Bree awoke to find that she had been placed next to Omoro atop a pallet on the floor. Omoro was unconscious. She drew away from him, feeling disgust that she had actually been lying beside him for the trip from Makonnen's compound. But she supposed there was nowhere else to put her. She felt almost human again. Swinging her legs out of the open door, she sat there a moment. Then, suddenly, she saw Ishi running across the field as if all the hounds of hell were behind him. When all that was following him was a gangly white man. That was when she heard what she thought was Dominic's voice uttering expletives. She got to her feet and walked around the helicopter. The sight of Dominic on top of Yusef Makonnen trying his best to kill him, plus the small crowd of people making their way toward her, nearly made her knees buckle. She slowly walked toward the scene, which seemed to be unfolding in stark surrealism. Was she really finally safe?

"Dom. . . ." Her throat was still raw and scratchy from her ordeal; therefore her voice's volume was lower than usual. "Dominic!"

Dominic had been possessed by a frenzied anger so intense, he didn't even hear her or notice her standing less than five feet from him. All he knew was, Yusef Makonnen had taken the most precious thing he had ever had in his life away from him, and he had to get it back. Clay and Alec pulled him off the bloodied and nearly unconscious Makonnen. That was when his vision cleared and he saw Bree being hugged repeatedly by her mother and her father and her sister. He didn't know where they had all come from!

"Oh, baby, look at you! Did they hurt you?" Tears sat in Toni's eyes at the sight of her younger child. Bree's hair was matted and filled with sand. Her lips were so chapped there were points of blood at the corners of her mouth. The black leggings and top she had on were filthy, and her Nikes would never be white again but would permanently be the color of desert sand.

Bree had tears in her eyes, too. She just wanted to touch all of them to make certain they were real. She clung to one of her father's hands and one of her mother's. Georgie came close by her side, supporting her while she held on to her parents. "Just another day in the exciting life of our heroine!" her big sister said jokingly. Bree laughed, even though her ribs hurt when she did so.

Everyone moved aside as Dominic went to Bree, picked her up and tenderly cradled her in his arms. Bree had never seen him cry before. But now she was a witness to a side of him that only made her love for him that much stronger. She wiped at his tears with dirty fingers. "I really look worse than I am, baby. I'm going to be fine. Truly." She looked back at the helicopter. "I don't know about the guy in the helicopter, though. He's been shot. Somebody better get him some help before it's too late."

Clay and Alec went to investigate.

"She's probably dehydrated," Hyde spoke up. In the excitement, they had forgotten he was still in their midst. "She needs medical care."

Bree said, "Everybody, this is Hyde. He's one of them, but go easy on him. He saved my life more than once."

Dominic cut a hateful glance at Hyde, but spoke to Bree. "Save your strength, baby." He turned and began walking with her in his arms toward the air terminal.

"Welcome back, baby girl!" Margery said, clasping Bree's hand momentarily as Dominic continued walking. Bree just smiled at her. She was worn out from saying as much as she had on Hyde's behalf. She and Dominic went on ahead while the others attended to Yusef Makonnen and the fellow they knew as Hyde.

Inside the terminal, Rupert and Salah were following two ambulance attendants as they rolled Mubara out to the waiting ambulance on a gurney. She had awakened and was handcuffed and strapped to it. Salah noticed that the majority of the terminal's passengers and even some employees were gathered around the double glass doors leading out to the landing area. She placed a hand on Rupert's arm. "Something's going on over there. You go with her. I'm going to see what's happening."

"Still haven't gotten the taste for intrigue out of your mouth, huh?" Rupert said. "Be careful. It can be addictive."

"You ought to know," Salah said as she hurried off.

By the time she managed to push through the crowd, they had begun to part for a tall, bald black man carrying a woman who looked as if she had been in a recent airplane crash. More curious than ever, Salah squeezed through the spot the couple had opened up when they had come through the door and walked out onto the tarmac. Several more people were walking toward the terminal. Four women were in front. Bringing up the rear were two men carrying another between them. Behind them were two more men. One supporting the other.

As the women approached, she thought she recognized one of them and realized it was Margery Devlin-Lincoln, the actress. "What happened?" she asked Margery. "Are you here filming? Did a stunt go wrong?"

Margery smiled at the beautiful stranger. "No, dear. Nothing like that. I only wish that it all was make-believe."

Confused, Salah asked, "Then, that woman the gentleman carried inside was indeed injured. Was there a helicopter crash?" If there had been, she couldn't make out the aftermath in the dark.

Georgie stepped between Margery and the curious woman. "Look. This is a private matter. If you're a news hound, get your story elsewhere."

"I'm not with the press," Salah denied. She couldn't tell the protective Amazon with the braids that her curiosity stemmed from the fact that she sensed her husband had something to do with this incident. It was crazy, this assured notion that Yusef was here somewhere. But she felt him. That was the only way she could explain it.

"Well, good," the braided one said, and she ushered the other women inside the terminal. Salah stood there and carefully observed the three men coming closer: A big, good-looking black guy in a duster like cowboys used to wear on the trail. A smaller, but no less muscular, white fellow with dark hair and eyes. They were carrying a black man who appeared to be dead. Pallid skin, purple lips. His shirt front was covered with blood. She studied his face, even though she knew she would have nightmares later. Drawing her eyes from him, she looked in the distance and her heart seemed to plummet to the pit of her already nauseous stomach. She knew Yusef's form anywhere. The realization that Rupert Giles had been right about her husband confused and sickened her. Her safe, sheltered world came crashing down around her ears. Then she saw his face, and even though she knew she and Yusef would never be the same again, she also knew she was as much to blame for the events of the last three days as her husband.

So it was that in the space of a few seconds, Salah Makonnen resolved to make everything right again. With this in mind, she went to Yusef and placed a supportive arm about his waist. Yusef couldn't believe his eyes. "Salah? Are you really here?"

"I am, my love. And I always shall be."

Epilogue

Bree had to remain in the hospital overnight. Aside from the dehydration, which was remedied with an intravenous mixture of glucose and a saline solution, she was perfectly fine. The next evening, she was well enough to attend a dinner in her honor held in the hotel restaurant. The hotel staff was extremely solicitous of her, expressing their happiness at her safe return.

Bree took it all with grace and aplomb but with an underlying sadness. Dr. Amlak hadn't phoned with any news of Pierre's condition in two days. She tried not to discourage the others, though, who were understandably elated.

They all sat around a huge, low round table on pillows. The waiters brought basins of warm water, soap and towels so that they could wash their hands before beginning. The traditional Ethiopian meal wasn't eaten with cutlery but with one's hands. The food was brought to the table in huge bowls, and diners reached in and scooped the savory meat dishes up with pieces of injera, a pancakelike bread.

Clay and Georgie fed each other. Next to them, Toni and Chuck also took turns scooping the entrée with the injera and feeding each other. Dominic wished he could make the last three days disappear. He cherished Bree, and as soon as he got her alone, he was going to propose and wasn't going to take no for an answer.

The professor, Solange DuPree, had become suddenly shy in Rupert's presence, and he made no secret of his interest, the way his dark eyes fairly devoured her. To take his mind off more carnal things, she asked him the question she had wanted to know ever since their first meeting in Miami: "Tell us, Rupert, how did you come to be involved in all this?"

Rupert smiled at her. He would rather sit there and admire the professor's lush body and imagine her lips all over him as she had promised they would soon be. But he satisfied their curiosity anyway. "I was assigned to the case after the first statue was stolen in Cairo," he said, swinging his long legs around and getting comfortable. "I was fortunate enough to get a lead on the thieves right away, at least on the men Makonnen had hired. They seemed to be following a certain pattern. So, I consulted an expert on African mythology, and he told me about the myth concerning the conception of a special child that had been attributed to the Queen of Sheba. The thieves were collecting the exact gods and goddesses listed in this myth. Why, I wondered, would anyone want to perform a ceremony in order to conceive a child in this day and age when fertility experts abound?" He looked into Solange's eyes. "It's because of a deep desire to procreate. This reasoning took me to a database of fertility experts, which, I might add, isn't available to the normal Web surfer. I was looking for the names of wealthy people who'd gone to fertility experts in the last few months. I came up with several. However, I narrowed the list down, finally, to Salah Makonnen, wife of Yusef. After I did this, I visited her doctor in California. Dr. Song was able to identify a photograph of Vera Chong, a con woman who poses as a mystic in order to bilk money from the wealthy. She has pulled many cons in the past. Sometimes promising she can speak to a dead loved one. Sometimes promising that she can insure you the man or woman of your dreams if only you'll listen to her." He gave the comely doctor another warm perusal. "Anyway, Vera Chong got close to the gullible, lovesick Dr. Song and was able to look into his records. She has already been identified by several of his other patients as the mystic who promised to help them conceive a child. Makonnen was the brass ring. If she had pulled that one off, she would've been able to retire."

Later that night, Solange stood in her room dressed in a sheer, white lace nightgown and eyeing the box that held the goddess. She thought of Salah and Yusef Makonnen and the great lengths to which he had gone in order to make her happy. And it had all been a sham. A con run on him by a woman after his millions.

Solange didn't want to be stifled by her fears any longer. She placed her hand on her flat belly. *So what if I'll never have a child. I can still be a happy person without experiencing childbirth.* She picked up the goddess and held it to her chest.

Suddenly, she heard a noise from her balcony. Startled, she turned and saw Rupert climbing over the railing, a rose clasped between his strong white teeth and a rakish grin on his face.

Over the next few days, events started to unfold. Harris, Makonnen's helicopter pilot, was found in his helicopter not far from Lideta Airport where Vera Chong had forced him to land. He had a bullet in his shoulder, but would pull through. Omoro wasn't as fortunate. He got blood poisoning and died from his wound. His partners in crime, Hyde and Ishi, sat in jail awaiting trial.

Yusef Makonnen was their very unhappy cellmate. But only overnight. His attorneys got him freed on a technicality the next day, whereupon he and Salah left Ethiopia, never to return.

When Jack Cairns got home after his stay in the hospital, still in need of cosmetic surgery, he found a hand-delivered letter had been slipped underneath his door. In it was a note from Salah Makonnen telling Jack how sorry she and Yusef were for his pain and suffering. Also included in the envelope was a cashier's check in the amount of seven hundred and fifty thousand dollars.

In late November, Toni and Chuck were married in the ballroom of Greenbriar. In attendance were myriad family and friends. Toni wore a Carolina Herrera cocktail dress in champagne-colored silk. Chuck wore a black tux by Armani. Toni's father, James, gave her away. Margery was the matron-of-honor and Georgie and Bree were bridesmaids which, technically, neither of them were since both were married women by then. The Shaw women never did anything according to tradition. Chuck's best man was his longtime friend, Dr. Lawrence Hamlin.

Following the ceremony, the reception was held there at Greenbriar. A caterer and extra servers were hired so that Cook, Carson, and the rest of the regular staff could join in the festivities.

Chief among the revelers was a little black dog who had the run of the place, much to the chagrin of the guests whose toes he ran over with a contraption that resembled a cart with two back wheels. His back end, still in a cast, was held safely in the tiny wagon while his hip healed. The good Dr. Amlak had built it especially for him.

Dear Reader:

I hope you enjoyed *A Second Chance At Love*. It was my most difficult book to write because it is the sequel to *All the Right Reasons,* a book I dearly loved. In *A Second Chance At Love,* I endeavored to answer your questions about Toni and Chuck, but also to give you an update on what has been happening in the lives of their daughters, Georgie and Bree.

I'm thinking of giving characters Dr. Solange DuPree and Rupert Giles their own story. Let me know what you think. Should they have their own book?

Write me at P.O. Box 811, Mascotte, FL 34753-0811 or if you're using E-mail at Jani569432@aol.com. You may visit my Web site at:
http://romantictales.com/janicesims.html.

Many Blessings,
Janice Sims

ARABESQUE

The Soul of Romance

Arabesque and BET.com
celebrate
ROMANCE WEEK
February 12 — 16, 2001

Join book lovers from across
the country in chats with
your favorite authors,
including:

- Donna Hill
- Rochelle Alers
- Marcia King-Gamble
- and other African-American
  best-selling authors!

Be sure to log on
www.BET.com
Pass the word and
create a buzz for
Romance Week on-line.